CW00822779

Secrets Beneath The Sea

Secrets Beneath The Sea

The Forsaken Series Book 4

Phil Price

Published 2020 by Evenfall – A Next Chapter Imprint
Cover art by Cover Mint

For Des Rogers.
One of life's good guys.

Prologue

They tore their gaze away from each other, looking out towards the pounding surf. A tiny figure stood there, frozen in time as the waves crashed a few yards away from her planted feet. She looked so fragile, so inconsequential against the raging sea. Yet they both knew she had an inner strength, borne out of the darkness that lurked hidden from view. Well, hidden for most. The woman rose to her feet above him, walking away towards the shore, her straw hat and summer dress buffeted by the warm winds from the Atlantic. He watched as she shrank further away until the woman was standing next to the girl, her white bikini and bonnet clearly visible across the expanse of sand. The man squinted, raising a tanned hand to shield his eyes from the overhead sun. He watched, fixated as both the woman and the girl both turned to their left, staring along the coast, towards the south. On any other day, the man would have followed, snapping several shots of the precious moment, captured forever. Not this time though. He grew uneasy as the sky to the south gradually darkened, thick clouds roiling up on the horizon, heading in their direction. A flash of lightning struck the sea, the two figures unmoved by its immense power. They looked entranced, seemingly hypnotised by an unseen force that beckoned to them. The wind picked up, blowing across his face as he shielded his eyes. Looking back to the surf, the two figures were accompanied by two more. Tall and willowy, with pale skin and dark clothing. He flinched, an urge to charge headlong down the beach towards them.

"She will never give you what you crave," a voice carried towards him. "Their kind can bear no fruit."

He looked around himself, seeing holidaymakers carrying on with their fun, the words lost to the stiffening breeze. His eyes returned to the sea as the beach became shrouded in darkness. The woman and girl no longer stood there. In their place, a shuffling group of figures, yellow eyes piercing the oncoming gloom. Bearing down on Jake's position.

Jake shot up in bed, the sheets damp with sweat, his body peppered with perspiration. Tears ran down his cheeks, his breathing elevated and ragged. He turned to his left, seeing the unmade side of the bed, two pillows plumped up like they'd been for the last six years. He looked out of the bedroom window, bright morning sun radiating in gently as the Atlantic breeze ruffled the curtains. Climbing out of bed stiffly, Jake kneaded his lower back as footsteps along the landing made him turn. The door flew open, an auburn-haired girl leaning against the jamb. "Hey, Dad," she said confidently.

"Hey, poppet," Jake replied. "What time is it?"

She smiled, her face transforming instantly. For a split-second, Katherine was stood in front of him. The moment passed, a dark shadow almost forming between them as Jake's loss tried to resurface. "Breakfast time," Alicia proclaimed jovially. The dark clouds blew past, Jake returning the smile to his only living daughter as she turned and headed downstairs.

"Put the kettle on, please. I'll be down in a minute."

"Okay, Dad," Alicia chirped as she skipped along the landing before she headed downstairs.

Two minutes later, Jake entered the kitchen, pulling on a dark blue T-shirt that matched his blue shorts. "What's on the menu?"

"Do you fancy a bacon sandwich?" his daughter replied as she poured boiling water into a teapot.

"Perfect. Just what the doctor ordered," he said, ruffling her long hair as he padded towards the fridge.

"Dad," Alicia began. "Were you having another bad dream?"

Jake sighed as the fridge door closed to. He placed milk, bacon and eggs on the counter next to the stove before dropping onto a wooden chair. "Yes, love. They come and go."

"Was it about Mummy, or Alana?"

"Alana," Jake muttered, the attractive face of the white witch appearing before him.

She walked over, wrapping her arms around him. He closed his eyes, inhaling her scent, the world melting away for a moment. "You'll be okay, Dad."

"Thanks. You've got an old head on young shoulders. You're wise beyond your years, like your mother."

"I wish she were still here, Dad. I have no memory of her at all? Even Alana, I hardly remember her either?"

Jake's eyes became unfocused, images appearing before him. First was his wife, Katie. She'd been killed several years before, along with his daughter Megan. *God. It's almost fifteen years,* he thought. A tall auburn-haired woman appeared next, dark eyes boring into his. He'd met Katherine years after his wife had died, in another world. A world that lay next to his own, but far removed in every other sense. Vampires and dark beings had lurked there, Jake stumbling across an age-old secret after his brother-in-law had sent him on a wild goose chase following a double murder. A goose chase that had started a chain of events that Jake had been helpless to resist against. He'd visited two other worlds. Two parallel dimensions that had almost cost him his life. Jake had barely survived, his mother, father and brother all perishing at the hands of the creatures that had inhabited the forsaken lands beyond his own. "I know, poppet," he replied sombrely. "The painful thing is, is that I remember them all." Alana appeared before him, her milky-white complexion flawless, dark hair cascading around her face.

"Who did you love the most?" Alicia asked inquisitively.

Jake chuckled, relieved by the change in mood that was threatening to engulf the kitchen. "You can't ask a question like that. I loved them all, for different reasons," he responded evenly. "I only thought I'd be with Katie. We were married and had Megan," he said, his chest constricting. "But then Katherine came along, and I also loved her dearly. When she died, I thought that was it. But life tends to throw you curveballs. Alana and I probably came together through grief and suffering. I'd lost Kath, she'd lost her kin. And it kinda went from there." He was suddenly cast back six years, remembering with aching clarity the look on the witch's face when she knew that she was dying. He remembered the blood, the screams and tears that had echoed through the house as the woman's pregnancy had come to an abrupt end, extinguishing the life of the mother and unborn son in a heartbeat.

"Well, I love you, Dad," Alicia confirmed, lightening the mood. "I'll give you all the love and cuddles that you'll ever need."

He opened his arms, welcoming his daughter's embrace as tears stung his eyes. "Thanks, poppet. I don't know what I'd do without you?"

"You too, Dad. You're my world."

Chapter One

Cornwall – 2019

"I love coming up here, Dad," Alicia said, her voice almost drowned out on the incessant wind. They both stood on a rocky headland, a few hundred yards away from a large hotel that loomed over the coastline.

"Me too," he replied simply, the wind ruffling his dark locks that were now showing the first shoots of grey. His neatly trimmed beard was also shot through with silver, giving the former police officer a distinguished look that he now embraced. He knew he was getting older, his thirties behind him, with another milestone appearing on the horizon.

"I can feel her, Dad. She's still here with us."

"Well, that's good. She loved this world. Your Mum felt at home here. Believe me, it's a million miles away from the life she was used to."

"When will you take me? I need to see all this for myself."

Jake pondered the question, nodding at his daughter. "Well, it's the school holidays. There's nothing to stop us going there."

"Tonight," she replied excitedly. "Come on, Dad. Please?"

The man smiled, wrapping an arm around his daughter. "Okay. We've got no plans for the weekend. I'll let Wilf and Jo know later."

"What will you tell them?"

"I'll think of something." A buzzing sound inside his pocket made Jake fumble around in his cargo shorts before retrieving his smartphone. It was an unknown number. Swiping his thumb across the screen, Jake took the call. "Hello?"

"Is this Jake Stevenson?" a female voice answered.

"Speaking."

"Hi. I found your name on the internet. My name is Emma Thorne. And I need your help. My daughter has been taken."

* * *

Two hours later, Jake pulled off the Atlantic Highway, weaving his way along tight country lanes in his black Volvo SUV. The hedgerows almost clawed at his wing mirrors as he headed ever downwards towards the sea as brooding clouds caressed the land. He'd dropped his daughter off with Wilf and Jo, promising to be back soon as the pouty nine-year-old had stood, hands on hips on the front doorstep. After a few minutes, a sign appeared, telling Jake that he'd arrived in his destination, Towan Point. The road squeezed in further an avenue of trees covering the road, making Jake's headlights come on, illuminating the dark tarmac ahead. After a few seconds, the car emerged into the main village, a handful of houses, shops and one pub presenting themselves to the private investigator. He crawled past the frontages, noting the name of the weather-beaten pub, The Narwhal. *Strange name for a pub,* he thought as the village passed him by, the SUV climbing a steep lane towards a headland. He slowed the Volvo some more as a large object caught his eye close to the sea. A large stone lighthouse sat brooding over the village, joined to the mainland by a raised rocky strip of land. *Nice,* he observed. *If a little creepy.* Jake depressed the accelerator, turning onto a grassy track a few-hundred yards further up the hill. The car trundled gently towards a stone cottage nestled amongst trees and tall hedges as the first drops of rain fell from the sky. He applied the hand-brake, switching off the engine as his eyes took in the solitary building. It was the quintessential country cottage, double fronted with two windows upstairs and downstairs, a white door sandwiched between them. The thatched roof completed the cosy picture, tendrils of smoke drifting into the sky from the chimney. As he donned his summer jacket, Jake suddenly felt uneasy, looking around his position furtively for signs of life. Thinking that his imagination was running away with him he was about to walk over to the house when he stopped mid-step. A few hundred yards away, close to the turn-off, a lone figure stood against blackening skies. Jake squinted as he tried to focus on the person at the top of the driveway. Low clouds drifted across the land, obscuring the person who was dressed all in black, a hood blocking out his features. Jake knew it was a man, of probably advanced years as he stood rooted to the spot. A distant rumble of thunder rolled across the sky as the figure extended a hand towards him. Even from that distance, Jake could see that the man was pointing a bony finger towards him, a shudder coursing through his body as the stare down continued.

"Mr Stevenson," a voice behind him called out.

Jake flinched, turning towards the cottage, a woman standing there, a check blanket draped over her shoulders. He turned back towards the road, the figure now gone as more thunder echoed across the land. "Err, hi," he replied tentatively as he walked towards her. "Nice place."

"Thank you," the woman replied. "Did the coordinates work okay?"

"Perfectly. Strange that there's no postcode for this place?" Jake replied as he extended his hand.

The woman took it readily, smiling up at him. "We're a bit off the grid here in Towan Point. Not many people visit and very few ever leave, except for a few. Come inside before the heavens open."

He followed her in through the front door, slipping his trainers off and depositing them on a mat next to an antique telephone table. She led the way, walking along a narrow hallway that opened up into a large kitchen orangery. "Now this is lovely," he said, walking across flagstone tiles towards the large bi-fold doors that opened onto a secluded rear garden.

"Thank you," she replied. "Would you like a drink?"

"I'd love a coffee."

"How do you take it?"

"Milk with two, please," Jake said, his eyes never leaving the garden. High hedges and trees gave the intimate space a magical quality, a little stream running through the garden. He noticed other things too. A trampoline, covered in dried leaves, along with a small bike that lay overturned on a gravel path next to a stout-looking shed.

A minute later, a familiar aroma drifted across the kitchen, the woman walking over towards him. "Here you go. Why don't we sit down?"

"Thanks," he nodded, walking over towards a kitchen table. Pulling out a chair, Jake seated himself, taking a sip of the heady brew. "Very nice," he stated before proceedings could begin. "So, why don't we start at the beginning?"

"Okay," she replied quietly. "I hope you've got an open mind, Jake. Because you're going to need it."

Chapter Two

"We came to the village a few years ago, my ex-husband, Joe wanting a more peaceful existence. We'd lived in London for ten years and wanted to get out of the rat race."

"Understandable. I've lived here for several years since moving down from Birmingham. I like the pace of life here."

She smiled, Jake studying her face. She looked to be roughly his age, dark curly hair showing the first shoots of grey. An attractive face looked back at him, the man noting the dark smudges under her eyes, along with a sallow complexion at odds with the warm summer that they'd been subjected to. "You may have heard of him. Joseph Thorne."

"The writer? Yes, I've heard of him. I've even read one of his books, *The Winding Lane*. It was very good."

"Do you like horror?" she asked inquisitively.

An image flashed before his eyes. A vampire lying beneath him. A memory from a distant place that was woven into Jake's subconscious. "Yeah. Kinda," he replied evenly. "Always fascinated me."

"Well, I'm more of an *Emily Bronte* fan. Don't like things that go bump in the night. Anyway, where was I?"

"You moved here a few years ago."

"Oh yes. Joe had recently hit the big time, with a movie deal in the offing. Because of the nature of his work, he decided that it would be better if we all moved to Cornwall to help him focus on his craft." Her voice was soft, with little or no accent that Jake could detect. "Our daughter, Lauren, was about three at the time. And for a long period, things seemed perfect."

"You mentioned that your daughter was taken. By whom?" Jake asked, the first tendrils of unease washing over him.

"When we came here, Joe was finishing another book. He began frequenting the village pub, hearing tales from some of the locals who would talk to him. Apparently, the lighthouse that you must have seen on the way here has been owned by the same family for generations. The Longford's. I believe that one of them took Lauren." She walked across the kitchen, picking up a framed photograph that she duly handed to Jake.

"Nice picture," he said, looking at the girl who sat staring back at him, an uneven smile on her face. She'd inherited her mother's looks, the same brown curly hair, the features very similar. It was a beautifully taken shot, capturing a carefree girl with a beaming smile. "How old is Lauren?"

"Nine. When she was taken, she'd just celebrated her eighth birthday. That was just over a year ago." She paused, taking a sip of coffee. "I was saying about the lighthouse. It's inextricably linked to everything and everyone in Towan Point. As are the Longford's. They also own the pub, along with a few properties within the village. Joe became fascinated by the local legends surrounding the family and decided to write a story based on them. He tried to make contact with them but was rebuffed on every occasion. However, he became friendly with a barmaid at The Narwhal, who offered him plenty of inspiration for his book, and a lot more besides. I found out about the affair just over a year ago."

"Oh. Sorry to hear about that. Sounds like you've been through the mill, Emma."

"You could say that. One of the Longford's henchmen turned up one day, pinning Joe to the front door, telling us that this Ciara had fallen pregnant. Joe tried to wriggle out of it, but as soon as I knew what I'd suspected, I ended it. They're a nasty bunch too, the Longford's. Joe managed to find out that they're involved in some pretty shady activities."

"Like what?"

"Smuggling. But he never found out exactly what they are smuggling. Could be anything. Drugs, weapons, people."

"So, where is Joe now?" Jake continued, his heartbeat beginning to increase as he was pulled into the web.

"He was told to leave the village, which he refused initially. When a group of them turned up outside, it turned ugly. They set about us all, Joe receiving the worst punishment. Lauren and I were hurt trying to protect him. A few days later when we arrived home from school, he'd gone."

"Have you heard from him since?"

"Yes. He's living in Spain. A place called Yegen, in Andalucía. Do you know the area?"

"Not really. I've been to the Costa del Sol a few times, but never ventured too far from the beach. What's he doing there?"

"Writing. And hiding."

"So, what happened to your daughter?"

"Honestly, I'm not sure. I involved the police, but they came back with nothing. She was playing in the garden while I was painting in here. That's what I do, I'm a full-time artist. Anyway, I went outside to call Lauren in for lunch, but she was gone. The police said that she'd probably ventured too close to the cliffs that are a few hundred yards away from here. They found one of her trainers," Emma said before emotions boiled over. She wept silently, burying her head in her hands.

Jake looked around the kitchen, seeing a box of tissues next to the sink. He grabbed the box, handing it to Emma who accepted it with a sniffle. "Take your time, Emma," he offered reassuringly.

"Thank you." She blew her nose, wiping the tears from her face before composing herself. "The police and local coastguard looked for her for a few days before abandoning the search. And since then, life for the village has returned to normal. No one ever talks about it. It's as if it never happened."

"I'm so sorry, Emma. A few years ago, my mother was swept out to sea in Tintagel. We went through a similar thing. After a few days, they called off the search. Her body was never found," he lied, knowing that if he explained how she'd been taken by a vampire and transported to a parallel world, the woman would eject him from the cottage very quickly.

"Oh no!" she exclaimed. "I'm really sorry, Jake."

"It's okay. It was a few years ago now. Anyway, we're here to talk about Lauren," he replied almost to brusquely. "Sorry, that sounded a bit blunt. I just want to get as much information as possible before we proceed."

"That's okay. I totally understand," she replied, smiling at him. "The girl that Joe had the affair with also vanished, around the time that Lauren went missing. Same thing happened, the police quickly brushed it under the carpet. There were rumours that she'd fallen pregnant, being banished from the village because of the shame she'd brought on her family. No one's seen her since."

"Do you speak to your ex-husband? Did he come back when Lauren went missing?"

"Did he fuck!" she spat, Jake shocked by the outburst. "He said that it was a tragic accident and that I should accept it and move on with my life. But how can I? My husband cheated on me, which to be fair, I can handle. But to lose my daughter, with no explanation as to how or why she vanished – well, I cannot move on from that."

"Okay. So, how do you want to play this?"

She smiled at him over the rim of her mug, placing it before her. "So, you're willing to help me?"

"I am," he stated. "Don't hold out too much hope though. It's been over a year and the police will not offer much information. And it looks like the locals may be a closed book too."

"I understand. The fact that you're willing to help is enough for me. The garden lit up, the flash of lightning followed a few seconds later by a crackle of thunder. The kitchen seemed to darken, the downlighters doing their best to ward off the gloom outside.

Jake shuddered, feeling the temperature in the kitchen begin to drop a few degrees. "You wouldn't think it was supposed to be summer," he remarked, nodding towards the garden.

"I know," she replied, walking over to the fireplace that sat on a far wall. She bent down, dropping a few logs onto the dying embers before walking back to the table. "You should come here in the winter. To say it can be bitter is an understatement."

Jake drained his mug, watching as the logs begin to catch, a degree of warmth emanating from the hearth. "It's the same in Tintagel. Lovely in the summer, desolate in the winter. But we love it."

"Are you married?" the question was blunt, taking Jake by surprise.

"I used to be," he replied. But not anymore. I live with my daughter, Alicia."

"Any family?"

Jake needed to be guarded, not wanting to divulge too much information. Information that only a select few people knew about. "No, except an uncle who lives nearby."

Sensing that the man didn't want to open old wounds, Emma changed tack seamlessly. "If you're going to help me, the best place to start is with Joe."

"Your ex-husband?" Jake asked, confusion spreading across his face. "But he lives in Spain?"

"I know. But you'll get no help from the locals. You may even find them unreceptive to you being here snooping around." Jake thought back to the lone figure who'd pointed at him earlier in the day. "Joe has never spoken to me about what happened. We've barely discussed Lauren's disappearance either. But he knows that I'll never travel to Spain. I'm terrified of flying and the thought of driving there is too daunting. I'm not much of a traveller y'see. Driving out to the local supermarket, or to Truro to sell my paintings is as far as I ever go. And Joe knows this. But if you turned up on his doorstep, you may be able to shed some light on the secrets that he's keeping from me."

"Flying to Spain is not going to be cheap?" Jake stated evenly, a feeling of uncertainty creeping inside him.

"I know. But I live a very comfortable existence, money-wise. Joe sends me fifty percent of his royalties every three months. Plus, I make a modest living from my paintings and sculptures. So, money is not an issue. All you have to do is agree to it?"

"Okay," Jake said, checking his watch. "I'll be happy to help you. I will need to speak to Wilf and Jo, to make sure that Alicia is taken care of while I'm away."

"Thank you, Jake. When can you start?"

"Monday. Is that okay?"

She nodded. "Perfect."

"Okay. I will book my flights when I get home and keep you updated as much as possible. I should imagine that I'll probably need to spend a few days in Spain, so I'll buy an open return."

"Whatever you think is best. Do you require an up-front payment?"

Jake smiled, shaking his head. "That's not necessary. I'll send an invoice at some point, but let's focus on the task in hand." Something came to him, a question that he'd not yet asked. "Can I ask you something?"

"Sure."

"What do you think actually happened to your daughter?"

Her face dropped slightly, the woman taking a deep breath. "This is where I need you to have an open mind, Jake. I think she's at the lighthouse. I think the

Longford's took her in revenge of what Joe did with Ciara. And I believe that she's still alive. My daughter is alive, Jake. Please find her."

Chapter Three

Jake pulled up outside The Narwhal, killing the engine. The village was quiet, save for a few people milling around the shops and front gardens. The main thoroughfare took up most of the village, a few side streets branching off on either side. There was a sign on the left, directing him to the seafront. *A walk around can't do any harm?* he thought as Jake climbed out of his Volvo. As he crossed the street Jake felt several sets of eyes focused on his every movement, a few people stopping what they were doing to stare at the stranger. He paid them no heed, heading down a winding lane that led to the sea. The rain had stopped, threatening clouds still looming overhead as the private investigator walked down the centre of the lane, tall hedgerows blocking any view. The sound of an approaching car snapped him out of his thoughts, a dark blue Land Rover heading his way, seeming to fill the lane in front of him. He found a small break in the foliage, stepping to one side as the vehicle approached. It slowed down, the driver peering to look at Jake who had pressed himself into the hedge.

Jesus, it's the same guy, Jake thought as a seated figure in a black hood regarded him for a few seconds before a bony finger pointed in his direction. He froze, an area of scarred skin on his chest beginning to itch. Instinctively, he looked down, scratching at his skin as the 4x4 sped away, spitting gravel against the private investigator's legs. Stepping out into the road, he watched as the Land Rover disappeared from sight, leaving the lane devoid of movement, the seagulls above bringing life back to his surroundings. "What the hell was that all about?" His fingers kneaded the skin on his chest, a faded scar where a black onyx pendant once hung. In its place, a purple stone from a distant land lay nestled amongst greying chest hair. He was cast back several years, remembering vividly how he'd received the scar. An image flashed in his mind of a grotesque creature who had appeared between two trees in a dark forest a few miles away from his home. The creature was a vampire called Anya, sent to kill him. Only blind luck and fortune had saved him as her fangs had lunged at him, the cross doing its job, sending the former human screeching into the night. Now as he stood there, a feeling of dread washed over him. *You can walk away,* he thought, weighing up his decision as another rumble of thunder stuccoed across the sky. *No. All the vampires were destroyed,* he thought, trying to reassure himself. *It was just your imagination running away with you.* He continued along the lane, coming out on a rocky beach a few minutes later. The clouds seemed to touch the sea, the top of the impressive lighthouse swathed in mist. The lane led out onto a rocky promontory, leading directly towards the stone structure that loomed over him. Jake walked onto the pebbly beach, seating himself on a low wall as his gaze drifted from the water to the lighthouse. A stout wooden door faced him, the rest of the building appearing impenetrable. Behind the main edifice, a low-slung section of building jutted out towards a jetty at the shore, steps leading down to the sea. *Probably fifty feet height difference between the front door and the sea,* he thought. *I wonder if the place has a basement? If it does, that's where I would hide someone.* He watched as a large bird of prey hovered on the thermals above him before Jake climbed to his feet, heading away from the lighthouse towards the village. A hundred feet above, a large glass window slid open, two men stepping out onto the gantry.

"Is that him?" the taller one asked, his features hidden beneath a grey hood.

"That's him," the shorter one replied, his face also hidden. "Who do you think he is?"

"I don't know. But I do know one thing."

"What's that, Lukash?"

"He's trouble."

* * *

An hour later, Jake pulled up at his parent's former home. They'd moved close to Jake and Katherine years before, just as Alicia had made her arrival. They'd spent a few happy weeks there, until Alison was taken on a stormy night by a vampire named Elias. The police had surmised that Jake's mother had been washed out to sea by the floods, her body never found. It was only a short time after that Jake and his father had discovered the truth. She'd been turned, Killing Douglas, Jake's beloved father. The house had lain empty for a time, until Wilf had taken up residence, liking the new world that he'd found himself in. Along with the house, the older man had found Jo, the first woman he'd ever been with. At the time of their meeting, Jo ran a local pub in the village, recently widowed. They'd struck up a rapport, the old, usually brusque man vanishing whenever she was close by, replaced by a genial older gentleman. Jake walked up the path as low cloud blanketed Tintagel in a perpetual mist, the temperature feeling more like late autumn than mid-summer. A familiar face opened the door as he approached, Jo beaming at the man through the glass sliding door. "Hello," she chirped, kissing him on the cheek before showing him in. "They're in the lounge."

"Thanks, Jo. Has she been good?"

"Kinda," the woman replied. "She's been giving Wilf a going over."

Jake stepped into the cosy front room, smiling at the sight of his daughter and the old man from another world. They were sat on the sofa, Alicia sat on his lap with a large book in her hands. "Have you tired Wilf out?" he began. "He's missed his afternoon nap."

Alicia slid off her great uncle, smiling up at her father as the older man levered himself upright. He walked over to Jake, clapping him on the shoulder. "She's been grand, reading me a story about three pigs and a big bad wolf."

"We need to get you some more books," Jake observed. "That story's for little children."

Jo walked into the lounge, zipping up her jacket. "I'm just off down to the shop. We're almost out of milk and I don't want to get caught in a downpour."

Jake nodded his head towards Wilf. "What would you do without this angel?"

Wilf stepped across the lounge, putting his arm around his woman, kissing her on the forehead. "She certainly is that," he concurred.

Jake looked at them, loving how happy they looked. They had found happiness, albeit late in life. Jo was a few years older than Jake, with an attractive girl-next-door look about her. She was tall, almost matching height with the grizzled man next to her. Wilf had melded well with his new home. Gone were the medieval-type clothes and long straggly hair. His grey hair was now cut short, his attire befitting a senior citizen. He looked at home. He looked at peace. "Well, we'll be off in a bit, Jo. Taking Alicia up to Birmingham for a few days. Show her my old stomping ground."

"Sounds like fun," the woman replied happily before giving father and daughter a farewell hug.

Moments later, the three of them sat together, the lounge seeming to darken somewhat as mist pressed itself against the windows. "So," Wilf breaking the silence. "Where are you really going?"

"Alicia wants to see Elksberg," Jake responded.

Wilf nodded slowly. Elksberg was the land that the man had spent much of his life. A simple, yet harsh existence, living in a large forest that had been blanketed in cloud for as long as he could remember. He'd worked the land with his older brother Cedric, ensuring the safety of the villagers until an outlander had appeared one day. That outlander was Jake, who'd found a doorway between his world and Wilf's as he'd tracked a vampire called Elias. That had started a chain of events that had eventually brought Wilf to Cornwall years later. Gone were the horrors, replaced by a serene existence that the older man never knew could have existed. "Are you prepared?"

"We are. Got everything that we'll need, just in case."

"How long will you stay out there?"

"Just a night. I was thinking of taking Alicia down to Shetland."

Wilf stared past Jake, lost in his memories. He pictured a spit of land, battered by an unrelenting sea. A place that he once called home. It had been called Shetland, after his grandfather, George Drysdale had settled there many moons before Wilf had come into existence. Wilf had never known him, hearing countless stories of his courage and adventures, handed down throughout the ages. "Give them my best regards. Tell them that old Wilf is doing well."

"We will," Jake replied, clapping the older man on the shoulder.

"Bye-bye, Papa Wilf," Alicia said, jumping into his embrace.

His face lit up as the young girl buried her face in the crook of his neck, squeezing her fiercely. "Now, you be good and listen to your Father. You may have vampire blood in your veins, but the land you're about to visit is not one to be taken lightly."

"I know," she countered, her face suddenly serious, her grey eyes peering up at him.

"Safe travels," he said simply, walking with them towards the front door. Wilf stood on the doorstep as the Volvo sped off down the road. "No more drama," he said to himself before closing the door behind him.

* * *

Hours later, Jake and Alicia sat in a darkened forest that lay at the southern edge of Birmingham. The Lickey Hills country park had been a constant in Jake's life, where he'd spent many years traversing its three hills as a youngster before finally realising that the trees held untold secrets that little or no one else knew about. He looked over at his daughter, who sat cross-legged on the bracken-strewn forest floor. *She seems so at peace in the darkness,* he thought. *She really does have Reggan's blood in her veins.* His thoughts drifted backwards several years. An image flashed before him, a huge beast a full head taller than Jake. Greyish skin and large tusk-like fangs floated before him, Jake remembering with startling clarity the moment when the vampire had literally taken a chunk out of him. Jake had barely escaped with his life, eventually destroying Reggan before beating a hasty retreat back to his own world with Wilf, Katherine and his dear friend, Tamatan the demon.

As if reading his thoughts, Alicia broke the silence. "You've told me so much, Dad," she began. "I can't wait to go through the doorway. I've seen it so many times in my dreams."

"Well, the door is due to open in a few minutes, I hope. It's been years since I was here. Let's hope the doorway still works."

"I'm sure it will. I wonder if anyone else has ever been through it?"

"No idea, love," Jake replied. "The last time I was here was to help Vicky help find her son. The doorway only opens for a minute or so, and at this time of night the forest is empty."

"Have you heard from Vicky?"

Jake smiled in the darkness. "Yes. I told her that we were taking a trip up here, but she's on holiday with Jasper. I'm sure we'll meet up with them both soon." Jake had told her about his involvement with Vicky and Jasper, who lived a mile away from their position. He remembered the face of the boy, floating in a bubble in front of him as he'd clung to life on a dark mountain. He was trying to get home, the vampiric virus inside him slowly taking Jake into an eternity of darkness. They'd made it home, Jasper eventually reunited with his mother, thanks to the help of Alana. It all seemed so long ago, almost another lifetime.

"Can you feel that?" Alicia said, standing up as leaves blew across the forest floor.

"Yes," her father replied. "The doorway is about to open." He walked over to a tree, kicking his motorbike off its stand before wheeling it back to his daughter as a blue doorway appeared in front of them.

"Oh my," Alicia blurted.

"Come on," her father urged. "Let's get through."

The girl walked forward, her fingers extended as she tested the doorway that shimmered in front of her. She felt a slight resistance, liking the warm feeling that spread up her arm. Without thinking, Alicia walked through the doorway, coming out on the other side a moment later. The forest that she now stood in was deathly quiet, no passing traffic, no animals scurrying around in the darkness. "Wow. It's real," she breathed as Jake leaned the bike against a stout tree trunk.

"You're finally here," he said as a thick mist roiled around their feet. "Come on. Wilf's old village is a few hundred yards over there. We'll sleep there tonight and go exploring when the sun comes up."

"Okay, Dad," the girl replied, following her father across Amatoll forest, the blackness of night pressing down on both of them.

Chapter Four

Eight hours later, Jake and Alicia rolled across the grassy expanses of Elksberg, heading towards a large ridge on the horizon. The land around them was desolate, save for a few bison and antelope that grazed on the stubbly grass as the sun began to warm the land. "Dad," Alicia shouted behind Jake. "What's that place?"

Jake looked ahead, seeing the small collection of buildings, obscured by a tall wooden fence. "That's Culnae. I've stayed there a few times, back when I first arrived here. We'll carry on, as I might not be too welcome there."

"Why?"

"Because the owner, Mungo, died helping me fight the vampires."

"Okay," she replied, her arms clinging onto her father as they sped past the small settlement. Not long afterwards, they were walking through a dimly lit gorge, the walls closing in around them. "Spooky," the girl observed, looking up at the red stone walls that towered over them.

"It is a bit. But we'll be out the other side in a few minutes. From there, it's a straight ride to Shetland."

"Great. I'm hungry, Dad."

"You're always hungry," Jake smiled down at her, ruffling her long hair.

The sun warmed their skin a few minutes later, Jake kick-starting the bike. "If you need to go, do it now as we'll not stop until we reach Fingles."

"Fingles?"

"Another small settlement next to the sea," Jake replied. "The Finglers have also helped me out on many occasions. They are a hardy bunch, as you'll see when we get there." As the sun began climbing into the sky, Jake and Alicia stopped next to a dark furious sea that battered the rocky shoreline. They dismounted, Alicia following her father towards a collection of wooden structures that reminded her of a Wild West movie set. "Strange," the man said. "The place is deserted." His eyes scanned the buildings, a cold feeling spreading through him as he noted burnt-out cabins and bones that lay scattered on the baked earth. "Something happened here."

"What?"

"Not sure. But it doesn't look good. Come on. Let's head over to Shetland. Maybe they can fill us in on what went down here." Climbing back onto the bike, Alicia hugged her father as he navigated the spit of land that stretched out into the grey sea. The bike made steady progress, climbing up grassy rises before dipping down towards the angry surf. A deep droning sound echoed across the land, the girl squeezing her father tighter as the rocky path narrowed to a point where she could see the crashing waves on either side of them.

"Don't crash, Dad."

Jake laughed. "Don't worry, love. I've been along this path many times."

The bike made its way down towards a stout bridge that spanned the gap between the peninsular and the settlement of Shetland. Alicia could see a carved wooden sign, welcoming them. "So, this is where Mum's buried." It was a statement rather than a question.

"Yes," Jake replied. "Something doesn't look right. It's too quiet. Come on. Let's go." They climbed up the rocky path on the other side of the bridge, Jake noting that some of the recently constructed buildings were mere husks, charred by flame. The farmhouse still stood proud, braving the perpetual elements that battered it from all directions. "No one's here," Jake observed. He was about to speak again when a man appeared at the far end of the settlement, a pitchfork held out in front of him. Jake waved, watching as the man advanced slowly. "Hello," he called.

The man lowered the weapon. "Jake. Is that you?"

"Yes. Toby, isn't it?" Jake replied as they closed the gap.

"Yes," the man called across the open stretch of grass. "I thought you were one of them?"

"Who?" Jake replied as Alicia snuggled next to him.

"I don't know who they were. But they came a few seasons ago and wreaked havoc."

Jake shook the man's hand as they came together, noting the dark smudges under his eyes. "What happened?"

"Men came from the south. Dressed in black. They took all the children and any able-bodied men. The women were all defiled and murdered."

"Jesus," Jake uttered, his heart sinking. "How did you avoid being taken?"

"I was away to the north with my family. When we got back, only Daria was still alive. She told us what had happened before she eventually gave out. We buried her and all the others next to the animal pens."

"I'm so sorry, Toby."

"It's just the three of us now. We've moved into the farmhouse and are just about managing to keep the animals alive. It's been tough."

"I'm sure it has. We passed by Fingles. It looks like these men did the same to them."

"Yes. They slaughtered all of them. After we got home, I went back out there to look for survivors. There were none. I've been back and forth ever since, taking tools and supplies to keep us going. Anyway, what are you doing here, Jake?"

Jake sighed, the horror of what had unfolded bearing down on his shoulders. "I'm here with my daughter," he said, nodding his head towards the girl. "This is Alicia, Katherine's daughter. Alicia, this is Toby."

"Hello," she said sheepishly."

"Hello," he replied, his face becoming sombre. "There is something you should know, Jake. Come with me."

They walked a few hundred yards across the peninsular, heading towards Katherine's grave. When they were within a few feet, Jake's face creased in confusion. "What happened?" he asked, his voice edged with disbelief as he looked at the churned earth.

"They took the body," Toby replied solemnly.

"What! Why?" Jake blurted.

"The leader stood by while the pillaging took place. This is what Daria told us. She said that the leader began sniffing the ground around the grave before he ordered his men to dig up the body. That's all we know, Jake. I am sorry."

Jake walked around the graveside, his fingers caressing the green leaves of the tree that now dwarfed him. "Why did they take you?" he said to himself, looking over at Alicia who was being buffeted by the sea breeze. He looked at the man opposite. "Did the leader have a name?"

"Lukash," the man replied.

"Lukash?" Jake repeated, the words dripping off his tongue like a bad taste. "How far to the south did they come from?" His voice was shaky, anger building within him. Anger he'd not felt for a long time.

"I don't rightly know," the man huffed. "It's a featureless place, with only one settlement of any significance. They called it Vrybergen."

"How far is it from here?"

Toby scratched his head as Alicia snuggled into her father, trying to fend off the cool breeze that battered the land around them. "On foot, it would take you at least two days. On your steel beast, it would be a lot quicker."

"We have time," Jake stated as he looked at his daughter. "If we leave now, I'm sure we'll make it back to Amatoll in time."

"Are you sure, Dad? It might be dangerous?"

"Your daughter is wise, Jake. No one from our kin has ever ventured close enough to see what darkness lurks there. From the accounts we've heard over the seasons, the place is not visible from the land. It lies underneath the rocks in a large sea cave, protected from the elements. Don't stray too close. We would hate for anything to happen to you. Enough people have perished recently, Jake."

"Don't worry. We'll just scoot past on our way home. And if there are any signs of danger, we'll be off like a bat out of hell."

The man's expression remained neutral, oblivious to the musical reference. "Just take care. We'll prepare you some food for the journey. When you reach Fingles, turn left and follow the coast. From what I remember, there is a large lighthouse close by, to warn approaching vessels of the dangerous rocks."

The hairs on the back of Jake's neck prickled to attention. *Lighthouse*, he thought, remembering his trip to Towan Point. Completely unaware that both places were connected. Like the silk threads of a spider's web.

Chapter Five

The sun had already begun its descent as Jake's bike pulled over next to a copse of trees. Alicia hopped off the saddle, removing her helmet, the constant wind ruffling her auburn hair. "There's the lighthouse," she stated as Jake propped the bike onto its stand.

"Yes. I had no idea that they would have such things in this world. In our world, yes, but not here. Come on. Let's take a look," he urged, eyeing the few hundred yards of open ground between the trees and the stone structure.

"I need a wee first," she stated, walking away towards the swaying trunks.

"Good idea. I'll see you by the bike when you're finished," her father replied as he found his own makeshift urinal. A few minutes later, they were huddled out of sight, Jake looking for signs of activity. "Okay. We'll proceed on foot. Now remember, if anything happens, run straight back here and we'll hit the road back to Amatoll. Agreed?"

"Yes, Dad. What time is it?"

He checked his watch, the luminous hands standing proud in the gathering darkness. "Almost seven. Don't worry, we have plenty of time. Stay close to me," he instructed as he tucked a pistol into his waistband.

They set off across the land, tall wispy grass rustling their clothing as they jogged towards the stone structure next to the sea. As they neared, Jake took out his smartphone, switching it on as a low mist rolled in from the sea. "No signal," he said, expecting as much. He selected the camera icon, snapping a few shots of the lighthouse, a sense of unease washing over him.

"Why are you taking pictures?" Alicia enquired.

"No reason," he lied, not wanting to divulge the story of the missing girl from Cornwall. "Come on. Let's explore." They walked the last few feet, coming up against a sturdy-looking door that led inside. Jake tested the catch, the door firmly locked. "I guess they aren't the most welcoming," he said, looking down at his daughter who smiled up at him. Away from the lighthouse, the land rose up sharply, a thin crag barely visible to the naked eye. "Let's go and take a look," Jake said, Alicia nodding in agreement. A rumble of thunder out at sea made the young girl clasp her father's hand as they entered the narrow rocky corridor.

"It's spooky, Dad," she breathed, squeezing his hand with renewed force.

"It's okay. I'm with you," Jake assured her. After a minute of progress, another narrow crevice presented itself to them, stone steps leading downwards into the gloom. "Right," Jake whispered. "Stay close and keep quiet." His daughter nodded, her face tinged with concern as she was enveloped in darkness. After a minute of descending, the steps came out on a rocky landing.

"Woah," Alicia exclaimed as her eyes took in the town beneath her. Clinging to a rocky ledge a hundred feet below her, a collection of hundreds of buildings lay nestled between the sea and the land.

"Tell me about it," Jake breathed, his eyes in sync with his daughter's. He took in the town of Vrybergen, watching as tiny figures bustled around the buildings and jetty, where a large galleon-type vessel gently bobbed on the tide. "I've never seen anything quite like this. In our world or others. It's certainly off the beaten track. You can see why it's remained hidden for so long."

"What shall we do now?" the girl said as Jake's eyes made their way back up from the town, following a rocky pathway that led to their position.

"Not sure? I don't want anyone to spot us. It's a good sprint back to the bike. I say we…"

His voice was cut off abruptly as movement to his left caused him to flinch. Out of the shadows, a large dog inched forward, spittle drooling from a mouth full of black teeth. Around its neck, a thick chain trailed off into a darkened rock-hewn doorway, a shadowy figure emerging a few feet behind the enormous hound. "You've taken a wrong turn, friends."

Jake looked up as the figure shuffled towards them, it's head almost brushing the rocky ceiling above him. The ex-policeman's stomach turned to lead as the strange form towered over them. "Sorry," he started. "We were just resting when we came across the stairs. We'll be on our way." He stepped backwards, taking Alicia's trembling hand in his own.

The dog snarled, its master pulling back on the chain as the beast advanced on them. "Easy, Tykor," the man rasped. "You'll scare them away. And they've only just got here. Be a shame to let them on their way without a tour of the old place."

"Really, we need to go," Jake insisted, his legs rubbery as sweat broke out across his forehead.

"No need to be scared, friend. We mean you no harm," the giant said as he edged closer.

"Dad, I want to go," Alicia said as the hound locked eyes with her. She stared at it, her eyes boring into black voids, partially hidden by matted fur. The dog let out a whelp, edging towards its master.

As the man looked down at the animal, Jake nudged his daughter. "Run," he whispered. "I'm right behind you."

"OI!" the cloaked figure hollered, Jake turning on his heels as he ran for the doorway. Out of the corner of his eye, he spotted several figures look up from the town towards his position before he disappeared up the rocky staircase. "Tykor. Kill!" a gargled voice hollered behind Jake as he broke out into open ground.

"Alicia, run," Jake shouted. "Get to the bike." He heard another whelp as the dog emerged from the split in the rock, running face-first into the ravine wall. Jake knew that had bought him a few precious seconds as his feet ate up the ground. He smiled thinly as he noticed his daughter already settled on the back of the saddle, her helmet in place as the sound of the approaching beast filled his ears. As Jake looked over his shoulder, the hound launched itself at him, the private investigator rolling into the grass as screams and hollers filled his ears. He came up on his haunches, pulling the gun from his waistband, firing two quick shots into the approaching hound's face, killing it instantly. The matted figure fell to its side as Jake cocked his leg over the saddle, firing up the bike as half-a-dozen large men ran towards him, the giant at their centre. "Hang on," he shouted, feeling Alicia's arms wrap around him as the bike lurched forward. Steering to his right, the bike sped away from the group, more shouts and curses dancing around them until they began to fall away.

"Dad," Alicia shouted. "You've forgotten your crash helmet."

"I'm not going back for it," he panted, a rasping laugh escaping his lips as the bike sped across the open land towards a lone mountain in the distance. *That was too close*, he thought. *No more adventures tonight. I need to get this little home safe.*

* * *

Hours later, Jake and Alicia sat next to two gnarled trees, a small fire barely illuminating the forest around them. "Dad. Who do you think they are?"

"I don't know, love. Whoever they are, they're not nice people. I shouldn't have taken you there."

"But they took Mum's body. I wanted to go."

Jake sighed. "I know. But too many people have died over the past few years. Before you came along, things were a little crazy."

"I know, Dad," she replied, knowing the stories and adventures off by heart. "But why take her body?"

"Reggan," her father replied cautiously.

"You think so?"

"It's logical. I was bitten by him and his blood ran through my veins for a long time. You also have his blood, and probably part of your mother did too."

"But I don't understand why they'd take her, Dad?"

"Nor do I really. But it doesn't matter right now. The doorway will open soon. We need to get you home, young lady."

"I can't believe that this is where Mum lived?"

Jake looked over at her, seeing the flames dance in her eyes as Alicia peered back at him. He was transported back a few years, when the forest was green and full of life, with green trees and birds occupying their upper branches. "She lived most of her life here. From a baby to the women that I knew. You would have loved her."

"I do love her, Dad. I just wish she were still here."

"I know. I wish that too," Jake said, a sudden melancholy sweeping over him. A skittering of parched bracken made him look up as a breeze blew through Amatoll, a faint blue light beginning to appear a few feet away from their position. "Come on," he urged, climbing stiffly to his feet. "We'd better get through. Best not to get trapped here."

"Okay," Alicia replied, walking through the blue portal that was gently pulsing between two ancient trees.

Jake wheeled the bike forward, meeting slight resistance as he passed from one world to the next, coming out in a darkened on the southern fringes of Birmingham. In the distance, a car wound its way lazily up Rose Hill, heading for the small town of Bromsgrove a few miles to the south. "We'll be back at the car in a few minutes. With any luck, you'll be tucked up in bed by three."

"I thought I'd be tired, Dad. But I'm wide awake."

"Well, I'm sure you'll fall asleep after a few miles. I'll stop and grab a coffee from somewhere. That should keep me going on the drive back to Cornwall. Come on, let's get out of here before the ghosts come out to play." A minute later, the motorbike rolled quietly through the forest, the blue door behind it vanishing once more. Until the next night.

Chapter Six

A world away, another blue doorway extinguished itself, a tall lone figure standing on rough flagstones as men gathered around him. "What news?" he said, his voice commanding.

"An outlander came," a man who matched his height replied warily.

"How do you know he was an outlander?" the hooded figure probed.

"Coz he was dressed like you, Lukash. He came with a girl. A little girl. We tried to capture him, but the man was clever. He took off and killed my hound before riding off on a steel beast."

"Steel beast?" Lukash countered, removing his hood. His pale skin shone in the torchlight, black hair shielding some of his dark expression. "You mean motorbike?"

"If you say so?" the man replied shrugging his shoulders.

"Lorcan, at first light, take the men back to the place we'd pillaged. Ask questions and don't leave there until you find the answers."

"Why there?"

"Do you remember the grave?"

"Y-yes," Lorcan hesitated.

"There was an engraving, written in English. No one from these lands can write, let alone in English. I'm guessing that whoever visited us, knows the people there. Find the answers, whatever it takes."

"Will do," the man said, retreating a few steps before another man handed him an object. "Oh. He left this behind," Lorcan offered, handing Lukash a black crash helmet.

The man turned it over in his hands, liking the sturdy feeling it gave off. "JS," he said, noticing two white letters embossed on the black exterior. "That could be his initials? Well done, men. You have done well. I know it's late, but head to the Narwhal. Free ale for all of you. Not too much mind. You've got an early start."

"Many thanks," Lorcan said, bowing reverently before they beat a hasty retreat across the quiet streets of Vrybergen.

Lukash strode across the stone floor, ducking into a doorway at the front of a large stone lighthouse that clung to the cliff's edge. He climbed the winding staircase, coming out onto a small landing where an old man sat in a rocking chair. "Papa," he whispered.

The old man in front of him, raised his virtually bald head, yellow watery eyes staring back at him. "Yes, Son. What news?"

"We've had an intruder."

"Intruder," the ancient male croaked, his head tilting upwards. "Go on?"

"He's an outlander. He came here with a little girl but was chased off by the town folk. We're unsure as to why he came here. But rest assured, I'm sending a gathering out to search for answers."

The slumped figure nodded as wall torches cast shadows across the dim interior as the sound of the sea filtered in through the open windows. "What news from Towan Point?"

"Nothing really of note, except..." Lukash stopped abruptly, something occurring to him.

"What is it, Son?"

"We've had a visitor. A man came a few days ago. He was there to see the Thorne woman."

"What is troubling you?"

"It just seems a coincidence that a man turns up in Towan Point, then we have an intruder here."

"You think they're related?" his father quizzed, rising from his chair, his wispy pate almost touching the low ceiling.

"Hard to tell, Papa. But it's worth considering."

"Why did a man visit the Thorne woman?"

"Honestly, I've no idea. Her man left long ago, moving away. She may have another man. Or maybe he's a reporter or someone who's there to help her look for the girl."

"Well, the girl is out of their reach. No one will ever find her, or the others that have made the voyage into the mist. If she had enlisted help, it will be a fool's errand."

"I know. But it is still troubling. Towan Point is our doorway to their world. And we've kept our secret for hundreds of years, Papa. Even the lawmen are prudent enough to leave us be."

"Go back to Towan Point as soon as you can. Keep an eye on the woman. If you suspect danger, do what must be done to keep our sanctuary hidden."

"As you wish," Lukash replied respectfully.

"Now. Come and embrace your father. I am growing ever more tired, Lukash. My time on this plane is coming to an end."

Lukash took two long strides, bending down to embrace the ancient being. "You just need to rest, Papa. You'll get your strength back soon. Maybe we need to move you away from this place? Even I find the conditions here unbearable sometimes."

"But this is my home. And it has been since the land was young. Before the forests came to be and before the influx of men and vampires tainted this great land."

"Maybe a few months at Towan Point might do you good? We have far more provisions there for you."

"Maybe. But there is work to do first. Go now. Let me rest, Son."

"I will see you soon, Papa," Lukash whispered before walking out of the landing area, taking the stone steps two at a time before he came out onto another circular landing.

A cloaked figure near the window turned towards him, her yellow eyes shining brightly in the dim confines. "Lukash," she said.

"Tilly," he replied, walking towards the vampire, the moon's glow illuminating her see-through cloak. "How are things progressing?"

Her lips parted, revealing grey canines and a black tongue. "Slowly," she answered, looking over at the stone coffin in the centre of the room. "But all is in hand. We've had word from the land beyond the mist. They are looking forward to receiving our gift."

Lukash looked into the coffin, the desiccated corpse inside bound in white cloth, a selection of healing stones and amulets placed around the body. A thin mist, violet in colour drifted slowly around the confines of the coffin, gently caressing the body. Lukash watched for a few seconds, relaxing slightly at the sight before him. "Are the spells having any effect?"

"Why yes," Tilly replied, smiling up at him. "If left here, she would rise from her slumbers within ten seasons. Once she has travelled to her new home, her new master will rouse her quickly."

He knew of what she spoke, nodding his head in agreement. "Good work, Tilly," Lukash replied, a smile transforming his face. "I must head back to Towan Point, but I will be back soon to check on you."

"Safe travels, Lukash," she purred. "We will take care of her."

"I know you will. Farewell, Tilly." He looked into the coffin, touching the corpse's shoulder, noting how it felt more substantial than before. "I will see you soon, Katherine Bathurst."

Chapter Seven

Jake stirred as the sound of nearby seagulls drifted in through his window. His eyes fluttered open, the man lying there as he came to, trying to recollect the fuzzy dreams he'd risen from. Grabbing his shorts from the floor next to the bed, he made his way quietly downstairs, flicking the kettle before pulling a large frying pan from a cupboard. Five minutes later, Jake was sat at the kitchen table, peering out at his back garden as bright sunlight began to warm the land. He typed a message to Emma Thorne, asking for her ex-husband's address, along with a picture and any other relevant information he'd need. A few minutes later, Jake placed his laptop on the kitchen table as a bacon-infused aroma drifted around the house, prompting movement from upstairs. As he checked flights to Malaga in southern Spain, Alicia walked into the kitchen, rubbing the sleep from her eyes. "Morning, poppet," he smiled. "Did you sleep okay?"

"I did," she replied, wrapping her arms around Jake, kissing him on the cheek. "What are you doing?"

"Booking flights to Spain."

"Spain? Why?" she said, breaking the embrace.

"A job, which I've just taken. I'll be gone for a few days. Jo and Wilf are going to have you over at their house while I'm away."

"But I'll miss you, Dad," she countered, placing a hand on her hip.

"Come here," he said, opening his arms. She complied, sitting on his lap, Jake loving the closeness they shared. "It'll be for a few days. I'll be home soon, I promise."

"Okay, Dad," she huffed, sliding off his lap before walking over to the frying pan. "Are you making this for me?" Alicia grinned.

"Go on then. It's ready to go. Just pop a few more rashers in for me please, love."

"You stay there, Dad. I'll cook it for you."

"You're a good un," Jake replied happily before selecting his flights. He then booked a hire car, along with a reserving a room at a small guest house in the heart of the small Spanish town.

A rap at the front door made Jake look up from the screen, heading towards the front of the house, grabbing a hoodie from the coat hooks under the stairs. A familiar face smiled back at him as he opened the door, Wilf appraising the younger man. "I've seen more meat on a cockerel's kneecaps," he smirked, looking at Jake's legs.

"Did you just come around to insult me, or did you smell the bacon?"

"Bacon," he replied readily. "You know me and bacon, Son," he replied, walking past Jake into the house. "Hello, you," he chirped as he walked into the kitchen, Alicia beaming up at him.

The girl skipped across the room, jumping into his arms, red sauce smeared across her lips. "Hello, you," she replied, kissing his weather-beaten cheek.

Jake handed Wilf a piece of kitchen towel. "Here. Wipe that off your face, or Jo will think you've been mugged."

Wilf did so, scrunching the paper in his hand before placing it next to Jake's laptop. "Jo asked me to pop to the shops to buy her a paper," he stated. "I thought I'd come and say hello on my way back."

"What you up to today?"

The older man shrugged. "Nothing much. Dinner and then that blasted television."

"I was meaning to ask you. Would you be able to look after Alicia for a few days?"

"Of course? Why?" he probed.

"I've got to travel to Spain for a few days, to locate someone related to a case," he replied, eyeing his daughter across the kitchen. "Come through to the lounge. Alicia, could you sort out the sandwiches while I talk to Uncle Wilf?"

"Man talk?" the girl replied, a pouty expression on her face.

"Something like that. Brown sauce on both, please," Jake replied, winking at her. Wilf followed Jake into the lounge, easing himself into the sofa as the younger man sat on the windowsill. "A young girl has been abducted in a fishing village to the south. The mother contacted me, asking for my help in finding her."

"When was she taken?"

"A year ago," was the clipped response.

"So, where is this Spain place that you're going to?"

"It's a few hours to the south by plane. I'll be flying tomorrow lunchtime, probably spending at least three days there, in hope of finding the father, who may be able to shed some light on what went on. And there's more."

"Go on," Wilf urged.

"We went to Shetland, or what's left of it." He saw the older man's expression change, ploughing on before the questions came. "There are only a few people left, Wilf. Men came from the south. They killed pretty much everyone on Shetland, along with the Finglers."

"Fuckenell," Wilf retorted. "Bastards!"

"My thoughts exactly. Tell me, do you know the land to the south of Elksberg?"

Before he could reply, Alicia appeared, handing both men a steaming mug of coffee before disappearing back into the kitchen. Wilf took a sip from his mug, eyeing Jake across the room. "I've never ventured there. It's a sparse land, devoid of life, except for a few settlements. I've heard tales of a place called, Vrybergen though. A hidden town next to the great sea."

"That's where we ended up. We headed south from Shetland, arriving there about an hour later. We saw the town. It is hidden from view. The whole place sits inside a huge cave, next to the sea. We didn't stay long as someone appeared and chased us off. Well, chased us anyway, with intentions to kill both Alicia and me."

"Fuckenell, Jake! You could have both been killed."

"I know. I shouldn't have taken her there, but I was curious to see the place. There is another reason why I wanted to check it out?"

"What's that?"

"They took Katherine's body."

His eyes widened, his mug shaking in his hand. "What!"

"I've no idea why, apart from what Toby told me. Said that the leader was sniffing and scratching at the ground before ordering the body to be removed. They took it with them, Wilf."

"The fiends! I've half a mind to head back there and raise hell."

"I know, but as you said, it's a dangerous place. And it looks like the place is very well guarded. Getting into the town would prove difficult. I just wanted to let you know."

Wilf slumped in his seat, suddenly appearing weary. "I miss her, Jake. There is not a day goes by that I don't think about Kath. Alice and Cedric too," he said, mentioning Katherine's younger sister who was killed a short while before Jake first ventured to Amatoll forest, along with his older brother, who Jake did meet.

"I know, Wilf. I miss her terribly. And Alicia does too. I just would love to know why these men wanted her body? It'd be of no use to them? Unless..." his words trailed off.

"Unless they knew about Reggan and Korgan." It was a statement, not a question, taking Jake by surprise.

"Yes. I thought that. The fact that they were sniffing the ground. Maybe these people can sense that kind of thing?"

"Maybe they can. But whoever they are and whatever reasons they had, they've taken our Kath's body and killed my kin. That cannot go unpunished."

"Well, let's park it for now," Jake replied evenly. "When I'm back from Spain we'll talk more about it."

"Okay, Jake. Whatever you think is best."

"Breakfast is ready," Alicia called from the kitchen.

"Come on," Jake urged. "Let's get some grub down us before Jo sends out a search party for you."

"Good idea," Wilf agreed. "She knows I like an adventure. If only she knew eh?"

Chapter Eight

The next day, Jake sat in the departures lounge at Bristol airport, a large cup of coffee next to his laptop. He'd driven up from Tintagel, the ninety-minute journey without incident as the West Country sat under sunny skies. He'd checked in, filing through airport security like a lemming before finding a coffee outlet close to his gate. His laptop was open, a file folder titled Lauren Thorne waiting to be clicked as he sipped at his coffee. He double-clicked the keyboard, a Word document and a JPEG image presenting themselves to the private investigator. He opened the picture, staring at Joseph Thorne's smiling face. He looked roughly the same age as Jake, a week's worth of stubble covering his chin. He wore steel-rimmed glasses, giving him a geography teacher look. Out of curiosity, Jake typed his name into Google, clicking on the Wikipedia entry at the top of the page. Originally from London, Joseph Thorne now resides in Cornwall with his family. *Strange*, Jake thought. *Not much information, for such a well-known author, who'd sold millions of books.* He closed the webpage, looking up at the flight information screen that told him he'd be boarding in ten minutes. Packing away at a leisurely pace, he sauntered over to the gate, holidaymakers and business travellers already lined up, itching to get into the air.

The flight was uneventful, Jake dozing off shortly after take-off. He was bumped a few times by a passing trolley, his eyes fluttering open for a few short seconds before he resumed his nap, the elderly couple next to him, gently snoring as the plane headed ever southwards. An hour later, he settled into his rental car, A Seat Ibiza, with the steering wheel on the left-hand side of the car. *I forgot about that*, he thought, trying to recollect the last time he'd driven in Europe before keying the destination into the navigation system. After leaving the hubbub of Malaga, he relaxed as the Andalucían countryside opened up before him a few kilometres after pulling off the main highway. The temperature outside the car was hotter than he was used to, Jake thankful of the air-conditioning. His eyes scanned the road ahead as he passed small villages and farms, the barren landscape giving way to forested valleys and the mountains of the Sierra Nevada beyond.

Three hours after touching down, Jake parked his car outside a small guest-house in the centre of the town. He lugged his suitcase and laptop bag up a steep flight of terracotta steps before thankfully walking into the cool interior. A middle-aged woman, with flame-red hair appeared from through a doorway, smiling at the man across the counter. "Hola, buenas tardes,"

"Buenas tardes," Jake replied. "¿Habla Ingles?"

The woman nodded. "Yes. But not so well."

"It sounds perfect to me," Jake responded, smiling. "I have a room booked for three nights, maybe more."

"Mr Stevenson, no?"

"Yes. Jake."

"Welcome to el hotel Limonero," she enthused. The woman rummaged around under the counter, asking Jake to fill in a piece of paper and provide his passport. He did so, appraising the woman. She was a good few years his senior, olive skin and a large mole under her left eye, which seemed to accentuate her Mediterranean looks. She was dressed simply, denim shorts and a yellow top with bare shoulders, Jake's eyes spotting a colourful gecko tattoo on her upper arm. "Here is your key, Mr Stevenson. Your room is on the first floor. Take the stairs next to the entrance. Desayuno - I mean breakfast is from seven till nine and the bar is open until midnight."

"Perfect. I'm pretty hungry. Can I get a bite to eat?"

"Certainly. We serve food until ten."

"That's great," he replied, noting that it was almost six. "I'll unpack and head back down in a bit."

"Okay. I will see you then. Enjoy your stay, Jake,"

"I'm sure I will..."

"Manuela," she replied.

"Thanks, Manuela. See you later." He headed for his room, a large wrought iron key clamped between his teeth as he navigated the narrow stairwell. Five minutes later, he'd hung all his clothes up and plugged his laptop in to charge. He looked around the spartan room, a large bed the centrepiece. Across the room, a large window opened out onto a narrow street, another white-washed building seeming only a few feet away. There was a large dark wooden wardrobe, dresser and flat-screen television on the wall above it. He looked in the full-length mirror, wondering if he should change out of his combat shorts and Fleetwood Mac T-Shirt. It'll be okay for tonight, he thought, grabbing his key and smartphone from the dresser before heading out of the room. He walked outside, dialling Jo's mobile number as he watched locals go about their business.

"Hello, Jake," a familiar voice said down the line.

"Hiya," he replied happily. "How's everything there?"

"All good. We're just cooking dinner. Alicia is out in the garden with Wilf, who is attempting to cut the grass."

"Bless him," Jake replied, smiling at the image floating in his mind. "I'm just calling to let you know that I'm at the hotel."

"That's good. How were the flight and drive?"

"Good. No issues at all. It's bloody hot here, although it's cooling off nicely now. Probably because I'm up in the mountains."

"Well, I'll let them know that you're safe and well. Do you want to speak to Alicia?"

"It's okay. She sounds like she's probably got her hands full."

"You're not wrong there. Okay. I'll let them know you've called. Have a cold beer on me."

He heard her chuckle down the line, his throat suddenly parched. "I intend to, very quickly. Take care and I'll give you a call tomorrow at some point."

"Okay, hun. Bye for now."

"Bye," he said, ending the call with a swipe of his thumb. Before taking that drink, Jake decided to take a quick stroll, to familiarise himself with the new town that he found himself in. He passed an endless procession of whitewashed buildings, adorned with wooden doors and shutters, the smell of olive groves and pinecones wafting through the town, relaxing the former police officer. Many outlets were still open, enticing aromas drifting his way. Elderly men sat drinking coffee, taking in the world through beady eyes and weather-beaten expressions. He took out his mobile phone, selecting the address given to him by Emma Thorne. Starting the directional mode, Jake ambled through the winding streets, his destination approaching with every step. After a few minutes and several left and right turns, Jake was standing outside a restaurant called,

Don Quixote. He pretended to dial a number, leaning against a lamppost, his eyes scanning the edifice and interior. Large hunks of Serrano ham hung from wooden rafters, as a lone waitress tended tables inside and out. The building had three storeys, some of the windows shuttered. He looked upwards, spying a man roughly his age leaning against a wrought-iron Juliet balcony before heading back into his apartment. *That's him*, Jake thought, happy with his detective work. Putting the phone back into his pocket, he walked back towards his hotel, a growling stomach making the man quicken his pace.

Five minutes later, he was perched at the bar on a stout wooden stool, waiting for Manuela to appear. As if reading his mind, she appeared from a doorway, smiling warmly at him. "What can I get you?"

Jake pointed at the tap in front of him, his throat aching. "A pint of Alhambra, please," he croaked.

"Sin problema," she replied in her native tongue, pouring the lager into a long-fluted pint glass before sliding it across to him.

He lifted it to his lips, enjoying the crisp taste as it cut through his thirst. "Boy, I needed that. Could I see the menu, please?"

She handed him a leather-bound menu, watching his expression as he tried to decipher the text. "I would recommend the wild boar. Raul brought on in this morning. It's been slow-cooked. Very peppery. I think you will like it."

"Sold," Jake said happily, taking another long pull on his beer.

"Okay then," Manuela replied, walking back through the doorway, Spanish words floating out of the kitchen towards him. "It won't be so long," the woman said as she began to stack glasses underneath the bar from a dishwasher. Jake drained his glass, Manuela placing another in front of him seconds later.

"Cheers."

"Salud," she replied. "So, what brings you to Yegen?"

Jake placed the drink on the bar, wiping the suds from his whiskers. "I've never been here before. I went on honeymoon many years ago in Benalmadena and thought I'd explore the interior a bit."

"It's very nice. You should visit Granada and the Alhambra. Very pretty. Is your wife not with you?"

A dark cloud passed over him, his face dropping slightly. "No. She died a few years ago."

"Merde!" Manuela blurted. Jake knew what it meant, watching the woman's expression change. "I'm very sorry, Jake."

"It's okay, Manuela. It was a long time ago. My wife would have loved it here."

Manuela regained her composure, smiling at the younger man. "It's a very nice place to live. It used to be a hive of activity. Have you heard of Gerald Brenan?"

"Doesn't ring a bell? Who is he?"

"He was a famous English writer, who lived in the village during the 1920s. He wrote a book called *South from Granada* about his time here. Very good, no."

"I'll have to take a look on Amazon," he replied politely.

"And now we have another famous English writer living in the town. Joseph Thorne."

The hairs on Jake's forearms sprang to attention at the mention of Emma's husband. "I've heard of him. He lives here?" Jake said, trying to keep his voice under control as the tension built inside him.

"Yes. For a year or so, I think? He's staying at the *Don Quixote.*"

Wanting to make the most of the unexpected development, Jake probed further. "Cool. Does he ever come in here?"

"He used to, but not for a few months. That idiota at the Quixote is taking his Euro's."

Jake chuckled. "I take it you don't like him?"

"He's from the north, Bilbao. Not a real Spaniard." A young couple walked over to the bar, taking Manuela away from Jake, letting him digest the information. *Oh well, it looks like a few pints at the Don Quixote is on the cards,* he thought mischievously.

Chapter Nine

The heat of the day had dissipated, locals milling about as Jake watched from a table outside the *Don Quixote.* A van had pulled up outside the restaurant a few minutes previous, two local men unloading several boxes as the diesel engine gently puttered its fumes into the Andalucían sky. "Hello," a female voice started, causing Jake to look up at a young woman with a pen and paper in her hands.

"Err, hi," he responded, smiling up at her.

"What can I get for you?" she asked, her lilting Spanish accent pleasing to his ears.

"Could I have a large cerveza and the paella de mariscos, please."

"No problem. I thought you were English," she stated, placing a hand on her hip.

"Do is look that obvious?"

"Not so much. I just know these things. There is an Englishman staying above. He's just ordered his supper," she said, inclining her head towards a lone figure underneath the awning. Jake looked over, his heart rate quickening as he confirmed Joseph Thorne, who was stood smoking a cigarette as he leaned against a lamppost.

"Well, I'll try and blend in. I'm Jake by the way," he replied in a friendly tone.

"Veronique," she added before turning towards the establishment. "I will bring out your cerveza in a few minutes, Jake."

He watched as the young waitress weaved between wrought iron tables, her long dark hair swaying behind her as she went. Jake returned his gaze to the street, watching as the van and its inhabitants slowly rolled off along the cobbled street. Iron chair legs scraped against stone making Jake turn to his left as Joseph Thorne seated himself at the next table, nodding towards the private investigator. "Evening," the man said simply.

"Evening," Jake echoed, seeing the man's eyes narrow slightly.

"You're far from home?"

Jake smiled. "Yes, you could say that."

The conversation stalled as Veronique placed a large glass of lager in front of Jake, turning to Thorne. "Another?"

"Please," Thorne replied politely, lighting another cigarette. He looked at Jake. "You don't mind?"

The other Englishman shook his head. "Carry on." He reached forward, sliding his glass towards him before taking the head off his pint, savouring the crisp taste.

"What brings you to Yegen?"

Jake had rehearsed his story over and over, hoping that the other man fell for it. "My late wife and I were married in Benalmadena a long time ago. I've never been back, so I thought I'd take a few days off to revisit and explore the interior a bit."

"Oh. Sorry to hear about your wife," Thorne muttered as Veronique placed a large glass of Rioja in front of him. "Gracias," he added, switching smoothly to Spanish before the waitress headed over towards fresh customers.

"That's okay. It was many years ago. How about you? Do you live here?"

Jake sensed a change in the man's demeanour, noticing his expression harden. "Yes. I've lived here for a while. I'm a writer."

"Oh, okay," the younger man added, his eyebrows raising. "Anything I might have read?"

"Depends on what you like to read," was the clipped response.

"I'll read anything, but I prefer horror and thrillers."

"Well, I write horror. My name's Joseph Thorne."

Jake's eyes widened, carrying off the shocked expression with ease. "Shit, really? I've read one of your books, The Winding Lane. I loved it."

He was expecting the other man to smile in appreciation of great feedback. Instead, Thorne ground his cigarette into the ashtray on the table and rubbed the back of his neck. "Not one of my best books, but thank you. Sorry, authors are usually wracked with self-doubt. I'm glad you enjoyed it though." He looked at the man across the cobbled pavement, his interest piqued. "So, what do you do?"

Jake added to his cover story, not wanting to alert the writer as to his intentions. "I run my own airport taxi service in Birmingham."

"Oh," Thorne muttered. "I bet you're busy," was all he could muster.

"Pretty much non-stop. It pays the bills and lets me have the occasional trip like this, or a week in Cornwall with my daughter."

He sensed a flicker of recognition in the other man's eyes. It was there for a split-second before Thorne regained his composure, taking a large glug of wine. "I lived there before I moved here. I was married, but it didn't work out."

"Oh, sorry to hear that. It's a lovely part of the world. I have family in Tintagel."

"Nice place," Thorne countered, the wine seeming to relax the author. "Love the post office on the main street. My ex-wife painted it. She's an artist."

"Cool," Jake said neutrally, trying to coax further information out of him. He drained his pint, motioning towards the other man. "Fancy another?"

"Why not," Thorne replied, smiling at Jake.

As empty plates and bowls were taken away from the table, more drinks were served as both men reclined slightly in their chairs, sated by the local fayre from the kitchen inside. Thorne lit another cigarette, blowing smoke into the ever-darkening skies. "What are your plans for the rest of your stay?" he asked.

"Going to drive to Granada tomorrow," Jake responded as he placed his beer in front of him.

"You'll like it there," Thorne stated, his speech starting to slur.

"And you? More writing?"

"Yes. I'm halfway through my latest novel. I'll spend a few hours on it tomorrow, followed by a wander around the local market."

"I may take a look at that myself. I should really get my daughter a little something. Do you have kids?" The question was casual but loaded. Jake watched the other man closely, hoping for a way in.

"I did," Thorne whispered, his voice barely audible over the passing traffic. "She went missing and was never found. The police think she drowned. Washed out to sea."

Jake's fake shock wasn't picked up by Thorne, the author taking another hefty gulp of his Rioja. "Oh God! I'm so sorry to hear that."

"It's okay," Thorne added. "After that, things went downhill. We never recovered and I came to live out here. You'd be surprised how a change of scenery can mask your grief."

"I'm really sorry to hear that, Joe," Jake soothed, trying to appear familiar in hope of extracting more information. "It's a lovely place, but the sea can be dangerous."

A stray tear fell from Thorne's eye, the author wiping it away quickly. "Yeah, the police told us. If only they knew the truth?"

Jake leant forward, sensing an opening. "What do you mean?" he urged.

"My daughter's not dead. She was taken, because of me."

"What? Who took her?"

The author quickly regained his composure, shaking himself free of his guilt. "Sorry. I've said too much. I'd better call it a night," he blurted, draining his glass. "Nice to meet you, Jake. Enjoy the rest of your trip." He got up on unsteady legs, zigzagging towards a door next to the restaurant's entrance.

"So, it's true," Jake said to himself. "She's alive."

Chapter Ten

The following evening, Jake sat at the same table, his belly groaning after a large fish stew the locals called, Cataplana. He took a swig of his beer as Joseph Thorne sat down next to him. Jake looked at him, seeing dark smudges under his eyes, along with unkempt hair and a stubbly chin. "I'm so sorry about last night," he began. "I let the wine and my emotions get the better of me. Let me buy you a beer." He signalled to the waitress, ordering two drinks before looking sheepishly at his new drinking partner.

"It's okay, Joe," Jake replied, seeing the anguish etched on the other man's face. He looked broken, utterly bereft of resolve. Jake decided to change tack and go for it. "I have something to apologise for."

"What?"

"I wasn't completely honest with you last night. Yes, my name's Jake. But I don't live in Birmingham, and I don't run a taxi company. Hear me out, Joe. You need to hear this."

"I'm listening," the older man said, his expression changing.

"I live in Tintagel. Your ex-wife asked me to come and see you." He saw the other man flinch, the wrought-iron legs of the chair grating against the stone floor. "I'm a Private Investigator. Emma has asked me to help find Lauren."

At the mention of his daughter's name, Thorne baulked, his eyes filling with tears. "How do you…" his voice trailing off.

"I've been to your house. Emma thinks that Lauren is still alive, and that someone in Towan Point knows where she is."

"It's bloody pointless," Thorne hissed. "She's gone!"

The policeman in Jake rose to the surface. "You said she was still alive?"

"Yes, I know… But she's gone to us."

"I don't understand, Joe? If she's alive, then there is a chance we can find her." Both men fell silent as drinks were placed on the table, the author gulping down half his glass in one go. "I can help you both."

"No, you can't, Jake. She is out of our reach and it's all my fault."

"Does this have something to do with the barmaid?"

Thorne nodded, realising that the man opposite knew his sordid past. "Yes. Ciara. It was a stupid fucking mistake that I'll regret for the rest of my life. I loved Emma. Hell, I still love her, but my head was turned by a pretty young thing."

"Don't beat yourself up. You're not the first and you won't be the last to do what you've done. Tell me about Ciara?"

Joe flinched again, reaching across the table for his cigarettes. He lit one, his hands trembling slightly. "She worked at the Narwhal. One of the only people in the village who gave me the time of day. I wanted to write a story about Towan Point and the family that has held it in their grip for generations."

"The Longfords?"

"Yes. Ciara is one of them, but friendly. Probably too friendly, if you know what I mean?" Thorne smiled, his face transformed for a few seconds. "None of the others would let me ask questions about the family, or the lighthouse that they've owned for hundreds of years. But Ciara did. She told me everything."

"Like what?" Jake probed.

Thorne looked around himself, assured that no one was listening to their conversation. "The Longford's have ruled Towan Point since the Dark Ages. The place is off the grid, as you've seen. Hardly anyone ever goes in, and even fewer ever come out. They are very powerful. Not even the police have the balls to question them."

"I've never heard of them," Jake countered.

"And why would you? As I said, they keep to themselves. Do you remember American Werewolf in London?" Jake's nodded response was enough for Thorne to continue. "Towan Point is like East Proctor. It keeps its secrets well hidden."

Jake took a swig of his beer, an involuntary shiver shooting up his spine, despite the warmth of the Spanish evening. "So, the police have closed the case and that's that?"

"Pretty much. When the Longford's found out that Ciara was pregnant, they came to the house and it turned ugly. I was ordered to leave. Emma was heartbroken and pretty much ended it there and then. So, I moved out, staying with my Mother for a few days before heading here."

"And what happened to Ciara?"

"That's the thing. She's vanished too. We'd been texting during our... affair, but once I left the village, her phone was disconnected."

"Might be a coincidence? After all, her family may have destroyed her phone?"

"Maybe," Thorne replied. "But she also went off the grid at the same time that Lauren went missing. Personally, I think the Longford's punished her for bringing shame on the family. She was terrified of Lukash, the leader of the tribe. Be warned if you're going to continue this. He's not one to meddle with."

"Lucas?" Jake said, a memory sparking within his subconscious.

"No. Lukash. Strange name," Thorne replied.

"I'm just gonna pop to the loo."

"Okay," the other man replied.

Jake stood up, his legs feeling rubbery as he made his way to the rear of the establishment. He shouldered his way into the toilet, his mind a tumult of thoughts. *Lukash. It must be the same guy who took Katherine's body. But what was he doing all the way out there?* He finished what he was doing, flushing the toilet and splashing cold water on his face before making his way back outside. "Now, where were we?"

"Be careful with the Longfords. They are dangerous."

Jake smiled thinly, not wanting to divulge too much information to the man across the table. "Well, I'm a former police officer and can take care of myself, Joe. But thanks for your concern. Is there anything else that you can think of? It might seem trivial, but anything may help track your daughter down."

"There is something. Something that I've told no one about, even Emma."

Jake leaned forward, his pulse quickening. "Go on."

"Just before the shit hit the fan, Ciara stayed behind after the bar had closed one night. She seemed spooked about something, but couldn't talk in the pub. Once she got off, she took me to the lighthouse, telling me that no one was there. We snuck in through a back door near to the rocks, walking down a flight of steps into a large basement."

"What was down there?"

"Not much, just boxes and old furniture. But there was another flight of steps that led further down. That's what she wanted to show me. She said that at the bottom of the stairs is another doorway. One that if you go through, you never come back."

The hairs on Jake's neck prickled to attention, sweat breaking out across his forehead. "Did you see it?"

"No," Joe sighed. "We walked halfway down the stairs into the darkness. It was freezing down there and damp. Then, a blue glow appeared far below us. Ciara wanted to show me, but a noise from above told us that we weren't alone. We scarpered. That was the last time I saw her."

Jake slumped in his chair, the author noticing the other man's pallid complexion. "What did you think was down there?"

"No idea. Another doorway perhaps. I don't know, Jake. Whatever it was, it had Ciara on edge."

"Okay, Joe. Thanks for the information. I will take it from here," Jake said, rising from the table.

"Where are you going?" Thorne asked quizzically, concerned by the other man's expression.

"I need to go home. I have work to do." He walked away from Thorne, Jake's heart hammering in his chest. *Another doorway,* he thought. *But where does this one lead to?*

* * *

Jake climbed out of the Volvo, heading across the main street towards the Narwhal. The weather had turned, dark clouds seeming to grip the Cornish coast. He ducked inside as the first droplets of rain from above hit the pavement around him. Inside, the small bar was almost empty, save for a few locals hunkered in the corner next to an open fire that radiated heat across the confined space. He walked over to the bar, seating himself at a stool as a middle-aged woman appeared from a doorway. She smiled hesitantly, shuffling over towards Jake. "Hello. What can I get you?"

Jake returned the smile, pointing at one of the lager taps. "Pint of Heineken, please. Are you doing food?"

"Just the lunch menu," she replied, handing him a small laminated card.

He quickly scanned the menu as his drink was poured. "I'll have a steak sandwich, please."

"Righto," she confirmed, her Cornish accent soft and light, at odds with her school mistress appearance.

He took a sip of his pint, eyeing the bar. "Nice place. Not been here for a while."

The woman turned around, scrutinising him. "You've been here before? You don't look familiar?"

"I was here last summer. There was a different barmaid on that day. Ciara, I think. Does she not work here anymore?"

"Malcolm," the woman called, her expression changing utterly. Jake heard heavy footsteps behind him as the barmaid addressed him. "Get out! We don't like outsiders sniffing around Towan Point. Get out and stay away."

Before Jake could interject, a large hand clamped down onto his shoulder, pulling him off the stool. He turned around, craning his neck at the figure in front of him. A large male, a full head taller than Jake stood there, motioning towards the door. One eye was milky white, his teeth discoloured and crooked, spittle hanging from purple lips. "Okay," Jake lamented. "I wasn't that hungry anyway." He stepped around the giant, heading out of the bar as beady eyes followed his exit. Shutting the door of his Volvo, Jake looked back at the entrance of the pub, Malcolm staring at him, a lop-sided grin on his face. "I wouldn't want to meet you in a dark alley. Or a dark lighthouse," he said before pulling away towards the far side of the village. Two minutes later, he knocked on the farmhouse door as the heavens began their deluge.

"Jake," Emma said, a surprised look on her face. "Come in."

"Thanks," he replied, slipping his trainers off before being ushered through to the kitchen.

"I'll put the kettle on." Jake seated himself, looking at a large canvas that stood proud against the far wall. It was partially completed, an ancient church surrounded by chocolate box cottages and fields.

"Is that your work in progress?"

"Sort of," she blushed. "Anyway, how did you get on? Your text had me up all night."

"Sorry about that. I was rushing to get to the plane and my phone was about to die. I have much to tell you."

Two minutes later, Emma placed a large mug of coffee in front of him, seating herself across the table. "Okay. What happened?"

"I met Joe. We shared a few drinks and he opened up about the whole thing. When I told him who I was and what I was doing there, I expected him to run a mile. But he didn't. He laid it all out on the table, so to speak." He looked across the table, seeing the anguish on Emma Thorne's face. "He deeply regrets what happened. He looks a broken man."

Emma let out a sob, Jake reaching across to squeeze her hand. "Sorry, Jake," she blurted. "Hearing you say that has opened old wounds."

"It's okay. I totally understand. He also agrees with you. He thinks that Lauren is still alive."

"What?" she countered, tears rolling down her cheeks. "He never said that to me. He just kept telling me to let it go and move on." She buried her face in paint-stained hands, Jake sat motionless, letting her grief flood out.

"He also told me about Ciara's disappearance. I know that this might sting a little, but Joe said that after he left the village, Ciara's phone went offline. He's not spoken or heard from her since."

Her shoulders slumped, the woman looking bereft of strength. "I know he did wrong. And I know that it takes two to tango. But I wouldn't want anything bad to have happened to her. She's someone's daughter after all."

Jake nodded. "On my way here, I stopped at the Narwhal. I wanted to test my boundaries, so to speak. I asked the barmaid about Ciara and was quickly ejected by an oaf of a man."

"Malcolm," Emma replied, shaking her head. "He's a wrong un, one of the mob that turned up here. Be careful, Jake. I want you to help me, but I don't want you to end up in hospital, or worse."

"Let me worry about that, Emma." He took a sip of coffee, the full-bodied taste to his liking. "There is more. And this is where I need you to have an open mind."

"I'm listening."

"Joe told me that just before you found out what was going on, Ciara took him to the lighthouse one night. Something had scared her, and she wanted to show Joe what it was."

"And what was it?" Emma urged, her face tense.

"Okay. This is where I need you to be open-minded. It was a doorway, underneath the lighthouse. A doorway that Ciara said you never come out of."

Emma got up from the table and began pacing the kitchen, her slippered feet scuffing the tiled floor. "He never mentioned the doorway, but he'd said some really odd things in the weeks before he left."

"Like what?"

"He'd walked past the lighthouse several times. Said there was something sinister about it and that he'd spotted the Longford's taking large bundles from a Land Rover into a door at the back of the lighthouse. He said that they looked like body bags. Naturally, I dismissed it at the time. But looking back, it does seem odd. What does this mean?"

"I'm not totally sure," Jake lied, knowing that a doorway between this world and another existed underneath the landmark. "But whatever is down there spooked Ciara and when Joe was talking about it, he looked scared. If there is a doorway down there. A doorway that no one ever comes out of, maybe Lauren is down there somewhere?"

Emma stopped, her eyes locking onto Jake's. "Okay. So, what do we do?"

Before Jake could answer, a loud banging could be heard from the hallway. "Are you expecting anyone?"

Emma flinched, shaking her head. "No," she replied, her voice quivering with fear. She headed into the hallway, Jake a few steps behind her. A large silhouette was on the other side of the partially glazed door, seeming to make the hallway darker. The woman opened the door, three figures stood before her.

Jake recognised the barmaid and giant from the pub, the other man new to him. He was tall, with pale skin and tousled black hair. "I hear you've been asking after Ciara?" he said, his voice making Emma shrink away from the doorway.

Jake stepped forward, his legs rubbery, his throat dry. "What of it?"

"Whoever you are, stranger, I would advise that you leave this place and never come back. Nothing good will come of it."

"And who are you?" Jake countered, taking a step forward.

"Lukash Longford. I spotted you at the lighthouse. What business do you have poking around my village?"

Jake sized the man up, wanting to extract answers about his beloved Katherine's body before choking the life out of him. "Your village? The last time I checked it was a free country. I can go wherever I like, mate."

The giant took a step forward, his knuckles whitening as he clenched his fists, ready for the attack. "Easy, Malcolm. We mean the stranger no harm. This is just a polite warning. Whatever the woman wants from you, be advised, do not interfere in our matters."

"I don't know what you're talking about. Emma is a friend of mine. I was just checking out the local sites on my way out of the village."

"You were asking about Ciara," the woman barked.

"And?" Jake huffed. "I just remembered her name last time I was here."

"Just be mindful, stranger," Lukash soothed. "We keep to our own here." He took a step forward, coming to within a few feet of Jake who held his ground. He was about to continue when his face changed. Changed utterly as he caught the scent of the man on the doorstep. Dark eyes were drawn to Jake's pendant, the head of the Longford clan seeming to recoil slightly. "We bid you farewell," he said, taking a step backwards, his eyes never leaving Jake's.

They watched from the doorstep as the three figures retreated up the driveway, turning right as they reached the road to the village. "Jesus!" Emma croaked. "What the hell was all that about?"

"Let's go back inside and finish our coffees, then digest what just happened." They walked back into the kitchen, seating themselves once more. "Well, that was interesting," Jake quipped.

"Interesting? More like bloody terrifying," Emma retorted. "I thought it was going to kick-off."

"So did I. But something stopped the leader in his tracks."

"Yes. I noticed that too. Do you know what?"

Jake reached into his shirt, twirling the pendant between forefinger and thumb. *What should I tell her?* "Look, Emma. I cannot say too much, in case I'm wrong. But I've met people like this before, many years ago. You're just going to have to trust me until I can tell you more."

"Why can't you tell me now? Come on, Jake. I need to know."

"Because, if I tell you, I cannot un-tell you. And if I'm wrong, you'll think I'm bonkers."

Despite the situation, she smiled over the rim of her coffee mug. "Okay. I will trust you, but you must tell me soon."

"I will. I'll head home after the coffee. But I'll be back in Towan Point tonight."

Her eyes widened. "To do what?"

Jake grinned. "To find the doorway that no one comes out of."

Chapter Eleven

"Just be careful," Wilf said gravely. "Remember what happened last time. We almost lost you."

"I'll be careful," the younger man replied calmly. "But if anything does happen, you know where I was when the shit hit the fan."

"Don't jest about such things. What would I tell Jo? She knows nothing of this. And Alicia needs you. We all do." Both men watched as Alicia hooted with joy as Jo pushed her higher and higher on the swings in the local playground. The older man smiled. "I never thought I would end up here, with a new family. Jo is the best thing that ever happened to old Wilf."

"She certainly is. She's one in a million. And she loves you, Alicia does too."

"And you," the older man observed. "We're a family, and families stick together."

"I know. Don't worry, I'll take precautions."

"This family…"

"The Longfords."

"Yes. The Longfords. You really think that they have the little girl?"

"I do. If there is a doorway underneath the lighthouse, chances are Lauren was taken through it. After that, she could be anywhere. I've no idea where I'll come out. Whether in your land or somewhere else entirely. But I've done this before. And I'll be home before you know it."

"You were younger then. You're getting on in years, Jake."

"I'm forty-two," he replied defensively. "You're a good twenty years older than me, but it's not stopped you chasing monsters."

"True. So, what time will you leave?"

"About nine. It's an hour drive and I'm not going to park too close by. There's another town a few miles to the north. I'll park there and head to Towan Point along the coastal path. I should be at the lighthouse by eleven, give or take."

"And if you do find a doorway, you'll be gone for at least one night."

"Yes. That's the plan to start with. I very much doubt that Lauren will be sat waiting for me to pick her up. So, I'll have to scout about wherever I end up before coming back through the doorway. If all goes to plan, I'll be back in Cornwall on Saturday morning. Just promise me one thing."

"What's that?"

"If I get stuck, don't come after me. You have Jo and Alicia to think about."

"You said you'd be careful, Jake. So, it won't come to that. You'll be home as planned. I know you will."

Jake slipped an envelope into the older man's hand. "Keep hold of this. Only open it if I don't return. Okay?"

"Okay. I will give it back to you in two days."

"Okay. And I want to find out why these bastards took Katherine's body."

"I agree. Whatever the reason was, one day they'll pay for it."

Several hours later, Jake killed the engine, sitting in the dark confines of his car as he checked through his gear. He knew he had everything he'd need but did one more check before climbing out of the Volvo, locking it. He looked around the sleepy village, pleased that his car would be safe before he headed towards the coastal path. As he walked, the sound of the Atlantic filled Jake's ears, calming him as the lights of Towan Point gradually came into view. He was dressed suitably, dark combat trousers, a thin black jacket and trainers making him almost invisible unless someone literally stumbled into him. After twenty minutes, a large stone lighthouse came into view, a solitary light shining from a stone window half-way up the monolith. *Someone's home*, he noted, grimly. *Let's hope they're off to bed soon.* The path began to descend until Jake was a few hundred yards from the lighthouse. A large fence blocked his view, the man coming to a stop. *Shit!* He moved to his right, walking the length of the fence before it ended abruptly at the cliff edge. He threaded his fingers through the links, swinging out over the abyss before scrambling up the other side. "They really don't like anyone getting too close," he observed before continuing his course.

Eleven thirty. Time to make a move. Jake walked as silently as he could across the shingle beach, thankful that the sky above was blanketed in cloud, keeping him in the shadows. As the shingle gave way to course wet sand, Jake broke out into a jog, covering the last hundred metres in less than half a minute. Next to the shore, a wooden jetty creaked gently as the swells rose and fell. He climbed up, following the rough wooden planks as they led him towards a doorway, cut into the stone structure.

"Please be a padlock," he whispered as he snuck into the recess, his eyes feeling for the lock. "Bingo." The stout wooden door was secured with a hasp and staple, a rugged-looking brass padlock barring his progress. Pulling out his lockpick set, he made quick work of the lock, a satisfying click telling him he still had the knack. Silently, Jake opened the door, stepping inside, a can of pepper spray in one hand. He turned, pulling the door to behind him before he took stock of his surroundings. He was in a large circular room, boxes and furniture piled in haphazard fashion. He flicked on his *Maglite*, finding a stone staircase to his right that fell away below ground. As Jake began walking towards it, the outer door was pulled open, a large figure piling in towards him.

"Here," a deep voice boomed, two hands reaching for the private investigator as overhead lights bathed the room in a flickering glow.

"Shit," Jake mouthed, as the giant from the pub lunged towards him, his one eye malevolent, his mouth hanging open. Without thinking, Jake brought the pepper spray to bear, emptying the contents into his attacker's face. It had no effect, two large hands seizing Jake by the throat, slamming him into the wall.

"I knew you'd be back," Lukash Longford cooed as he walked down a flight of stairs towards the grappling duo. "And I knew you'd be trouble."

Jake fired a punch at Malcolm, his fist bouncing off a solid jawbone as the giant glowered at him. "No," Malcolm said flatly as his master came to stand next to him.

"Put him down," ordered Lukash, Jake landing in a heap on the dusty floor. "You've made a big mistake, my friend. I warned you, but alas, it's too late to change things now."

"Fuck you," Jake croaked defiantly, large hands dragging him to his feet.

"Such colourful language," Lukash muttered. "But it will do you no good where you're going. Malcolm, take him beyond the mist." Before Jake could speak, a flat hand chopped him underneath the ear. Then, the world went black.

* * *

Jake's eyes opened slowly, his vision blurred. He closed them again, the sound of the sea and creaking timbers filling his ears. He rolled over, opening his eyes once more, a large wooden barrel a few inches from his position. "Ugh," he groaned, sitting up slowly. "Where am I?" He looked down at his ankles, dread consuming when he saw the iron shackles that held him firmly. *Where the fuck am I?* A few torches flickered on the deck around him, a thick mist creeping across the rough planks as the man tried to focus. *I'm on a boat.* He could smell the tang of the ocean, the galleon rising and falling gently on the unseen swells beneath the keel. Gingerly, Jake stood up, gripping a thick wooden rail, his held together. "You're far from home, boy," a male voice heckled. He turned to his right, seeing a wiry man approach, a large sword dragging across the deck.

"Where am I?" Jake rasped, his throat like sandpaper.

"You're in our world now," the man teased, the point of his sword, snagging Jake's jacket.

"W-what? Who are you?"

"Kurt," the man replied. "Captain of the Tilburg."

"The Tilburg?"

"Me bleedin ship. Fuck, Malcolm must have dislodged yer brain, boy."

"So, I'm on a ship. I take it, this isn't Cornwall?" Jake asked, dreading the answer.

"No, lad. We set sail from Vrybergen. You're heading for your new home, beyond the mist."

Panic seized Jake's chest, his first thought, Alicia. "You've got to let me go. People will come looking for me."

"Let them come. No one from your land knows about this place. Best get comfy and enjoy my soft deck. Because where you're heading is gonna feel like hell compared to this." Before Jake could answer, the man slapped him hard across the face. He fell backwards, his skull bouncing off the deck before darkness consumed him once more.

He woke up sometime later, his head lolling to one side as he woke up. The deck was empty, the large mainsail above propelling the ship forward. Standing up, Jake looked dead ahead, an impenetrable mist slowly creeping towards him. "What the hell," he breathed, catching sight of a rugged coastline in the thick fog. He stood there, rooted to the spot as a huge sea cave came into view, the ship's sail suddenly hanging limp as the sea breeze seemed to drop off. The mouth of the cave swallowed them up, darkness spreading across the deck until Jake could barely see the forecastle ahead of him. A jetty came into view, lanterns barely able to fight off the cloying blackness. "Oh fuck!" Jake blurted as a huge blue archway reached out towards the vessel. Slowly, the Tilburg bumped into the portal, Jake almost knocked off his feet as the inertia rocked the ship. Two men landed on the rough planks, one wrapping a huge rope around an anchor point on the deck before disappearing from sight. "This can't be happening," Jake said as the rope went taught, the Tilburg pulled through the portal, into the unknown.

Chapter Twelve

Three days since their last conversation, Wilf paced the lounge, constantly looking out of the bay window. Jo walked in from the kitchen, seeing her partner walk up and down the dark carpet. "I was making a cup of tea, hun. Do you want one?"

"Huh?" Wilf replied, turning to face the woman who was regarding him from the doorway. "Oh, yes please, love."

"You okay? What's up?"

"Jake should be back by now," the grey-haired man observed.

"I'm sure he will be. He's only gone to Plymouth. Maybe traffic is bad? Maybe the job is taking longer than he first thought?"

Wilf knew where the man he considered a son had gone. And something deep inside him knew that something had gone badly wrong. "He's not contacted us with his telephone?"

"True," Jo agreed. "Maybe he's just really busy?"

Wilf slumped onto the sofa, an overwhelming tiredness spreading through him. He pulled an envelope from his cardigan pocket, handing it to his woman. "Read that for me, please."

Jo's expression changed, a frown appearing on her face. "What is it?"

"Jake gave it to me when he left, just in case he ran into problems." Jo sat down beside him, gently taking the paper packet from Wilf, breaking the seal with her finger. "Before you read it, love, I'm truly sorry that we've kept this secret from you for so long. That was never our intention, Jo. I hope one day you'll understand?"

"Wilf, you're scaring me. What is going on?"

"Read and you may find out."

Jo looked at the page, clearing her throat.

Dearest Wilf. I only wanted you to open this if something happens to me. I told you not to come after me, wherever I end up. All I will tell you is that I was heading for the lighthouse at Towan Point, trying to find a young girl called Lauren Thorne. Her mother's address is on the other side of the page. Her name is Emma Thorne.

If this is the last time that I see you, just know that I've grown to love you. The void left when Dad died has been filled by you. I know we were never meant to meet each other, but I'm so glad we did. You're a good man, Wilf Bathurst and I know you'll look after Jo and Alicia.

Tell them I love them, and I always will.

Your friend, Jake.

Jo looked up from the page, seeing the tears that were rolling down her man's face. "Wilf, what's going on?"

"He's gone. I know he has."

"Gone. Gone where?" she replied, panic welling up inside her.

The old man took her hands, pulling them into his lap. "Have you ever wondered why I cannot read your words?"

"You told me that when you grew up you never went to school?"

"That's true. I never did, yet I understand your tongue. Where I grew up there were no schools and no cities like you have here. My world is very different, Jo."

"Your world? What are you going on about? You're starting to freak me out."

"I'm from another world, Jo. A world connected to yours by a doorway. That's how I met Jake. He came through the doorway near my village, hunting for vampires."

Jo laughed, then checked herself as he looked into Wilf's eyes. "What, have you lost your mind? What's going on, Wilf? Is this some kind of joke?"

"It's no joke," Alicia said from the doorway into the hall. "Wilf, where's Dad?"

"He's gotten lost, love. I think he's gone through another doorway and he's not come back yet."

The little girl ran across the lounge, hurling herself across Jo and Wilf's lap. "We have to find him. Please, Papa Wilf, please go and find him." Tears welled up in the girl's eyes, breaking the old man's heart twice in as many minutes.

"What's going on?" Jo urged, rising from the sofa.

Alicia focused on her, wiping her eyes. "Jo, Wilf speaks the truth. He is from another world. One next to this one. You have to believe us. It's all true."

"Sit down, love," Wilf soothed, his voice unusually calm. "Let's start from the beginning. And please, don't run screaming from the house."

* * *

"Do you really expect me to believe all this?" Jo asked, her voice quivering.

"No. But in time you will, I hope. Jake is lost, maybe trapped and we have to get him back."

"I'm losing my mind," Jo whispered, dropping onto the sofa, head in hands.

"Think about it, love." I cannot read. You remember when we first met? When I said I had to go away to visit my kin?"

Jo nodded. "Yes."

"Well, my kin live in a place called Shetland. It was named after the man I told you about. George Drysdale. I did visit them but have never returned since. Because I met you. Because I fell in love with you. I've never loved a woman before. And I know I'll never love another woman that's not you. You have to believe us."

"I don't know what to believe. My world has just turned upside-down, Wilf. Doorways to other worlds. Vampires. It's ridiculous."

"But it's not. It's real. Look at Alicia. A vampire's blood runs through her veins, albeit a little. She's never been sick. She never cried as a baby. She's different. Surely you can see that?"

"Well, yes. She's never been sick and come to think of it, I've never seen her upset or hurt. But that doesn't mean I believe all this?"

"What will it take?"

Jo looked past them both, staring out of the window for a few seconds. Finally, she stared into Wilf's eyes, a look of determination in her eyes. "Show me. I want to see this with my own eyes."

* * *

Jo's Mazda pulled up outside the isolated farmhouse as the sun warmed the Cornish landscape. They all stepped out, looking over at the property, unsure of how to approach their task. "So, what do we do?" Jo asked.

"We do what is needed," Wilf replied, striding up to the front door. He knocked twice, his knuckles wrapping against the firm oak as Jo and Alicia joined him.

The door opened, a woman peering out at them through the six-inch opening. "Yes?"

"Hello," Wilf began. "Are you Emma Thorne?"

"Who's asking?" the woman shot back defensively.

"My name is Wilf. This is Jo and Alicia. We're looking for Jake and may need your help."

The gap between door and frame opened slightly, the woman's expression changing. "What's happened?"

"He's gone," Alicia countered. "My Dad has gone."

Emma hesitated, unsure of the strangers on her doorstep. "How do I know that your Jake's family?"

Jo pulled her phone from her jacket pocket, showing the screen to Emma. "Does this prove it?"

Emma looked at the phone's wallpaper, a picture of Jake, Wilf and Alicia smiling back at her. She nodded, opening the door fully. "Please, come through." They filed in, walking along the hallway until the four of them were stood in a large kitchen. "Sit down and I'll put the kettle on."

Five minutes later, Alicia was playing in the back garden, bouncing on the trampoline, the sound of the springs stretching filtering in through the open doors. Emma looked at Wilf, seeing the anguish in the older man's eyes. "So, what's happened?"

"When did you last see Jake?"

"A few days ago. He was going to check out the lighthouse. My daughter has been missing for just over a year. I asked Jake to help me find her."

"We're really sorry to hear that," Jo said, seeing tears forming in the other woman's eyes.

"What else did Jake tell you?" Emma probed.

Wilf blew out a breath, his shoulders sagging. "He thinks that someone took your daughter. The lawmen have not been able to find her, so you turned to Jake."

Emma's brow creased at the mention of 'lawmen'. Something was not quite right about the older man across the table, but Emma could not put her finger on it. "That's right. She vanished just after her eighth birthday and I've not seen her since."

"We're so sorry to hear that," Jo repeated, squeezing the other woman's hand. Emma smiled, glad of the fleeting contact. "Wilf told me something this morning that has flipped my world upside-down." She looked at her man expectantly.

"Okay," the gruff old man said, clearing his throat. "Not many people know about what I'm about to tell you. As Jake would say, keep an open mind."

Twenty minutes later, Emma drained her mug, placing her head in her hands as Wilf and Jo looked on nervously. Her fingers trailed down her face before she laid her hands out on the table. "I should be freaking out right now, but I'm not. As crazy as your story sounds, it kinda fits."

"And it looks like the people who took Lauren also defiled my Katherine's grave. I don't know what the connection is, but it all leads back to the same family," Wilf stated.

"It's all so unbelievable," Emma added, looking across at Jo.

"Believe me," Jo started. "I'm still unconvinced. But I know Wilf would not lie. As mad as it sounds, I'm starting to believe him."

"Tell me, Wilf, where do you think Jake is?"

The older man shrugged. "I've no idea. I've been through a few doorways. Some between this world and mine. Others led to different worlds. Jake could be anywhere. All I know is that he was heading for the lighthouse, to look for the doorway that no one comes out of…"

The words hung in the air, the gravity of the situation apparent to all three of them. "So, what do we do?" Emma asked, not really wanting the answer.

"We find him," Wilf replied, a steely determination in his eyes. "The last time he got lost, Jake had someone with him. This time, he's all alone, maybe hurt, maybe worse."

"Try not to think the worst," Jo responded, holding his hand. "But how do we do this?"

"I'm not sure, love. Jake is cunning. He has tools and tricks and would know how to get inside this lighthouse. We're going to struggle to do the same, unless."

"Unless what?" Jo urged, seeing a smile spread across the man's face.

"Unless we have help."

Chapter Thirteen

"I can't believe we're doing this?" Jo said as the foursome hunkered down a few hundred yards from Towan Point's lighthouse.

"It'll be okay," Wilf soothed, wrapping an arm around her shoulder.

"The doorway opens in ten minutes," Emma whispered. "Are we set?"

"Yes," Wilf nodded. "We've got supplies and your bolt-cutters should make short work of any locks we find, I hope." They made their way across the open ground as quickly as possible, pressing themselves against the stone structure with only a few minutes to spare. Wilf shuffled towards the door, smiling when he saw a large chain and padlock that had been used to secure the door against any uninvited guests. He motioned for Emma, who handed him the cutters. With barely a grunt, the lock snapped, falling into Emma's hands without making a noise. "Right, let's go. And go quietly."

They entered a large circular room, a set of stone steps leading down into the ground. Across the room, another staircase led to the main body of the lighthouse. "Spooky place," Emma muttered, the sound of the surf wafting in through the open doorway.

"Come on," Wilf urged, heading down the stone staircase, the others following close behind. After thirty seconds, they were presented by a wall, blocking their path.

"Now what?" Jo huffed.

"We wait," Wilf observed as a low drone echoed up the staircase, causing the two women to flinch. Before their eyes, a faint blue outline appeared, growing stronger until it gently pulsed in front of them.

"Jesus Christ!" Jo started, Wilf shushing her gently.

"Oh my God," Emma said, walking towards the portal. "It's true."

"Come on," the older man ordered. "We need to get through before someone comes." He pulled a stake out of his backpack before taking a step forward. "Everyone hold hands. Alicia, you go between Emma and Jo, I'll go first."

Jo and Emma gawped open-mouthed as Wilf disappeared from sight, Alicia nudging Jo from behind. "Come on. The doorway will close any second." It was all the motivation she needed, walking through the doorway, into another world. She came through the other side, Alicia and Emma a few paces behind her. The three females took in their surroundings, a large lighthouse dominating the small settlement in which they now found themselves.

"I've been here before, Papa," Alicia stated, looking up at the rocky path where they'd met the giant and his hound.

Wilf looked skywards; the huge sea cave's ceiling partially hidden in the darkness. "Okay. We need to hole-up somewhere. Alicia, is it easy to get out of here?"

"Yes, Papa. There are steps that lead outside up there. If we can get out of here, we're not too far from Shetland."

Wilf looked at the two women, noticing the fear that was seeping through them. "Get your weapons out. We're not in your world now. There are no laws here. If someone challenges us, we need to silence them. If not, we're in the shit." His words seemed to galvanise the women, who opened each other's packs, handing out wooden stakes. "Right. Let's move."

They moved quickly, weaving around the deserted streets of Vrybergen, keeping to the shadows. After a minute, Wilf pulled them into an alleyway as men spilt out of a tavern a few yards ahead of them. They stood quietly, waiting for the rabble to pass by their position. "That was close," Jo whispered, her pulse racing.

"I know. We're outlanders here. We do not look like the locals. If they see us, they will raise merry hell. We need to keep well-hidden." They carried on further, a large ship moored next to a wooden jetty making the two women stare in awe.

"Bloody hell!" Emma said. "It looks like the *Golden Hind* that's moored at Brixham. I wish I had my camera."

"No time for that," Wilf chided. "I can see the path out of here." The foursome pushed on, pleased that none of the locals had spotted them as they made their way ever closer towards the ceiling of the cave, a small passage to their left. Two minutes later, they were out in the open, catching their collective breaths.

"That's where they chased us," Alicia pointed out. "Dad's bike was over there."

"Alicia," Where is Shetland from here?" Wilf asked as his breathing returned to normal.

"That way," she pointed, Wilf nodding in satisfaction.

"Okay. Whatever happens, we're stuck here until midnight tonight. If what Alicia says is true, which I'm sure it is, my land is that way. We should set off now."

"And then what?" Emma asked, a feeling of dread seeping into her bones.

"Then we use the doorway to get back home. Well, you three will. I'm staying here to search for our helper."

"And who is that?" Jo began. "You mentioned help, hun, but who is it?"

"Tamatan," Wilf replied. "If anyone can help us, he can."

"You mentioned the name earlier," Emma said. "You said he's a demon."

"Yes. But a friendly one. He and Jake are linked, and I know that Tamatan will give his life to help us."

"So, where does this Tamatan live?" Jo asked.

"The last time we saw him, he was heading for the western seas and the lands beyond. That's where I will find him."

Jo grabbed his hand. "You can't go alone. We must come with you?"

The grizzled man shook his head. "I must go alone. It will take me half a moon's cycle to make my way to the farthest edges of Mantz forest. That's no place for the three of you."

"I'm not leaving you here, Wilf," Jo argued. "I'm not going through another doorway without you. So don't try and change my mind."

"But what about Alicia?" he countered. "She'll be going back to school soon. She's needed there."

Jo tried to bat something back at him, realising that Wilf was right. The school term was due to start in a few short weeks, and questions would be asked if she were not there. "Then come back with us. We'll figure something out, hun."

He shook his head. "I must go alone. You three can head back through Amatoll. Jake's friend Vicky lives close to the doorway. Tell her that I sent you. She will make sure you all get home safe."

She walked over to him, her eyes pleaded in the darkness. "You can't do this. I'm not losing you."

Tears ran down the woman's cheeks, Wilf wiping them away gently. "Love, this is my land, my home. I know it well and I know how to take care of myself. I must do this alone and cannot risk putting you and Alicia in danger."

"I'm staying with you," Emma stated. "I've nothing to go back for. If you're going to do this, I'll do it with you."

Wilf looked at the dark-haired woman, seeing the resolve in her eyes. "Fine. As long as you don't mind living off the land. Our supplies will not last forever and this place is fraught with danger and hardship."

"Beats sitting on my arse at home, doing nothing."

"Fair point. Come on. Let's head for Amatoll."

* * *

Three days later, tired and hungry, the foursome collapsed on the stubbly grass outside Cedric Bathurst's former home. Wilf made a fire as shadows began lengthening across the village green. "What time is it?" he asked.

"Almost seven," Jo replied as began laying out some food and drinks next to the fire. "There's not much left. Are you sure that you want to do this?"

"Very sure," he countered. "I've told you where Vicky and Jasper live. Once through the doorway, you'll be safe. Emma and I will head west, towards the sea. It will be a long road, but there will be animals out there that old Wilf can catch. We'll not go hungry."

Alicia gathered up the rest of the provisions, tucking them into Wilf and Emma's backpacks. "You need this more than us, Papa. I'm sure Vicky and Jasper will be able to give us food."

He bent down, lifting the girl into his arms. "You're a good girl, like your mother."

Alicia squeezed him, burying her face in his chest. "I love you, Papa Wilf."

"Now don't start me off," he choked. "We'll be back home before you know it."

They sat around a makeshift fire, chatting about anything and everything with Wilf describing his upbringing and the battle with Korgan and Reggan, the fallen vampire kings. Jo and Emma sat next to the crackling fire, listening intently until Emma checked her watch. "It's getting close to midnight."

"Then let's make a move," Wilf suggested, climbing slowly to his feet. They walked in silence through the forest, tendrils of mist caressing tree trunks as they made their way towards their destination. A few minutes later, the four-some were stood in front of two gnarled trees, their trunks disappearing into the darkened canopy above. "Now. You both know what to do?"

They nodded, Jo walking over to him, wrapping her around his neck. She kissed him, a sob escaping her lips as Wilf held her tightly. "Just come home to us. Both of you."

"We will. You have my word," he replied. "When you get to Vicky's house, you must give her your telephone number, just in case we come back this way. I would rather try and use the door that we came through, but we will need to have Tamatan with us to stand any chance."

Jo and Alicia hugged him, Emma watching on as emotions boiled over. Wilf knelt down, taking the little girl's face in his hands. "Go swiftly, little one. Take care of Jo, and let her take care of you."

"Yes, Papa Wilf," she snuffled, wiping tears from her eyes.

Bracken and twigs rustled on the forest floor, a low humming sound making them all turn towards the trees. A blue outline appeared, the doorway gently pulsing in the darkness a few seconds later. "Take care," Wilf croaked, kissing Jo one last time. "I love you both."

"We love you too," Jo replied, her voice faltering as she hugged him tightly. She walked over to Emma, embracing the other woman. "Take care. And look after each other."

"We will," she replied, not knowing what else to say as the two figures walked towards the doorway. They turned around, tears streaking both of their faces before they stepped backwards, disappearing from sight.

Wilf and Emma stood there, waiting for the doorway to disappear for another night. "Are you tired?" Wilf began.

"Not really. Kinda wired."

"Well, whatever that means, shall we begin our journey towards the west?"

"Why not," Emma agreed. "I'm keen to see all the wonders of your land."

"Well, let's hope we don't encounter all of the wonders," he smiled at her in the darkness before shouldering his pack.

Chapter Fourteen

They walked for hours, eventually collapsing from exhaustion next to a large gorge with a log cabin nestled next to the sheer cliffs. As the sun began its descent, Wilf and Emma ate some of their rations before continuing through Monks Passage, keeping as close to the shadows as possible. They seemed to lose track of time and days as they stopped to rest at the fringes of Mantz forest, Emma's eyes trying to find a way through the densely packed trees. "Jesus! Is it like that all the way through?"

"Yes," the old man responded. "We fought the Cravens many moons ago, this was their lair."

"The Cravens?" an icy finger running down her spine.

"Heathens, preying on anything that came across their path. We won out, destroying their leader and most of the clan. Any stragglers would be scattered by now. Or dead."

"Let's hope they're dead. I don't fancy meeting them, especially in there." They walked a few hundred yards into the forest, finding an abandoned settlement of roughly hewn cabins. Wilf lit a fire, setting a snare for any unsuspecting animals that were close by. Hours later, they were pulling apart the freshly cooked carcass of a large bird, both of them tearing tender flesh from greasy bones before they fell into a deep sleep on musty hessian blankets.

The next morning, they set off, keeping conversation to a minimum as they weaved through densely-packed trees. The hours seemed to fall away, Emma's determination and resilience clear for the old man to see. He kept pace with her, listening out for animals or danger. They found the former, a young deer with a snapped hind leg. Wilf stroked the animals flank, uttering soft words before snapping its neck swiftly. Emma looked away, the sickening crunch loud in the silent forest. Securing the dead animal to his backpack, Wilf led the way, looking for another place to set up camp.

* * *

Two weeks later, tired and hungry, they slid down a steep incline, bringing them out on a wooden jetty. The watery sun reflected off the grey sea as Wilf and Emma stared across the misty expanse. "Now what?" she asked expectantly.

"We eat," the old man observed. "And soon. Wilf's belly is in need of sustenance." He walked along the wooden structure, testing the stout boards with his feet. "We may be in luck," he beamed, pointing towards a makeshift raft that had been tied up and left next to the lapping waves.

"Maybe someone left it there and are on their way back?"

"It matters not. Let's skewer some fish, then continue our journey. We'll need some branches that I can sharpen."

As the sun dropped below the horizon, they sat in silence, crowding around the fire, discarded fish bones succumbing to the flames. "That's better," Emma croaked, wishing that she had a nice glass of wine to wash down her meal. "Do you know where we're going?"

"No," Wilf sighed. "All I know is that Tamatan lives in the land beyond the sea. I do not know how long it will take us to reach it, but I'm hoping no more than a few days. Come on, let's make a few oars and head out into the sea."

"Okay," Emma agreed, a feeling of anxiety washing over her as she stared out at the darkening waves.

Days later, soaked through from the perpetual sea mist, Wilf and Emma staggered onto a pebbly beach, looking for signs of life. They pulled the raft away from the shore, hiding it amongst the long grasses that separated the sea from the interior. "Which way?" Emma prompted, looking at the older man who she'd been huddled next to for most of the voyage.

"That way," Wilf urged. "I can see smoke in the distance. Let's hope someone lives further along the coast." They made their way slowly along the beach, walking a few yards inside the grasses to speed up their progress. After a short period of time, they came across a clutch of wooden buildings next to the sea.

As they neared, a stout-looking man appeared from a newly-built cabin. He eyed the couple warily as they approached. "You look a long way from home?" the man said evenly.

"Yes, we are," Wilf replied. "We're looking for someone and I think he resides in this land, or the lands beyond."

"Who is it you're looking for?"

"Tamatan," Wilf stated, seeing the man's expression change.

"Why are you looking for him?" the man said, flinching slightly at the name.

"Do you know him?" Emma urged, watching as the stranger weighed them up.

"Maybe I do. Maybe I don't. Not many people venture to the Unseen Lands and even fewer head into the interior."

"My name is Wilf. This is Emma. We are friends of Tamatan, and we need his help."

"What kind of help?"

"My friend, Jake has been taken. Tamatan is the only one who can help me find him." At mention of the name *Jake*, the man flinched once more, knowing that the diminutive demon's son shared the same name. "You do know him, don't you?"

The man sighed, wiping a damp hand across his pate. "Yes. I do know him. My name's Sica. I've known Tamatan and his kin for a long time. The last time I saw him he was heading through the Pagbob towards his land, Marzalek."

"Do you know how to get there?" Wilf asked, hoping that the stranger believed their story.

"Not fully. I dropped his kin at the large lagoon along the coast. They would have made their way home from there. Tell me, Wilf. What is Tamatan's sister called?"

"Veltan," Wilf replied confidently.

"Well, that settles it. Any friend of Tamatan's is a friend of mine. How did you get here?"

"We found an old raft at the fringes on Mantz. We sailed over on it."

"Well, you both look like you could do with a jug of cyder and a hot meal. Come inside, I have some fillets cooking on my grill and the fire will warm your bones."

"Thank you, Sica," Emma smiled, following the man towards the wooden structure a few yards away.

Emma's nose wrinkled as they entered the cabin, the smell overpowering. After a few deep breaths, her mouth began to water at the sight of thick hunks of yellowy fish that sat gently spitting and sizzling on a wrought-iron griddle.

Flames gently licked at the flesh from underneath, warming the confines. She looked around, fascinated by the interior. A large skull of an unknown sea creature stood proud on the one wall, a collection of tools and bones littering the wooden worktops. "Nice place you have."

"I give thanks," Sica chirped as he poured two mugs of cyder. "It's taken me many seasons to build, but finally it's all done. After the winter is over, I'll start work on my boat."

Wilf lit his pipe, sucking smoke into his lungs. He offered the pouch of tobacco to Sica who took it warily. "Try this," he offered.

"I give you thanks," Sica replied, pulling a wooden pipe from a pocket on his waistband. His thick fingers stuffed the coarse tobacco into the bowl, lighting it with a twig from the fire. He took a long draw, the tobacco glowing, lighting up his features. "That's some good weed," he exclaimed.

"Keep it. I have some more in my pack."

"I offer more thanks, friend," Sica responded. "Now come. The fish is ready, and the fire will dry you off before we set sail for the lagoon."

"Are you sure it's no trouble?" Emma tested.

"Not at all. I just need to load up my boat with a few things. You two can sit by the fire until I call you. Then we will cast off."

Chapter Fifteen

Jake stirred, a noise in the darkness bringing him out of his fitful slumber. "Wake up, lad," a hoarse voice commanded. "Time to clean up before you meet your new master."

"Where am I?" Jake croaked, his throat devoid of moisture. He'd lost count of the days he'd been on the ship, sleeping fitfully on the rough planks as it stopped at unknown ports to offload and take on cargo.

"The Grey halls of Kenn," the figure above him stated flatly.

Jake sat up gingerly, seeing the captain of the Tilburg. "Who's Kenn?"

"What?" Kurt replied, his brow creasing.

"Kenn. Who's Kenn?"

"Kenn is a place. Your new home. For now."

"Right," Jake replied warily, watching as the rocky cavern seemed to press down on top of them.

Kurt bent down, removing the shackles that had kept his prisoner in place. "No need for them now. You're not going anywhere unless Grey decrees it."

"Grey?"

"Your new master."

Despite his situation, Jake stifled a laugh. "So, the halls belong to Grey and the place is called Kenn?"

"Problem with that?" Kurt boomed, taking Jake under the armpit, steering him towards the edge of the vessel.

"No. Sounds peachy," he countered, looking down at the dark waters next to a stone jetty.

"Jump across."

Jake did so, landing in a heap, his strength sapped from the uncomfortable journey and little in the way of sustenance. A few minutes later, they were walking side-by-side, heading deeper into the cave system. He took everything in, trying to find any escape option. Sadly, none presented themselves as they came to a large wooden door. The dull thud of Kurt's knuckles prompted a response from the other side, the sound of approaching footsteps filtering under the door. A shutter creaked open in the door, beady eyes peering through in the darkness. "Kurt."

"Moke. Got our master a little gift," the captain said gruffly.

The door opened inward; Jake being shoved through by the burly man behind him. "Jesus Christ," he breathed, the gloomy expanse opening up before them. Hundreds of columns rose towards a dark rock-hewn ceiling, their rows disappearing into the darkness.

"Walk," Kurt ordered.

He obeyed, not wanting to raise the bigger man's ire, his body already feeling the effects of Kurt's blows. They walked for a few minutes, Jake spying cloaked figures, heads bowed as they shuffling between the massive stone structures. He never spoke as they descended a winding rocky staircase, flickering torches barely able to illuminate their surroundings. At the bottom, two tall figures approached, both wearing flowing grey robes, hoods obscuring their faces. "Hi," Jake said, the figures silently appraising him.

"An offering from Vrybergen," Kurt added, Jake noticing how the bigger man's demeanour had changed. He could see it clearly, Kurt looked spooked.

"Come," One of them said, a robed arm pointing the way.

As Jake walked through the doorway, Kurt's retreating footsteps echoed through the anti-chamber where he now found himself. The space was small, round in shape with strange animal heads adorning the stone-hewn walls. None of them looked familiar to him, dead eyes staring back at him, frozen in time. At the far end of the space, a figure sat on a large iron chair, its backrest stretching towards the rocks above. The figure face was obscured by a grey hood, tendrils of breath escaping an unseen mouth. "Step forward, Jake Stevenson," a low warbling voice uttered.

"How do you know my name?" he replied, a spidery coldness creeping down his spine.

"I am Grey. I know such things. I know everything."

Jake's eyes opened wider as the figure removed its hood. An old man looked back at him, white unseeing eyes crinkling at the corners. The man's skin way the same colour as the hood that now lay draped across wide shoulders, small pointed teeth that looked at odds with the large nose and prominent brows above. "So, who are you and how do you know so much?"

"I am eternal. I have sat on this chair since the dawn of time. Before the mountains rose from the seas. Before men like you roamed the many realms above us."

"So, what do you want with me? I'm just a man."

"You're more than that, dear Jake. I know your past. I know that you lost your kin at a young age. I know that you battled the vampire kings and won through. A mere man would not have done that. A mere man would have succumbed. And even though the white witch cured you of the darkness, I can still sense the essence of the beast within. The mountain, they called Reggan still occupies a small piece of your soul, and your daughter's soul too."

"Jesus," he exclaimed. "You really do know everything."

"It's my business to. Have you often wondered who controls the countless doorways that you've passed through?"

Jake shook his head. "I thought it was Korgan and Reggan."

"A simple but reasonable guess," Grey replied, drumming his bony fingers on the arm of the chair. "But incorrect. It is I who controls the doorways. I have done so since I came to be."

"Why?"

Grey chuckled. "To have control. You see the pool over there?" He extended his arm, Jake's eyes following. Next to the wall, a large pond lay within a raised stone wall, its surface like blackened glass. "That is my window to the realms. Through that I see everything. I see your world with its machines and technology. I see other worlds, where heathens roam the landscape, battling with the indigenous beasts. I see demons, vampires and many other dark creatures, all vying for position. My power, my secret if you like, is that very few know of my existence."

Jake took a step forward, coming to within a few metres, a rank smell stopping him in his tracks. "So, you're all-powerful, but nobody knows it."

"Yes."

"So, what's your goal. You control everything but nobody knows it. Doesn't make sense?"

"Oh, but it does. You see, I have an army of close aides who ensure that I remain hidden. An army who does my bidding."

"And what is that?" Jake replied becoming more and more curious, despite the grave situation.

"Why, lives of course. From far and wide, my helpers bring me children. They bring me things of value that I can barter with. There are many powerful forces across the planes. Some who want a blonde-haired boy, or a demon as a plaything. Some want precious metals and gemstones. Or the healing stone that hangs around your neck. I make sure that they get what they want. In your world, you'd call it a supply chain. An endless stream of trade that keeps the wheels turning. But we've spoken enough for now. The Longford's brought you to me to do my bidding, not so we could converse like old women."

"What do you want me to do?"

"You are a resourceful man, Jake. One who is adept at finding people. Special people. There is someone that I want you to find. Although I have many helpers, there is someone who has always eluded me. I want you to find them and bring them to me."

"Who are they and where would I even start?"

"She resides on this plane, well almost. Her name is Jubella."

"Jubella," Jake repeated. "And who is she?"

"She is a mongrel. Part human, part demon. I need her essence to wake a sleeping soul. A soul that will sit next to me in my sanctum, keeping me company throughout the ages."

"Let's say I find her and bring her back to you. Then what happens to me?"

"You return to your kin, Jake. To Cornwall. People are already looking for you, but they will never find you here. The chasm is too great, even for them. Do as I bid, and you will see their faces again, one day."

"And if I say no?" Jake replied, wondering who was searching for him.

"Then you'll end up the plaything of someone I know. Someone that you really don't want to become acquainted with."

Chapter Sixteen

"Papa, what's wrong?" Jake said as his father sat down heavily.

"I feel something close by. Something I've not felt for a long time."

"What?"

Tamatan looked up at his offspring, his orange eyes dimmed. "An old friend, who's in pain." They set off across the forest, the diminutive demon closely followed by his large son, his loping strides covering the uneven ground as he kept pace with his father. They crossed the Obtab river, the shimmering spires of Katarzin now visible in the distance. A short time later, father and son arrived at the home of Bikabak, Tamatan's mother. The front door was open, letting the air out into the warm cobbled street. "Hello, Mama?" the demon called.

"In here, Tama. You have guests."

Tamatan hurried into the rear living space, Jake a few steps behind him. As he entered, an old man with a ruddy face and grey hair rose from a wooden chair. "Hello, old friend," Wilf said, embracing the advancing demon.

"Wilf," Tamatan exclaimed, his face dropping when he saw the old man's expression. "It's Jake, isn't it?"

The man took a step back, looking to his left. A woman took a step forward, her eyes appraising the demon. "This is Emma. She's a friend."

"Hello," she said evenly, smiling at Tamatan and Jake.

"Hello, Emma," he replied. "Wilf, what has happened?"

"I will make some lunch," Bikabak stated. "Emma. Would you like to help me as Veltan's not due back until later and old Bikabak isn't as strong as she once was."

"Of course," she replied, following the shuffling figure towards the kitchen at the front of the house.

Wilf sat down, a weary look etched across his face. "Jake's been taken."

"Taken by whom?" Tamatan asked.

"A powerful family close to where he lives. We found another doorway. One that this family has used for its own means. A young girl was taken a few seasons ago. Emma is her mother and Jake was trying to find her when he went missing."

"We will finish our lunch then set off immediately."

"I will come with you, Papa." Jake said in earnest.

"The road will be dangerous, Son. One that you've never travelled before."

"I'm coming with you."

"No, you're not," the older demon ordered. "You're to stay here with our kin. If there is trouble ahead, you need to be here. I will hear no more on it."

* * *

"I am so sorry to hear about Katherine," Tamatan said as they made their way from Katarzin. "She was a good person, and good people should not die like that."

"That she was," Wilf agreed. "And she went out protecting her kin, which is of little comfort to old Wilf."

"At least she was taken back to the land of her ancestors. Now she is at peace."

"Well, she was, but when Jake was last there, he found out that someone had desecrated the grave and taken her body."

The demon stopped in his tracks, looking up at the grizzled man. "There are ill forces at work, Wilf. Why would someone take her body? It would be of little use to anyone?"

"That's what we thought. But the more I think about it, the more I think it's linked to what happened to Jake. After all, Katherine had vampire blood in her veins. Maybe someone knew that?"

"Well, we need to find Jake. And quickly. We almost lost him once, we cannot let that happen again. Tell me more about the place where he was taken."

Wilf recounted the tale, Emma chipping in as they made their way through the dense forest called the Pagbob. Trees seemed to squeeze together, Emma feeling more and more claustrophobic with every step as the old man next to her gave the account of Jake's disappearance. After a while, they came to rest as the forest began growing darker. "We rest here tonight," Tamatan began. "We have provisions in our packs that will help on the way to the sea. Hopefully,

Sica will provide more before we carry on the journey through the vast forest that leads to your land."

"If we're lucky, we should be back in Amatoll by the new moon," Wilf countered as he sank down onto the soft earth.

"And how much longer until we reach this Vrybergen?" Tamatan asked, stretching his legs out in front of him as hundreds of fireflies circled above them.

"A few more days. Truth be told, even though we know the way there, once we arrive, I've no idea where Jake is. Or how we're going to find him?"

"Leave that to me, Wilf. Jake and I are joined. If he is out there, I will find him and bring him home."

"I know. That's why we had to find you. I'm getting on in seasons and while Emma is willing, she does not know our lands and the monsters that lurk in the shadows."

"Tell me more about this family. The Longfords."

Wilf lit his pipe, Letting the heady aroma fill his lungs before he began recounting what he knew about them. Tamatan sat in silence, as both Wilf and Emma supplied him with more and more information. Finally, after several minutes, the demon's eyes glowed red in the darkness. "Well. We must find Jake and your daughter. Then when all that is done, we need to right the wrongs that have befallen you."

Chapter Seventeen

Jake looked across the cell where he'd sat for the past two weeks. The first few days he'd spent walking up and down the confines, staring out at the subterranean cave and the waters beyond. As the days rolled out, he did push-ups and sit-ups to maintain a level of strength, lying on his straw mattress for long spells, his mind wandering. He heard footsteps approaching, the bolt on the door opened noisily, making him flinch. A figure emerged from the darkened hallway, stooping to fit under the stone lintel above the opening. "Jake."

He craned his neck, his eyes opening wider as he assessed the thing in front of him. It looked to be male, with pale skin and yellow feral eyes. Eyes that were very similar to the monsters of his past. The figure was dressed in black, pallid breath escaping its thin lips. "Uh-huh," he replied warily.

"I am Jed, your guide as it were."

"My guide?"

The figure chuckled, perfectly white teeth being displayed for the first time. Sharp teeth. "Didn't Grey tell you? How else do you think you'll be able to travel to the place where she resides?"

"Jubella?"

"Yes, the one and only. I will help you find her. Then, we will bring her back to Grey."

"Forgive me for asking but look at the size of you. Why do you need me to bring her back here? Surely you are more than able?"

"You have something that none of us have, Jake."

"What's that?"

"Life. You are from the light. You walk with the healing stones and you've risen from the darkness. You will be more than a match for her. Not even Grey would attempt to venture into her land. It's a paradox, is it not?"

Confused, Jake's brow creased. "How do you mean?"

"She's a mixture of darkness and light. The darkness is all-powerful, the light even more so, as it keeps the likes of us from her door. Grey has been watching her over the ages, calculating when he will strike. Now that his future mate has arrived, the time has arrived."

"His mate?"

"Yes. Someone who was found. Someone who is special. Jubella will awaken her. Then your deed is done and you may travel far and wide."

"Well, I guess I have nothing better to do. How far is it to Jubella?"

"Oh, not far, as the birds fly. But where we're going there are no birds."

"I don't understand?"

"Jubella lives underneath our land. A dark place where the rivers hiss and boil. A place that not even Jed cares to venture. But venture we must if we're to please Grey."

"Okay. Let's go."

"First, you eat."

"Eat?" Jake replied quizzically.

"Yes. Best not set off on an empty stomach. Our people are preparing you a meal and will give you provisions for the journey."

Jake's mouth began to moisten. "Okay. You're the boss. I am rather hungry."

* * *

"In there?" Jake asked, not wanting the answer.

"Yes," Jed replied, a smile appearing on his lips. "This portal is unlike the ones you're used to. Once we dip below the cool waters we will appear on the other side in a similar pond."

"Whatever you say," Jake said, lowering himself into the frigid water. He caught his breath as the pond licked at his chest and arms. He took a deep breath, sinking lower into the depths, expecting his feet to land on the bottom. However, the bottom never came as Jake felt himself swirled around in the darkness. Mildly concerned, he swam to the surface, breaking the pond as he gasped for air. "What the…"

"A nice place," Jed joked, climbing out of the pond, shaking his robes and long dark hair.

"I wouldn't go that far," Jake replied as he took in his new surroundings. The pond sat in a forest, the likes of which he'd never seen. The trees around him were completely white, even the leaves that dangled from the branches were the colour of freshly fallen snow. "What is this place?"

"The White land of Kenn," Jed whispered.

"Kenn, like the Grey halls of Kenn?"

"Yes."

"Sorry, I don't mean to laugh, but Kenn is a name where I'm from. Never heard of a place called Kenn."

"Well here, Kenn means power and in the land above us too."

"Okay, I get it now. The Grey halls of power."

"You are correct. Now come. We have a long road ahead. One that will not be easy." Reaching into his robe, Jed pulled out a short axe with a leather handle. "Here. Take this, Jake. It will be of use here. Don't hesitate. Use it when you need to."

"Where's your axe?"

"I have these," Jed replied, holding up his huge hands, curved fingernails pointing menacingly at Jake. "These have served me well over the ages."

"So, which way to this Jubella?"

"That way," Jed stated, pointing deeper into the forest. "We must pass through a few settlements. Hocken then Pinemoor. Both are places where being seen will cause us problems. We must stick to the shadows."

"Fair enough," Jake agreed. "I've had enough rough and tumble to last me a lifetime. Can we not skirt the settlements?"

"Unfortunately, not. There are fortifications as you enter with ravines on each side. Jubella has made it that way, to stop Grey's followers from attacking her. So, when we get to Hocken, we must rest up to see how the land lies."

"What are these places like?"

"Hocken is a dark place where children are put to work. They mine the precious stones underneath our feet. Pinemoor is a smaller place, where weary travellers can rest before setting off in either direction. Both are strongholds of Jubella. She has her soldiers stationed all over the forest."

"How big is the forest?"

"It covers the entire plane. That's why it took me so long to reach you. I set off once the messenger arrived. Beyond the forest is the sea which leads to my land, Sumera. I was resting there, knowing that someone or something would arrive at my gates."

"Okay. So, shall we set off before I freeze to death?"

"Follow me," Jed replied evenly, taking a path close by.

Jake kept pace with the giant, looking at the gleaming forest around him. No animals could be seen or heard, the occasional puff of breeze ruffling the strange bushes and plants that littered the forest around him. "What's that?" Jake said as his eyes picked out movement in the distance.

"Get down," Jed whispered. "It's a sentry, one of Hocken's lookouts. He's heading our way. Be ready and don't make a sound."

Jake hunkered down, letting a large fern cover his whole body. He could see a figure approaching along the same path that they were travelling on. Slipping the axe out of his waistband, Jake primed himself for action, his heart beginning to pound in his chest. He looked across the path towards Jed's position, a cold knot forming in his stomach as his companion slid further from sight. He looked at Jake, running a finger across his throat. Jake knew what that meant and what was expected of him. He waited patiently as the rustling footsteps approached, hearing rather than seeing his foe before he made a move. As quick as he could, Jake launched himself across the path, his axe scything down the unknown sentry, a sickening crack carrying across the forest. The man fell soundlessly, killed instantly by the blow just below his ear. "That was indeed impressive," Jed stated as he rose from his position. "He never knew what hit him. I congratulate you, Jake. You are indeed formidable, a worthy ally to have on such an escapade."

"I'm getting too old for this kind of stuff," Jake replied, dusting himself down. "Let's hope we have no more trouble."

"A hopeful thought, but I'm guessing the closer we get, the more people we'll have to deal with. Added to that, this man will be expected back soon. When he doesn't return, people will be wary. People will be on guard. Come, let us quicken our pace before the sun drops away."

"How long until we reach Jubella?"

"Not long. If we make it through Hocken and Pinemoor without too many hold-ups, we'll be there before morning."

"Lead on then," Jake urged. They travelled quickly as the forest darkened around them. Jake spotted glowing white eyes up in the trees, peering down at them as they passed by. After a while, the forest seemed to narrow, the sound of crashing waves carrying to their ears. In the twilight, he could make out to large wooden structures that funnelled everything towards a large stone archway, covered in white lichen.

"We are here," Jed said as he slowed to walking pace. If anyone stops you, tell them that you're travelling to Pinemoor to look for passage across the sea to Windorp."

"Windorp?"

"Yes. It's another land, similar to my own. There are ships that travel to-and-fro every day. You will not arouse too much suspicion."

"But look at me, I'm not going to look like anyone else. People will think I look odd."

Jed pulled a robe out of the bag he was carrying, handing it over to Jake. "Don this. It will hide your human garments."

Jake did so before something occurred to him. "Hang on, you said if I get stopped. Are you not coming with me?"

Jed smiled in the darkness. "I'll be right by your side, but no one will know that." Jake's eyes opened wider as the giant's form began to dissipate, shimmering motes cascading around the forest until he disappeared from sight.

"Bloody hell!"

Two large coins dropped at Jake's feet. "Take these. There is an inn towards the far end of Hocken. Those coins will get you a hot meal and a mug of ale. I will scout on ahead whilst you eat. Don't get into any trouble but listen to the other patrons. You might pick up a few titbits of information."

Jake bent down, dropping the coins into his pocket. "Okay. Let's do this." He walked on, looking up in awe at the stone archway that led into the settlement. Wooden walls reached up into the canopy, a feeling of claustrophobia washing over Jake as he made his way along the main thoroughfare, his eyes constantly on the move. People milled about him, groups of unsavoury looking men watching as he walked on by. At the centre of the settlement, a gated wooden structure stood out amongst the other building.

"That the entrance to the mine," Jed whispered next to him. "See, the children are coming out."

"Where do they go?"

"To their quarters until the sun comes up. They are fed a meagre dinner before they bed down for the night. The weaker ones don't last long. That's why they constantly need young ones to carry on the work."

"Sounds lovely," Jake whispered, trying to keep his face hidden as much as possible. Ahead, a large woman dragged three girls to one side as the children filed past her. Jake could see the woman issuing orders to the girls, whose tear-streaked faces nodded in obeyance. "What's that all about?"

"This is a regular occurrence. Some of the girls head to the inn to entertain the customers."

"Entertain?"

"I've seen many horrors in my time, Jake. I have committed many myself. However, nothing is as dark and twisted when the young are subjected to such evil. It is something that I try to block from my mind. You must too when you're inside the inn. Just observe, keep your head low and fill your stomach."

"Jesus," Jake breathed, his stride never faltering as he made his way past the entrance to the mine. All around, lanterns began to glow, bathing Hocken in an almost festive scene. For a brief moment, Jake forgot about the task ahead, almost enjoying the warm and friendly scene that played out in front of him.

"Over there," Jed signalled. "The inn is the last building on the left. I will wait outside and take a scout around."

Jake took in the building, noting a gang of swarthy-looking men who stood outside the from porch, plumes of smoke drifting from their pipes into the darkening skies. "Okay, I'll be back out in a bit." He made his way up the front steps, drawing suspicious looks from the large men. One spat on the wooden floor just as Jake was about to crest the steps. The others laughed, a raucous chorus that made Jake quicken his step slightly. A minute later, he seated himself at a small table next to a side window, surveying the room. It was half-full, tables of men swigging ale and slapping each other on the back as young serving maids squeezed between them. Jake smiled as one of the young women swatted a lecherous hand away, drawing howls of laughter from the men around her.

"Come here," the man bellowed, dragging the woman towards him. In one fluid motion, he'd pinned her to the tabletop, yanking up her dress before entering her roughly. Jake looked away, his eyes closing in pain as the girl's screams mingled with the men's encouraging chants.

"What can I get you," a voice beside him asked.

He looked up, trying to smile at the woman, who had a pinched look on her face. "What have you got?"

"Pie and tatties are popular tonight," she responded, her blackened teeth and pock-marked skin giving her a degree of protection from the clientele.

"Sounds good to me," he replied quietly, handing over the two coins.

"That's plenty. I'll bring you a few extra jugs of ale to cover the cost. Someone will bring yer grub shortly."

"Thank you," Jake said, drawing a raised eyebrow.

"Not many people thank us around here."

"I'm not from these parts."

"I can tell," she smiled, softening slightly. "If there is anything else you need, just give me a nudge. Or if you prefer something a bit fresher, I can get you a girl, or a boy if you fancy?"

"The food and ale will be just fine."

"Suit yerself," the woman huffed, slouching back towards the bar area, leaving Jake to his thoughts. Across the bar, the assault had been concluded, the girl tossed onto the floor as the men clinked mugs to toast a mighty conquest. Jake looked away, something building inside him. Rage. He averted his eyes, looking out of the window as a young girl approached.

"Mug of ale," she said warily.

"Thank you," Jake replied, taking the drink. He looked at the girl, his stomach twisting some more. She was no more than eight, with blond curly hair and an olive complexion. She smiled at him, a small gap in between her teeth making Jake smile back. "What's your name?"

"Scarlett," she replied meekly.

"Where are you from, Scarlett?"

"From another land. Near the place with the big cave."

"Vrybergen?"

She hesitated, unsure. "I think so. I lived on the sea with my kin. They were killed by the nasty men. They burned down our farmstead."

"I'm so sorry to hear that. When was this?"

Scarlett shrugged. "A while ago now. I can't rightly remember. Anyway, I'd better get back to the kitchen before they come looking for me. I'm only doing this because they hurt one of my friends last night because we went outside for a pee."

"Oh no. Did they hurt her badly?" Jake quizzed, his blood beginning to boil once more.

"Not sure. She didn't work today. Think she's hurt her leg. I hope she's going to be alright. Lauren's my best friend."

The hairs on Jake's forearms crinkled to attention. "Lauren! Did you say Lauren?"

"Yes, Lauren."

Jake moved closer to the girl, motioning for her to step forward. "Tell me, what colour hair does Lauren have?"

"It's brown. And it's curly, just like mine."

A few patrons looked over towards the window as Jake's mug smashed on the floor before a member of the kitchen staff dragged the girl away from him.

* * *

Jake walked out of the building, leaning on a braced gate as people milled about him. His mind was whirling, many pieces of the jigsaw falling into place. *The Longfords took her and brought her here. The bastards.*

"Have you satisfied your hunger?" a voice asked close by.

Jake flinched slightly before adopting a relaxed stance next to the invisible figure. "I have. I just need to go to the toilet before we set off."

"Toilet?" Jed enquired.

"Yes. Y'know. I need to relieve myself."

"But of course. I'll wait here. There are stalls at the rear of the building."

Nodding to no one in particular, Jake scooted around the rear of the building, finding half-a-dozen ram shackled stalls. He stepped inside the closest one, his nose wrinkling as the pungent aroma enveloped him. "Fucking hell!" he gasped, quickly emptying his bladder into a pit in the ground. The stench intensified, Jake trying not to gag before beating a hasty retreat to relative fresh air. He looked around for activity, slowly inching his way around the rear of the inn. His breath caught in his throat as he caught sight of Scarlett who was sat on a log near the edge of the forest. He hurried over, the girl looking up at him nervously. "It's okay. I'm not going to hurt you. I need you to do something for me, Scarlett."

"What?" the little girl replied.

"When you see Lauren, tell her that I'm a friend of her mother's. Tell her that I will come back for her and take her home."

"But if you take her home, I will lose my best friend," the girl pleaded, tears forming in her eyes.

"Don't worry. I'll take you home too, I promise," Jake assured her before heading back to the waiting Jed.

Chapter Eighteen

"Well, what shall we do now?" Wilf said from behind the copse of trees next to the sea.

"We wait," Tamatan said. "I cannot sense Jake close by. That's not to say that he isn't, but we should do anything rash. Best to wait until the sun goes down. There may be lookouts posted."

"Good point," the old man replied, sliding down the nearest trunk before lighting his pipe. He let the aroma fill his lungs, blowing it out as he rubbed at his beard. He looked across at Emma, who was arching her back. "How are you?"

"Well, my legs have never been this hairy, my roots must be coming through and I'd kill for a hot shower and a glass of red. But apart from that, I'm in pretty good shape, better than I thought I would be after a month in a strange world."

"You have an inner-strength, Emma," Tamatan began. "I sensed it the first time we met. You're strong, where many people are weak. You will come through this and we will find your daughter."

Tears brimmed in the woman's eyes before sliding down her pink cheeks. "Thank you, Tamatan. I never thought that demons existed. But if they're all like you, then it can't be bad."

The creature chuckled, his eyes glowing orange in the ever-dimming evening. "Thank you for the compliment, but I wasn't always so agreeable. I have had my moments over the ages, and I've done some pretty roughish things. But even demons grow older and wiser, mostly. All that is now behind me. I have Veltan and Jake and they keep me on a straight path, even if I do veer off now and again."

Silence descended between them as the shadows lengthened. They were all lost to their own thoughts until Wilf spoke. "Look on the horizon. It looks like a ship."

The others followed Wilf's outstretched arm, spotting the approaching vessel. "I wonder if Jake is on there. Or if he was on there?" the demon enquired.

"Well, there is only one way to find out. We need to get down there. And soon," Wilf replied.

They covered the dark grass as quickly and quietly as possible. Tamatan took the lead, Emma and a panting Wilf bringing up the rear. They inched down the stone staircase, coming out on a rocky landing above Vrybergen. "We need to keep talk to a minimum," Wilf whispered, trying to regain his breath.

"I agree," the demon said. "If we come across anyone unfriendly, leave them to me."

"Guys," Emma started. "Over there."

Wilf and Tamatan looked over at a small nook in the corner of the landing. A large man lay on the ground, the occasional snore escaping his chapped lips. The demon signalled for the others to be quiet as he approached, his feet making no sound. He knelt down next to the man, noting the ruddy complexion and lesions on his face and skin. Tamatan grasped the man's ponytail, rousing him from his slumber. "If you say a word, I will snap your neck. Nod if you understand." The man nodded, fear replacing the groggy look in his eyes. He looked up at the demon, his bladder voiding as he took in his emerald complexion and glowing eyes.

Wilf stood over him. "Did a man called Jake pass through these parts?" The man felt a tightening hold on the back of his neck, sweat breaking out across his forehead. He nodded simply.

"Did he go on a ship?" Tamatan continued.

"Yes," the man rasped.

"I said no talking. But if you whisper you may see the sun rise once again. Where did they take him?"

"Through the mist, to the land of the Grey."

"The Grey?" Wilf replied. Before any more questions could be answered the quivering man let out a hoarse cry, Tamatan stifling it with his hand.

"Thank you, friend. You've been most accommodating," the demon replied before snapping his neck in one swift motion. Emma looked away, closing her eyes as the sickening crunch reached her ears.

They moved over to the wall, watching as supplies were being loaded onto the vessel hundreds of feet below them. "Well, it looks like Jake has been taken prisoner," Wilf said. "And if he has, god knows where he's ended up?"

"Well, our only option is to follow him. On that," Tamatan replied, pointing at the Tilburg far below. "But first, we need to get rid of him," he motioned towards the now-cooling corpse.

Wilf peered over the ledge, grunting. "If we drop him off here, he'll be hidden by the rocks."

Tamatan dragged the body by its feet, hefting the great weight onto the lip. With a nudge, the dead lookout fell to the rocks below, coming to rest silently, hidden from prying eyes. "Now that this business is taken care of, let's be on our way."

* * *

"How far to Pinemore?" Jake asked as they followed an unmarked trail away from the main pathway.

"Not far," Jed replied as the darkened forest came alive around them. Above them, spirits and wraiths floated across the upper canopy, their shrieks and wails drifting down to the two outlanders.

Jake's mind was working overtime, trying to hatch a way to broach the subject that was gnawing at him. "Do you know the Longfords?"

"I do. They are servants of Grey, bringing him children and wares that he uses and trades."

"I met their leader, Lukash. Seems like someone who you don't cross."

"He is powerful. But alas, he's only a man, unlike his father, Berndt."

"Berndt?" Jake asked, wanting to keep the conversation going.

"Berndt is the head of the Longfords. He's a warlock, and a dark one at that. But he is old. When he dies, Lukash will assume his place and take his power."

"Sounds like an ambitious man."

"He is, and not one that I would trust. Berndt serves Grey, but I've always thought that the rest of them follow Lukash."

"So, what will happen when this Lukash takes power?"

"Hard to say. He will be summoned to see Grey, who I'm sure will have plans for him and his cohorts."

"So, the Longford's only supply to Grey?"

"Yes, why do you ask?"

"Just wondered," Jake replied, feigning interest in the exchange. "So, what is the plan once we reach Jubella?"

"Take this," Jed said, handing Jake a large necklace with a gold pendant at its centre. "I'm sure you're familiar with this."

Jake held the cross in his hand, liking the coolness the gold metal gave off. "It's a crucifix."

"Yes, although in different places it has different names. It is a symbol of the light, casting away the darkness. Once we have her, you must put this around her neck."

"Me?"

"Yes. Until you've done that, I'll be unable to get too close to her. The darkness within her will be too much for me. With the necklace on, she's just a woman, one who we can carry back to Grey."

"So, I'm going in there alone?"

"No. I'll be next to you, although no one will know it."

"Fair enough. That makes me feel a little better."

"Pinemoor is to our left," Jed whispered. "We will skirt the settlement until we reach the Hax river. Once we're across, Grimholt will be almost at our feet."

"Grimholt?"

"Jubella's stronghold. A place that no other, with dark creatures within."

"What kind of creatures?"

"Vampires. Hideous fiends that are age-eternal. Another reason why you have the pendant."

"Great! I thought I'd seen my last vampire," Jake huffed.

"Believe me. You've not seen anything like this before."

He let out a sigh. "Let's just get there. The quicker we're in, the quicker I'm home."

Jed smiled. "But of course."

Chapter Nineteen

"They're loading stuff on board," Wilf whispered from their position a few hundred yards away from the Tilburg.

"So, what do we do?" Emma asked expectantly.

"We need a way of getting on board," Tamatan added. "The shadows will be our ally. All we need is a distraction."

"Like what?" Emma replied, eyeing the diminutive demon.

"Leave that to me and wait for my signal." He scooted off along the alleyway, leaving Wilf and Emma huddled behind large fishing baskets.

"If anyone can create some chaos, its Tamatan," Wilf said dryly.

The demon stuck to the shadows, looking for any opportunity. He shrank away as three men came out of a nearby inn, slapping each other on the backs as they made their way to the waiting vessel. On the deck, Tamatan spotted a large man, barking instructions at his crew, a leather belt hissing through the air as he became more and more frustrated by the lack of urgency. He could hear curses drifting to his ears as the three men each grabbed a box and made their way up a stout-looking gangplank. Tamatan looked up at the large sails, noting how they started to fill. A whistling wind entered the giant cave from the sea, whipping around the walls before blowing back out to sea nudging the vessel against its moorings. "I can see why he wants to cast off. The wind is primed, and the ship is ready to fly." He saw the lighthouse up ahead, skirting around wooden building until he was only a few feet from the gangplank.

"Hurry up, ya mangy pack o' bastards," Kurt yelled. "All of you head to the lighthouse to fetch the last of the trinkets. The Tilburg is ready to go, and the wind will die down soon. Move!"

The demon watched as a dozen men exited the ship, filing past his position as they hurried towards the large stone structure. "Here goes," Tamatan said to himself, his eyes fixed on two barrels next to the lighthouse. He knew what they were, cane spirit. His eyes shone brighter until they seemed to engulf his head, a jet of red light crashing into the wooden barrels. He braced himself for the explosion, which came almost instantly, rocking the buildings around the quayside. The demon sprang from his position, bounding onto the deck with ease, noticing Wilf and Emma running towards him.

"What the hell was that?" Kurt bellowed as he came onto the deck. Before he could react, Tamatan snatched his sword, bashing him just below the ear with the hilt before running over to the gangplank.

"Cut the ropes," he called to Wilf, who dutifully took the sword. "Emma, head to the wheel and guide us out."

"What! I've never steered a ship before."

"We have no time," the demon shouted, noticing men appearing from the lighthouse, a look of consternation on their collective faces.

Wilf jumped onto the deck as the ship moved away from the dock, following Tamatan towards the wheel. "Here, let me take it," he said to Emma who moved aside readily.

"OUTLANDERS," the men of Vrybergen screamed as they tried in vain to chase the departing vessel, a few of them falling into the black waters below.

"Wilf, stay here while I go and fetch the captain."

"Okay," he replied as he turned the wheel urgently, the side of the Tilburg narrowly missing the jagged rocks at the mouth of the cave.

A minute later, Kurt was dumped unceremoniously in front of Wilf and Emma, sitting up groggily. "What the..." his voice trailed off as Tamatan's eyes shone above him. "A devil!" he screamed, the front of his britches darkening as he tried to scramble backwards, his ragged fingernails digging into the deck.

"Not a devil," Tamatan started as thick mist blew across the ship. "A demon. Now, do as I say, if you value your soul."

"Who are ya, and what do you want?"

"We're looking for our kin. He sailed with you recently. His name's Jake."

"Never heard of him," Kurt countered gruffly.

"Really?" the demon replied, his eyes blazing. "The last soul who told an untruth to me is now in damnation for eternity. Is that where you want to be?"

"I'm tellin ya. Never heard of anyone called Jake."

"Well, if you're no use to us, we've no need for you to be on this ship," Wilf rasped, pricking the captain's skin with his own blade. "On your feet. You're going for a swim."

Kurt looked left and right, trying to seize any opportunity. He knew it was fruitless. He was about to die. "Okay okay. Maybe I do know him."

"What is your name?" Tamatan asked.

"Kurt."

"Well, Kurt. Start talking."

The captain climbed to his feet, standing unsteadily. "I need to take the wheel. No one knows these waters like me."

"Very well," Wilf acquiesced. "But if you try anything daft, your sword will skewer you. And not where you'd think."

Taking the threat seriously, Kurt took the wheel, thankful for something to lean on. "He came aboard a few weeks ago. The Longfords brought him to me. He's gone through the mist to the Halls of Kenn."

"Kenn," Wilf replied. "Who's Kenn?"

"Not what, where. It's a place, where he lives."

"He. Who's he?" Tamatan asked inquisitively.

"I don't know his name. I've heard whispers that he goes by the name of Grey," he stated, bending the truth. "Jake was being taken to him."

"I've never heard the name," Tamatan started. "But over the ages, I've heard tales about an all-powerful being that lives on a different plane. A being that controls everything."

"Not sure about that," Kurt countered. "But I know the Longfords answer to him. And if they do, he must be very powerful."

"How long to reach this Kenn?" Wilf asked.

Kurt shrugged his shoulders. "Depends. We never usually sail straight there as we drop off and pick up along the way. If the wind is fair and we encounter no bad weather, we could be there by tomorrow evening."

"Good," Tamatan replied, relaxing slightly. "If you hold to your word, we'll not harm you. Take us to Kenn and let us find Jake."

"I guess I have no bleedin choice, do I?"

Before anyone could answer, a jet of water shot into the air, a black behemoth breaking the surface of the water next to the Tilburg. The four of them watched as the giant creature sunk beneath the waves, its black jagged tail scything through the air before being consumed by the frigid water. As they watched in fascination, a deep drone rumbled across the expanse of water, raising goosebumps across Emma's arms. "You have a choice Kurt," Wilf started. "Help us and live. Or go swimming with the fishes."

Chapter Twenty

"We're here," Jed whispered, motioning for Jake to halt his progress.

The private investigator looked through the forest, his stomach tightening at the sight below him. A huge castle-like structure, white in colour sat brooding amongst the trees. It rose high, above the upper canopy its stone walls seeming impenetrable. "Looks lovely," he began. "So, how the hell do we get in there?"

"Good question. I've never ventured this far. But I can feel its power. Since entering the forest, every step that I've taken I can feel my power ebbing away. So, from here, I must hide my form. Don't worry, I'll never be more than two steps away from you, Jake."

"Good to know, I think."

"You can do this. You've defeated vampire kings, Jake. You have your axe and your pendant. They will serve you well."

Jake took the cross out of his back pocket, placing it over his head. It nestled next to the healing stone, comforting him somewhat. "Let's get this over with." They headed downhill, weaving in and out of the trees, both eyes searching for a way in and any signs of life.

"Over there," Jed breathed, "pointing towards a rising bank of mist. "It looks like some form of moat, surrounding the keep. There's a gate on the other side."

As they neared, Jake could hear the bubbling of water close by, waves of warmth buffeting him. "How do we get across there? It must be thirty feet wide?" On the far side, a gravel path wound its way around the stone structure on either side of the gate. No signs of life were present which made Jake nervous.

"Brace yourself," his invisible guide whispered, taking Jake under the arms. With a grunt, Jed leapt forward, Jake closing his eyes as they flew over the boiling waters, landing heavily next to the sloping walls. "I must rest for a moment. That took it out of me."

"Jesus!" Jake exclaimed, dusting himself down. "You could have warned me."

"Let's move before someone or something sees us," Jed commanded. Jake felt an invisible tug at his gown, moving towards the large iron gate. Jake's eyes opened wider as the metal bolt securing the gate silently slid to one side, the door swinging inwards. "Now keep quiet and have your axe and trinkets ready."

Whereas the exterior of the castle was white, the interior was utterly black. Jake looked up at the vaulted ceiling that ran off in all directions, stained glass windows high up in the walls offering only the merest indication of light from the outside world. A hacking sound off to Jake's left made him flinch, his eyes searching for somewhere to hole-up. Out of the shadows, a figure emerged, the private investigator's legs turning rubbery. "Jesus Christ," he murmured as it drew closer. It was taller than Jake, dressed in a black robe, tied at the neck. Its head was devoid of hair, its ear gnarled and pointed. Piercing yellow eyes sought him out. Ancient eyes, looking for prey. As it neared, the vampire hissed, a black tongue pointing out through long sharp incisors. As the hiss ended, a low growl filled the hall, Jake taking a step back. Time seemed to slow, the room seeming to tilt at an unusual angle as fetid clouds of breath reached him. "Stay back," he croaked. A coldness washed over him as his teeth began to chatter.

"The trinket," Jed urged, the vampire's eyes moving away from Jake, breaking the spell on him. As quick as his shaking hand would allow, he tore off his cloak, the cross immediately glowing white, the creature falling back a pace, its bluish brow creasing in pain. Jake heard the thud of something close by, not understanding what made the sound. He looked at the vampire, noticing a small hole in the front of its cloak, watching in stunned silence as the being crumpled before his eyes. "We must move quickly. The others will be alerted to our presence."

"How many are there?" Jake asked, his heart hammering in his chest.

"No idea. Let's go. The quicker we find her, the quicker we can escape this nightmare place."

They hurried along a large hallway, Jake noting with dread other vampires, similar in form to the one that they'd encountered. None of them seemed to follow, the ancient creatures shuffled slowly around the castle as Jake hurried past. "There are stairs up ahead," he said.

"I'm with you, Jake. Keep up the pace."

He needed no coaxing as growls and hisses echoed through the building. At the first stone step, Jake looked back across the hallway, counting several sets of yellow eyes slowly bearing down on their position. "Fuck! I hope there's another way out of here."

"Let's worry about that once we've captured Jubella," Jed answered. "Move."

Jake sprinted up the winding staircase, ducking as flying creatures whistled past his face. He tried to focus, his lungs beginning to burn as he wound his way ever upwards until he reached a large landing. He guessed the distance to a large door at the far end to be at least fifty metres, dark archways spaced evenly on either side. He began walking, the cross thumping against his chest as growls and hisses echoed up to their position. "Do you think…" Jake's voice was cut off as a huge white hand grabbed him around the throat, the arm connected to it slamming him into the wall. His vision exploded into a million points of light as his skull bashed against the wall, his feet hanging in mid-air as the life was choked from him. He regained his sight after a brief second, a single yellow eye staring at him, long yellow fangs advancing towards him. And then, he was tossed to the ground, gulping in stale air as the pressure on his throat gave way. Jake sat up, seeing the creature rolling around on the floor, an unseen enemy battling with it. "GO!" Jed screamed.

He took off, careering into the walls as he clumsily bounded towards the heavy wooden door, screams and curses at his heels. His shoulder hit the door first, crashing it open as he skidded to a halt on the floor. "Greetings, stranger," a lyrical voice called out. It was female, light and full of life, at odds with the room that he now found himself in.

Gingerly, Jake climbed to his feet, his shoulder tingling as the battle raged behind him. "Jubella?" He looked around the dark space, candles on the table and walls casting shadows across the flagstone floor.

"So, you know who I am. If you know that then you're not here for pleasure. Who are you and why are you here?"

Jake could not see where the voice was coming from. It seemed to shift around the dark space, tables and chairs close by beginning to rattle gently. "Where are you?" He looked over at the only window in the room, a faint hue from the moon barely able to penetrate the glass.

"Why, I am everywhere and nowhere," the voice soothed. "Did Grey send you?"

The commotion in the corridor beyond seemed to be inching closer, the familiar hisses and groans of the approaching hoard seeming to press down on Jake as he tried to clear his mind. "Yes. I'm sorry, but I have no other choice."

Light footsteps echoed around the room as a figure emerged from the shadows. Jake could see that it was female, small and delicate dressed in a flowing silver robe. Her skin was almost translucent, her red hair reaching down past her waistline. Jubella's eyes were as white as her skin, a lopsided grin spreading across her full lips. "Now I can see you, and what a fair sight you are. Surely, one as fair as you is not in league with that old monster?"

"I have no choice," Jake repeated. "I'm sorry."

Jubella's grin slipped away, a scowl spreading across her face. "Do you think I'm just going to skip through the forest with you, Jake? Do you really think I will go willingly?"

"You know my name?"

"Grey's not the only one who knows things."

Before Jake could speak, Jed crashed through the door with the creature, landing awkwardly. The beast gave one last guttural cry before succumbing to the darkness. Jed appeared, seeming to shrink back as his eyes met Jubella's. "Jake, the pendant."

Jake turned back to the woman, his eyes widening in horror at the sight before him. Gone was the white skin and red hair. Jubella was now a desiccated black form, her skin the colour of scorched earth, her hair grey and straggly. "You will never leave this place," she hissed. "My clan is almost upon you."

Jake glanced behind him, his stomach turning to stone as the first set of searching eyes came onto the landing. They gleamed, bright yellow in the darkness as a low moan drifted towards him. The hallway seemed to close in on itself, the floor sliding towards him like an ancient travellator. Another pair of eyes appeared, searching for the intruders. A footstep close by made him spin around as Jubella made her move. Tiny hands locked around his upper arms, forcing Jake backwards until he hit a stone wall. Shaking and dazed, he made the mistake of locking eyes with her. Eyes that now resembled dark pits, flecked with red. She opened her mouth, a rank stench washing over him as he tried to pry her vice-like fingers from him. He was losing, firing a punch into her face, his arm and shoulder jarring at the impact. "Jed, help!"

"I can't," a voice cried. "They are coming for us. Use the pendant."

Jake whipped the gold chain off his head, a scream exploding from Jubella's mouth. He felt the grip loosen slightly as he slipped the chain over her head. "GET THIS OFF ME!" she hollered as Jake finally broke the hold.

He was frozen on the spot, unsure of what to do as the figure in front of him began changing before his eyes. The puckered blackened skin began morphing, becoming lighter as Jubella's hair slowly returned to a lustrous red colour. "What shall I do?" he called over to Jed who was facing down an army of the undead.

"Hit her," he shouted back.

"Shit," Jake mouthed, not liking the answer. He turned, facing the woman once more, steam rising from her skin and robes. *Okay. It's not a real woman,* he reasoned before firing a right hook that struck Jubella just underneath the ear. She went down, landing in a rustle of garments. He turned to Jed. "We need to find another way out of here." Howls echoed down the corridor, the vampires sensing their master was in trouble, their pace suddenly quickening.

"Jake," you take over here. I will secure her for our journey back."

"But she's wearing the cross," Jake said, watching in fascination as Jed smashed a huge fist into the first vampire to enter the room.

"Use your smarts."

Jake looked around the room, seeing nothing of help apart from a table and half-a-dozen chairs. Hang on, as a thought pinged in his mind. He raced over to the nearest chair, tipping it onto its high back. Propelling his foot downwards, he snapped two legs from it, gathering up the sturdy pieces before turning towards the gathering hoard. He made a makeshift cross, the wood beginning to warm in his hands.

"NOOOOOOO," A vampire yelled as Jake approached. "You cannot escape, human," it cursed, bright yellow eyes burning in the darkness.

"Get the fuck back," Jake commanded, walking forward. The creatures gave way, backing away into the corridor. He stole a glance behind him, happy to see Jed securing Jubella's hands with rope. "We need to find another way outta here."

"I will find a way. Follow me."

Jake retreated, the baying pack spitting and hissing at him as the cross began to sting his palms. He kept his eyes on them, stealing a glance back every few steps as he headed towards an open door. *Gotta make a break for it.* He stepped into another corridor, pulling the door closed behind him. *Thank fuck for that*, as he slid a large bolt into place, locking the heavy wooden door. He turned, seeing Jed at the far-end of the corridor, Jubella hung lifelessly over his wide shoulder. Bangs and scratches from the other side of the door spurred him into action as he broke into a jog, making his way along the narrow hallway. He concentrated on the retreating figure, averting his eyes from the strange-looking animal heads that adorned the walls. A minute later, he came out on a square terrace, the upper canopy of the trees above his head, some of the thicker branches invading their space. "Thank God for that," he panted, looking over at the giant.

"Jake. This is where I leave you."

"W-what?" he blurted.

"I'm telling you before I go, Jake. I'm not deserting you, but Jubella will awaken soon and I must get back to Grey as quick as possible. You will slow me down, but you know the way to the pool. Head there as quick as you can, and we will meet again."

"You can't just fucking leave me…" His sentence trailed off as Jed leapt over the wall, vanishing before Jake's eyes. "For fuck's sake," he cursed as a heavy wooden door nearby began splintering under incessant blows.

Chapter Twenty-One

"Lauren, wake up," Scarlett whispered, gently shaking her best friend out of her slumber.

She rubbed her eyes, sitting up on the straw mattress. "Scarlett? What's wrong?"

"Shh," she warned. "The guards are outside. A man came to Hocken tonight. He told me that he was a friend of your Ma's and that he was coming back to take us home."

Lauren flinched, edging forward. "Who was he?" she urged as her eyes opened wider.

"He said his name was Jake. He was having supper at the inn. I served him and he was talking to me. I was dragged away by Ursa and beaten. Then a little while later, he found me at the back of the inn and told me that he will return for us."

"But that's impossible. I come from another world, Scarlett. How could he have found me?"

"I do not know. But he knew who you were, and he made a promise."

Lauren absorbed the news, sitting in silence as her best friend got comfortable on the mattress. She sighed, her shoulder drooping. "But even if he does return, there are guards all over Hocken, and in the forest too. I think it will be too difficult for him." She looked across the dormitory, dozens of small children huddled together before the sun rose and their work continued. Lauren suddenly felt weary, her young body feeling heavy despite the constant work that had strengthened her limbs and back. It had also strengthened her spirit. She'd seen many of her friends' wilt and die inside the mine, only to be dragged away by the elders, who dumped their bodies in the nearby river. Lauren held onto the hope that one day, her mother would come for her, spiriting her away from the nightmare that she found herself in, returning her to Cornwall and her wonderful garden and toys. The news should have buoyed her spirits. However, it had the opposite effect, knowing that no one could free her from her forested prison. "No one can save us, Scarlett. We're stuck…"

Her sentence ended abruptly as a deep rumbling echoed through the forest. "What's that?" Scarlett looked into Lauren's eyes, both girls edging closer as the horn-like sound washed over them.

"No idea. I've never heard it before." They both crawled over to the shutter, peering over the ledge as men ran around the settlement. "What are they saying?"

"No Idea," Scarlett added. "But it looks like trouble." They both watched as a group of men, all armed with axes, pitchforks and swords headed off towards Pinemoor, the gloomy forest swallowing them up within seconds.

"Someone's in trouble," she observed, a knot forming in her stomach.

"Oh well, as long as it's not us."

* * *

"What the hell is that?" Jake said to himself as he walked to the wall where Jed had made his escape. The sound seemed to be coming from inside the castle. "Oh shit. It's a call for help." He peered over the edge of the wall, the drop to the forest too far for him to jump. Added to his predicament, the boiling river bubbled below him, surrounding the fortification like a ring of hot steel. *How do I get down?* Before an answer could present itself, the door holding the vampires gave way, a splintering sound carrying out onto the terrace. Tucking one of the chair legs into his waistband, Jake grabbed the closest branch, testing the weight before dangling himself over the drop.

"Human," an ancient voice spat, Jake glancing to his left as they spilt out of the doorway, several sets of eyes seeking him out.

"Bollocks," he cursed, propelling himself across the branch that led to the larger boughs and the main trunk. His arms burned after a few seconds, the exertion sapping his reserves. *Keep going*, he willed himself, grabbing another branch which allowed him to place his feet on another limb for a brief respite. Sounds invaded his ears, the baying crowd just out of reach as they growled and moaned at him. Jake looked down, the river right below him. *I've got to get down, somehow?* Voices drifted through the forest, the shouts and hollers of men bearing down on the castle. "Shit! That's all I need," knowing that reinforcements were heading his way with one intention. To kill the outlander. Carefully, he made his way across the giant tree, placing each step carefully on the smooth bark, knowing that one slip would be the end of him. Behind him, the vampires filed back towards the doorway, their shuffling steps more urgent than before. *Where's Tarzan when you need him?* Jake crossed from one giant tree to another, climbing higher as several figures charged towards the castle in the darkness. He could see the men were armed with an array of deadly weapons, all of them with his name all over them. *Got to survive this. Got to get back home.* He rested on a huge limb, watching as a bridge was lowered across the steaming river. Several undead creatures emerged, their leader advancing on the men for what looked to Jake like a discussion on what had happened. He heard a loud roar go up from the men, weapons clanking together. Jake renewed his efforts, leaping and crossing the forest, moving away from the castle towards Pinemoor.

"He's in the trees," a voice hollered, the men training their eyes into the canopy.

"Shit! They'll catch me in no time up here." As quick as he'd dare, Jake began dropping through the trees towards the forest floor. He landed in a heap, ensuring that his axe and makeshift stake were at hand before taking off towards Hocken. Towards two little girls that needed his help. A deep laugh echoed through the dark forest, the hairs on the back of his neck prickling to attention. It seemed to taunt him. Telling Jake that all his efforts would be in vain. He weaved his way through the trees, looking for signs of danger. However, none presented themselves, Jake surmising that all the lookouts and potential foes were several hundred yards behind him. His jog turned into a brisk run, hoping that they were mostly out of shape, not being able to match his pace. Even as Jake had entered his forties, he exercised regularly, taking long walks with his daughter and even longer runs across the criss-cross of Cornish pathways that littered the English county. As he entered Hocken from the forest, he spotted a sentry stood outside the inn. *Shit, where would Lauren be?* At the inn or somewhere else? He decided that the man would give him the information or die.

"Who goes there?" a gruff voice called out.

"Jubella's been taken," Jake called back, seeing the man's confused face as the outlander approached with ill news.

"Hold it," he shouted, Jake seeing the whites of his eyes. He saw panic and uncertainty.

The man never saw the punch coming. It landed on his jaw, stunning the large man, who sank to his knees. Jake grabbed a handful of hair, lifting the man's head up. "Where do the children sleep at night? Answer quickly or I'll slit your throat."

The man's eyes darted left and right, looking for salvation. No one was going to save him. "Please, don't hurt me."

"Tell me where they are and I'll let you live."

"The cabin next to the mine. They all sleep in there."

"If you're lying, you'll be the first to die."

"I swear," he cried, meaning every word.

"Thank you," Jake replied, bringing the flat head of the axe down onto his head. As the man fell sideways onto the dirt, Jake was already moving, heading towards the mine, ready for anything. Judging by the hollers from the forest, Jake guessed hoped that he'd made ground on the angry mob. He hoped that it might just give him the advantage he'd need if he was to make it out alive. A few seconds later, he dropped a large woman with a single punch, kicking a wooden door open that led into a low-slung dormitory. "Lauren. Scarlett. Are you here?"

"Yes," a voice called out as two girls ran towards him.

She looked just like the picture Emma had shown him, except the girl now looked older, her hair much longer. "No time to talk. I'm a friend of your Mum's. We need to go. Now."

"Okay," Lauren replied, a glimmer of hope in her eyes that her nightmare was almost at an end.

"Let's go. There's an angry mob and a pack of vampires following." The three of them made a break for it, Jake looking back as several children ran out into the night in all direction. *Diversion*, he thought, hoping that the fleeing youngsters would give them a few more seconds advantage.

"Do you know where you're going?" Scarlett panted as she struggled to keep pace.

"I think so, why do you?"

"I know the fastest way to the pool. That way," she pointed to a right-hand path.

Jake veered off his course, striding through the forest hearing his heart pumping rapidly. "Keep going, girls. It can't be too… "

"Lookout," Lauren screamed as a dark shape flew past Jake, the private investigator losing his footing and rolling amongst soft ferns. The girls dragged him to his feet, Lauren handing him the axe. "Thanks. What the hell was that?"

"Don't know, replied Scarlett. "Looked like a giant bat."

"Jesus. Well, whatever it was, let's keep going. I can hear the men behind us." The forest seemed to come alive as they ran on. Spirits floated past them, misshapen faces morphing and sneering at the trio as they pushed on.

"Almost there," Scarlett huffed, Jake noting that the girls were beginning to falter.

"Come on. We're nearly there."

A few minutes later, Scarlett slowed to a trot. "There it is. We've made… "

Her words died in her throat as they spotted a dark figure kneeling close to the pool, their back to them. As they neared, both girls panting and wheezing, the figure rose to its feet. The head was devoid of hair, almost bluish in colour. As it turned towards them, Jake's stomach clenched, knowing what stood between them and their way home. A vampire. A large, ancient creature, its bright eyes burning into his as purple lips peeled back over misshapen incisors. It spread its arms out wide, curled talons sprouting out of its black robe. "Jesus. This guy makes Elias look like Mary Poppins. Girls. When you get chance, dive into the pool. Don't wait for me."

"But you saved us, we can't leave you."

"Do it," he commanded as the creature advanced on him, loping strides eating up the space between them. It growled, the noise making Jake break out in goosebumps. He gripped the axe and chair leg, hoping they would be enough to win through. "Move around the other side of the pool," he whispered to the girls, both of them edging away from him as the vampire readied to attack. It lunged, Jake moving out of the way, a long talon narrowly missing his face. *He's slower than Elias,* Jake noted, striking the creature across the back with the axe. Slower or not, Jake's arm jolted as the axe bounced off the cloak, the vampire turning around unaffected. "GO," he shouted, hearing the splash of water as the girls dove into the black water. The vampire charged once more, faster than before. As Jake dodged to his left, a vice-like grip encircled his throat, the creature snaring him. His feet left the bracken-strewn floor, swaying gently as he faced the ancient being. It smiled at him, chapped lips cracking as its fangs moved closer. Cold, rank breath washed over Jake, who gargled helplessly in the beast's grip.

"Jubella," it hissed, Jake's vision beginning to darken as blood was cut off from his brain.

His heels banged into the wall that surrounded the pool, Jake lifting his legs up quickly before lowering them into the frigid water. They scraped up and down, his trainer finding an indentation. He pushed his foot deeper, anchoring himself before striking the chair leg into the vampire's chest, penetrating its cloak and skin. It let out a howl, Jake feeling the grip on his throat lessen slightly. That was his cue as he hurled himself backwards, the vampire caught off-guard as its massive frame plunged into the water on top of him. The world went dark and cold before Jake was cartwheeled over and over, locked in a deadly embrace from which there was no escape.

Chapter Twenty-Two

"We're making good time," Kurt bellowed, his chains holding his arms and legs in place. Despite complying with the outlander's wishes, Wilf thought it prudent to secure the large man to the wheel, not wanting anything unforeseen to take place out on the open seas.

The trio sat on sacks of wheat on the lower deck, Wilf nodding at the positive news. "Just keep us on tack and you'll enjoy a mug of ale when all this is over."

"At least he's doing what he's told," Emma observed, a cool mist making her zip up her fleece top.

"For now," Tamatan countered. "Once we're at our destination, we must find a way to keep him aboard. If he sets sail for his home, we'll be stuck out there."

"If the Longfords are behind all this, there may be a chance that Lauren is out there somewhere."

"True," Wilf agreed. "But we've no idea what to expect. If Jake is out there, he will know more than us. Maybe he can cast some light on the goings-on."

The deck creaked as the ship ploughed on, its sails filled with incessant gusts of wind. A deep drone drifted across the Tilburg, as behemoths of the deep swam alongside. Tamatan looked up at Kurt, his eyes shimmering a deep orange. "There are dozens of barrels of cane spirit onboard. When we reach our destination, one of us must stay with Kurt."

"Why?" Emma asked, her brow creasing.

"The ultimate threat to him. If anyone tries to board the Tilburg, or if Kurt makes trouble, we blow up the ship."

Wilf nodded, blowing smoke into the air before it was consumed by the gale that pushed them ever forwards. "I'll stay. I have no issue with keeping him in line. Forgive me, Emma, but he may see you as a soft touch."

"Whatever you think is best, Wilf," the woman replied, smiling at the grizzled old man. "I'm sure Tamatan will keep me in line."

The demon chuckled. "My kin may disagree with you. I have my hands full with them both and they make sure that I am kept in line."

The sun broke through the low clouds, bathing the Tilburg in water light. Wilf walked over to the ship's rail, trying to discern if they were close to landfall. "It's like pea soup out there, as Jo would say. I have no idea if we're close, or if that rascal has turned the ship around and is heading back to Vrybergen."

"We're on course," Tamatan declared. "I can feel something on the wind. Like a dark web, pulling us towards it. Whatever it is, we are drawing near."

* * *

Jake broke the surface of the water, gasping for air. A growl close by, made him flinch, remembering who was sharing the pool with him. He ploughed through the water, dragging himself over the lip before landing heavily on the stone floor. He wiped his eyes, focusing on the ceiling above him a figure loomed over him. Their eyes locked once more, Jake's body relaxing as the vampire climbed out of the pool, its cloak dripping water onto his upturned face.

"You have done well, Jake," a voice close by said, the vampire breaking the hold. Its feral eyes shifted, opening wide at the unseen figure.

Jake scrambled to his feet, seeing Grey and Jed approaching, deep growls emanating from his dark foe. "I barely made it, no thanks to Jed."

"We can discuss the whys and wherefores later." Grey looked at the creature, a smile spreading across his weathered features. "Talack. It has been many years since we last met."

"Grey," Talack hissed. "Where is Jubella?"

"She's where she needs to be. In my care. You, however, are far from home." The vampire took a step forward, teeth bared. Grey lifted his hand, a long finger pointing towards Talack, who froze mid-step. "This is your end, Talack, baron of the dark forest."

Jake looked on in amazement as the vampire began choking, its blue complexion turning darker, red-rimmed eyes bulging from their sockets. Jake heard a sound like the snapping of twigs as the giant form collapsed in on itself, its dark cloak settling on the floor becoming still. "Jesus. I could have done with you on the other side of the pond."

Grey chuckled, removing his hood. To Jake, the all-powerful being looked like a regular old man. His hooded eyelids and prominent nose would not stand out back in his world. A memory flashed before him when the Wizard of Oz was unmasked, a little old man the actual protagonist. "I was watching, Jake. Yes, Talack is the chief amongst his brood. An ancient vampire, who has roamed various planes for millennia. You handled yourself very well. Jed would not have left you without the reassurance that you'd make it back. Both of us watched your journey through the forest. We commend you, but I have a question."

"What's that?"

"The children. Who are they?"

Jake was suddenly at a loss for words. He didn't know whether to err on the side of caution or lay it all out on the line. He chose the latter. "Where are they?"

"They are close by. And they are safe. Someone is preparing them a bowl of broth."

"Okay. The one girl is called Lauren. She is from my world. That's the main reason why I'm here."

"Go on," Grey replied, his eyes focused on the young man.

"Before I do, can I ask you a question?"

"It should be Grey asking the questions. But I will allow that. After all, I am in your debt, so to speak."

"The children that the Longfords bring to you. Do they only bring them to you, or do they supply them elsewhere?"

Grey walked over to the side of the pool, resting his ancient body against the stone. "We have an agreement. They only supply to me. Berndt and I have an understanding that I know he would never break."

"Okay, you're not going to like this. The girl called Lauren was taken from her mother by the Longfords and was sent to the mine at Hocken."

Grey's face transformed from inquisitive to a deep scowl, his eyes seeming to darken. Jed shifted uncomfortably, understanding the gravity of Jake's statement. "Impossible," spat the robed figure. "Berndt would never betray my trust."

"I don't know Berndt, but I've met Lukash and his gang. They basically own a small village where I live. It was only by chance that I came across Lauren. But It's true, ask her yourself."

"Jed, bring the girl to me."

Jake waited as the giant left, feeling Grey's constant gaze, the silence between them deafening. A minute later, Lauren appeared next to Jed, looking up expectantly at Grey. "Yes," unaware of just who she was speaking to.

"Dear child. Tell me, how did you come to be on this plane?"

"They took me."

"Who?"

"The Longfords. I was playing in my garden when I heard a voice through the hedge. When I climbed through, a big man grabbed hold of me. I think his name was Malcolm. He said that my Daddy would pay for what he'd done."

"And they brought you here?"

"Yes. I came on a big ship. Then, they asked me to hide in a large box that was full of stones and pretty gems. It was scary and I couldn't breathe very well."

Grey walked over to Lauren, his face softening. "Dear child. I am sorry for all you've endured. Do you miss your Mummy?"

"Yes, I really miss her. I want to go home."

Grey weighed up the situation carefully, looking from Lauren to Jake, then back to the little girl. *He did what I asked him. He delivered Jubella to me.* Glancing over at Jed, Grey made up his mind as the giant nodded at him. "Very well. Jake, I had further plans for you. Not that I would renege on our deal, but I wanted to keep you a while longer. However, this little girl needs to be reunited with her kin. The Tilburg is heading our way. It will be here by nightfall. Once the goods are unloaded, you both have free passage back home."

Jake sighed, relieved that their ordeal was over. "Thank you."

"What about Scarlett? She's my best friend and she has no family."

"Well, what kind of nasty old man would keep you apart. Scarlett will go with you. Jed, take Lauren back to her supper, she looks hungry."

"Yes, Grey. I will rest afterwards. The journey into the forest has sapped my reserves. I will check that Jubella is secure then find a bunk."

"Very well. I will rest too. My prize is heading towards me and I will need all my strength for when she arrives. Jake, go with Jed. He will find you a place to rest."

Jake nodded, walking away with Lauren and the giant. A nagging doubt tugging at his mind.

Chapter Twenty-Three

"Kurt, how much longer?" Wilf barked, his stomach rumbling.

"We'll be there by nightfall."

"We're starving. Is there any more grub?"

"Aye. Check the galley."

Wilf stood up, stretching his stiff limbs. "I'll go and forage for our supper. You two can wait here." They both nodded, the older man making his way through a door underneath where Kurt was stood. He made his way along a musty corridor, turning left through a small doorway into the ship's galley. After routing around for a few minutes, Wilf laid some dried hunks of meat, salted biscuits and two jugs of what smelt like ale. "That should keep us going," he smiled, placing all the provisions in a hessian sack. "What else is on this tub?" He walked out of the galley, moving towards the rear of the ship. His boots scuffed along the wooden walkways until he reached a large door. Must be the hold? The door opened noisily, Wilf taking a few steps inside. There were windows on either side the room, grey light filtering in from outside as he made his way past crates and barrels. The Tilburg creaked gently, hanging hams swinging gently as the ship ploughed its way across the still sea. He came to the far wall of the storeroom, a large rectangular casket sitting alone on a sturdy-looking stand. "Looks like a coffin," Wilf said to himself. He ran his rough hand across the top, the old man appreciating the craftsmanship. I wonder whose inside, he mused, deliberating whether to take a peek. His mind made up, Wilf gently prizing one section of the lid off, turning to lay it next to a wooden barrel. He took a step back, standing over the incumbent inside. "Fuckenell," he blurted, falling backwards into a shelf full of jars, sending them skittering around the room noisily. He sat on the floor, his breath ragged, his heart pounding against his sternum. "No. It can't be," he cried before dragging himself to his feet. He looked down once more, a ragged sob escaping his throat as he stared down at the corpse.

"Wilf, what is wrong?" Tamatan called, seeing the pallid colour of his friend's face.

The old man looked at the demon, tears streaming down his face. "Come with me. Emma, keep an eye on that rogue. If he does anything mischievous, slice his throat."

Tamatan followed Wilf to the rear of the ship, his eyes glowing brightly in the confines as the ship pitched and yawed gently. Entering the storeroom, the demon's pulse quickened, a distant memory flooding back to him. He stood next to Wilf, looking down into the casket. "Oh my…"

"Yes. It's Katherine. My Katherine."

Tamatan looked at what was once Katherine Bathurst. He did the calculation in his head, knowing that she'd been dead for several years. *She should be just bones.* The form that lay underneath them looked like the woman they had both known. Her hair was the same auburn colour, almost as vibrant as they'd both remembered. Her skin was white, the only indication that she wasn't sleeping. The demon reached out, placing his hand on her chest. The skin was cool to the touch, yet he felt a deep stirring within. "This is the work of a warlock. One who has the power to bring the dead back to life. But why would he have done this?"

"Remember I told you that they'd desecrated her grave. My betting is that whoever has Jake wants Kath too."

"You may be right, my old friend. She's not yet alive. Maybe this Grey has the power to wake Katherine from her slumber."

"Well to hell with that. If he's going to do that, then we will take her home with us. She's not going to dwell in a dark place away from her kin. Her place is with us."

"I hear you, Wilf. Really, I do. But for now, we must place the lid back on the casket and pretend we've not seen her. We must only act when the time is right, or risk not waking her at all."

"You're wise, Tamatan. I know I like to bolt off like a prize cock, but your plan makes perfect sense. Let this Grey wake her, then we will act."

"Let's just hope that she's the same Katherine that we knew before. Let us hope that She's not been tainted. Or turned."

* * *

Grey stood alone, the pond's surface a black mirror on nothingness. He raised a hand, the surface shifting, rotating until the body of water resembled a mini whirlpool. His watery eyes shone, casting light over the body of water, an image appearing. It was a ship, the Tilburg. "My prize is almost here. I've lived too long in solitude. Maybe now, I can have some company in my winter years." His brow creased. "Something is not right," Grey muttered, seeing an empty deck, save for the captain and another figure close by. "Where are the crew? And who is… " His voice trailed off as the figure next to the captain turned, her long dark hair blowing in the breeze. In her hand she held a sword, its tip pointed towards the man at the helm. "What devilry is afoot?" He stood stock-still, watching in earnest as two figures emerged from below decks. One was a man, aged in years, the other a strange-looking being, shorter than his accomplice, its eyes glowing green. "A demon, heading for Kenn. This can only be ill news. Are they here to take Jake to his salvation? And do they know about my prize?" He dropped his hand, the water returning to normal, ripples lapping at the stone wall. *It looks like my plans must change. It looks like they won't be going home after all.*

* * *

"We're here," Kurt boomed.

The others climbed to their feet, all conversation ending abruptly as they stared at the huge sea cave ahead. "Bloody hell," Wilf exclaimed as the Tilburg was consumed by darkness, a blue portal shining brightly a few hundred yards ahead.

"Right. We all know what we must do. Emma, are you ready?"

"As ready as I'll ever be," she replied evenly, pulling the striking stones out of her pocket, twiddling them between her fingers.

They made their way up the ladder, the demon addressing Kurt. "Right. We have told you what we are going to do. Make no mistake, Emma will blow this ship to pieces if you try anything. Is that understood?"

"Aye. Don't fret, you'll get no trouble from me."

"Good. Emma will guard you closely. Don't make me regret leaving her with you. If you hurt her, I will hunt you down, wherever you go. I will find you and take your soul."

The ship hit the portal, slowing it down to crawling pace. Two large men appeared on either side of the vessel, attaching thick ropes to the rail before disappearing back through the portal. They watched as the ropes became taught, the Tilburg edging through the portal into another plane. "I have an ill feeling," Wilf uttered.

"We will win through, my friend. Just keep your wits about you and your sword primed. We know not how many will be on the other side."

The ship lurched forward once free of the portal, the ropes guiding the Tilburg towards a stone jetty. A swarthy-looking man approached, a neutral expression on his face. "Are all the supplies on board?" he said to Wilf and Tamatan.

"Nothing will be unloaded until we have spoken to your master," Wilf huffed.

The man looked at him, his gaze flitting across to Tamatan. He saw steel in their eyes, knowing they would not yield. "Very well. Come with me."

"Our friend is onboard," Tamatan added. "No one is to go near the ship until we've returned. If they do, boom," the demon said, his eyes lighting up like twin flames.

"Understood. Follow me." They fell in line behind the man, walking towards a huge wooden door. He rapped twice, a small hatch opening after a few seconds.

Beady eyes peered out, regarding them suspiciously. "Yes."

"They are here to see Grey. Open up, Moke." The hatch slammed shut, the door opening after a few seconds. "This way," the man said, holding a long meaty arm out.

"Thank you," Tamatan smiled, walking into the huge hall beyond the door. Wilf followed, his hand on the hilt of his sword, his eyes looking for danger. They followed the man, walking past endless stone columns, their footsteps echoing loudly.

"This all seems too easy," Wilf whispered.

"I know. But let's play along. They don't know that we know. And let's keep it that way until the moment arrives."

Torches flickered on the columns, casting shadows across the endless cavern as the threesome descended a flight of stone steps. At the bottom, two hooded figures stood barring a large door. "They are here to see Grey," Moke stated, his voice quivering.

"This way," one commanded, leading Wilf and Tamatan through the door into a circular room.

At the far side, a figure sat on a large chair, a grey hood obscuring its face. "Welcome to Kenn, Wilf Bathurst and Tamatan."

"How do you know us?" Wilf replied as they neared the figure.

"I know such things. You're from Heronveld, in the land of Elksberg. You've killed vampire kings and for that, I commend you." The hood moved a few inches. "And you are Tamatan. From the land of Marzalek, beyond the unseen lands. You are both here for your kin, Jake."

"Well, at least that cuts out the introductions," Wilf shrugged. "Where is Jake?"

"He is here, resting after his latest adventures. Tell me, it that the only reason why you have arrived at my door?"

Both of them stole a glance at each other before the demon spoke. "Yes. Jake was taken. We are linked. He was taken and brought here. What reason did you have to bring him here?"

"All in good time," Grey chuckled. "I bid you no harm. Or Jake. I did not ask specifically for him. The Longfords sent him to me. And I'm glad they did, for he is a gifted man. A man who walks in the daylight but is equally at home in the shadows. I asked him to run an errand for me. And run he did." Grey clapped his hands, a robed figure approaching from the doorway. "Bring Jake before his kin." The figure strode off, leaving the three of them in silence.

A minute later, a door creaked open, Jake walking through it. "Wilf, Tamatan," he blurted, racing over to his friends. They embraced, a mixture of relief, tears and surprise emanating from them. Finally, they broke the embrace, Jake clapping them both on the shoulders. "How..."

"It's a long story," Wilf began. "I got your letter, Jake. Then Alicia, Jo and I visited Emma. It went from there. We found the doorway under the lighthouse and then Emma and I travelled across the sea in search of this rascal."

Jake took a step forward, embracing the demon once more. "I never thought I'd see you again, my old friend."

The demon's eyes lit up, salty tears running down his green face. "It is so good to see you, Jake. It has been many moons since our last adventure."

"So, you are all reunited," Grey announced. "Come closer. Let us talk." The trio approached, Grey's mind working overtime. *My prize is aboard that ship.* "So, you must stay here with me until sunrise."

"Why?" Wilf countered, his body tensing at the news.

"Because, Wilf Bathurst, the wind will not return until then, and the tide will not allow the Tilburg to set sail. There are provisions on board. I will have it unloaded whilst you all rest up. I believe that is fair and you will find me a most gracious host."

"Okay," Tamatan agreed. "Our journey has been long, and we could use some hearty food and somewhere to lay our heads."

"It will be done," Grey commanded, shifting his frame nervously.

Jake noticed it, seeing the look in the ancient man's eyes. *Something's not right,* he thought as the door opened once more, a cloaked figure beckoning them to follow.

Chapter Twenty-Four

Lukash Longford strode into the low-slung room, his father rising to meet him. "Don't get up, Father. You need to rest."

"Rest," Berndt spat. "How can I rest? Tell me!"

"What do we know?"

"Three outlanders took control of the Tilburg. They sailed towards the mist with the Grey's prize on board."

"Fuck! Do we know who they were?"

Berndt shuffled over to his chair, seating himself. "No. All we know is that there was a man, a woman and a strange-looking creature."

"A woman," Lukash mused. "If I were a betting man, I'd wager the woman was Emma Thorne."

"Well, it looks like your gambling has not paid off, Lukash."

The dark-haired man bristled. He was being spoken to like he was a child. Only his father had the authority to do that. "When is the Gull due back at port?"

"Today," Berndt replied. "Why?"

"Because, we can load it up with enough men to follow the Tilburg and make sure that not only the prize is where it needs to be, but also to bring the outlanders back here."

"Do not fail. If the Grey does not get his prize, we'll all pay. There will be nowhere to hide from his reach. Not even in Cornwall. Do you understand?"

"Yes, Father. I will assemble the men now. As soon as the ship docks, we'll head off."

Lukash left the room, the old man resting in his chair. *We need a backup plan,* he thought. *A way out of this mess if the prize is lost.*

"I want twenty men ready for when the Gull hits the dock," Lukash ordered, a large man standing before him.

"Is this because of the bastards who stole our ship?"

"Yes, Markus. They have taken something very precious. Something that belongs to a far greater power. If we do not get it back, we're all done for."

"Okay. I'll get twenty of the toughest bastards in Vrybergen ready for when the Gull arrives."

"Good. I will prepare a few things myself and meet you on the deck when it arrives." Lukash hurried back to the lighthouse, climbing the winding staircase, bypassing Berndt's quarters. When he reached his own living space, he bolted the door, striding over to his bunk. Reaching underneath, he pulled out a small wooden chest, studded with black rivets and a metal clasp. Unlatching the lock, Lukash opened the chest, his pulse quickening. The interior was a dark velvet, an object nestled on the soft fabric. He pulled it out, holding the dagger by its handle before swishing it through the air. The blade was made from a mineral unknown to him, red flecks embedded along its length. He remembered Jubella's words. *This is the only weapon that will kill him. It was forged by the dark maesters when the world was still green and young. Use it wisely, fore you will only get one chance as he is blind to its power.* Lukash slid the blade into the scabbard at his waist, a leather clip securing it snugly in place. *My insurance policy. I just hope I'll never need it.*

Lukash stood on the deck of the Gull, a hoard of men in front of him. All were armed, some with swords, others with axes and pitchforks. "The outlanders who took the Tilburg have said beyond the mist. They wish to cause havoc, which will affect our relationship with the people on the other side. We set sail immediately. Here my voice," he bellowed. "No one is to kill them. You may have some sport with them, but I will deliver the killing blow to all of them, one by one. Do you understand?"

A collective roar rose from the deck, echoing around the giant sea cave. A tall man with a patch over one eye approached Lukash. His unruly dark hair fell beyond his wide shoulders, a black beard laced with silver hanging all the way to his belt buckle. "We must sail at once. The wind is just right for a speedy passage. There is no cargo, so we will ride high, cutting through the waves with ease."

"Very well, Tybork. I am grateful for your efforts. I will head to my cabin and let you get us underway."

"Aye, Lukash. I'll see that the cook brings you something hot and wholesome once the crew are about their business."

Lukash took his leave, heading for his cabin. Once his boots hit the wooden floor, he stretched out on the long bunk as he felt the ship come away from the jetty. *I will make you all pay. I'll make you watch as I defile the woman before removing her head. Then, the crew will defile you before your heads are added to my collection.*

* * *

"Mummy," Lauren shrieked, running towards the Tilburg.

"Lauren," Emma blurted, not believing the sight below her. "Oh my God, sweetheart, is that really you?" She shot down the ladder, hopping over the ship's rail before catching her daughter as Lauren jumped into her arms. They crumpled to the floor, wracking sobs echoing around the cave as the others looked on happily. "I thought I'd lost you forever," Emma cried, her voice shaky.

"Me too, Mummy. But Jake saved us."

They remained on the floor, the woman holding her daughter's face in her hands, marvelling at how much she'd changed. She was heavier, with longer limbs. Her once curly brown hair seemed straighter, hanging almost to her waist. and Emma looked up at the private investigator, mouthing a silent 'thank you'. He nodded, a lump rising in his throat. "Well, you're safe now, sweetheart. Tomorrow, we'll head home. This will be our last adventure."

"I hope so, Mummy," Lauren chirped, wiping tears from her eyes. "I want you to meet someone." She waved the other girl over. "Mummy, this is Scarlett. She's my best friend."

"Hello, Scarlett," Emma said happily. "Pleased to meet you."

"Hello, Lauren's Mummy."

"Please, call me Emma. Where are you from?"

The little girl's face dropped. "I lived with my kin close to the eastern sea. The nasty men killed them and brought me here."

"Oh no. I'm so sorry to hear that." Emma made a snap decision, knowing it was the right thing to do. "Well, you can come home with us, if you'd like to?"

Scarlett looked at the woman, then Lauren who hopped up and down on the spot, a wide smile on her face. "I'd like that," she replied, embracing Emma tightly. Lauren joined them, the three of them sitting together on the jetty, everything else momentarily forgotten.

Wilf hopped onto the deck, climbing the ladder. "We're staying here tonight, Kurt. Things have gone to plan, so all is well. If I take these chains off do you promise to behave?"

"Aye," the bigger man replied gratefully.

The older man busied himself, freeing the ship's captain from his shackles. "Someone will be unloading the ship very soon. You will come with us and spend the night in our quarters."

"I'd rather be on me ship."

"I know you would. But that's not possible. You've had a long journey and you must be tired. Come with us and your belly will be filled."

"Aye," Kurt replied, knowing that when the moment was right, he would take his revenge.

Chapter Twenty-Five

Jubella opened her eyes weakly, sensing others close by. As her vision focused, she took in her surroundings. The cave was small and warm, steam rising close by, its vapour caressing her skin. In front of her, two figures stood. One was a wizened old creature, the other a giant, almost twice the height of his partner. "Grey."

"Welcome back from your slumber," the ancient being soothed. "You remember Jed?"

"Yes."

"He and Jake have done me a great service. They have brought the all-powerful Jubella to my door."

"And what plans do you have for me? A slow death?"

"Why no, my dear. I am to give you a new life, albeit in another vessel. Look."

Jubella followed Grey's eyes, noticing a figure laid out to her left, the flickering torches around the cave illuminating the prone form. "Who is that?"

"She was called Katherine Bathurst. A simple girl who crossed paths with vampire kings. Alas, she died many seasons ago, but she has the chance at life once more. Your life, to be exact."

"W-what?" she stammered. "You don't mean…"

"Yes," Grey smiled. "Your essence will fuel her body. When she arises, Jubella will be no more. Only Katherine will remain."

She struggled against her bonds, a growing panic coursing through her. "They will never let you do this," she spat. "They will be coming for me."

"Alas, Talack already tried. Tried and failed, my dear. And he was your most powerful sentinel. The rest are just a hoard of shuffling bones, no match for my kin."

"You monster!" she hissed, trying to break free. She knew it was futile, the pendant on her chest sapping her dark energies. She was helpless, and she knew it.

"Hush now. You've lived a long life, Jubella," Grey replied, his watery eyes beginning to turn darker. "Jed, move her close to Katherine, then bring that bunk over for me to rest on."

The giant nodded, lifting the crude wooden frame that held her as if it were a sack of feathers. Loud footsteps thumped against rock before he placed her gently close to the cloaked form. He then did the same with the small bunk, placing it in between Jubella and Katherine. "Sleep well," he mocked, moving away as Grey approached.

"Please, Grey, I beg you. Don't do this."

The ancient being could see how she fought against her bonds, albeit with no success. "Sleep well, Jubella. He looked at the giant as Grey positioned himself on the bunk. "Silence her."

Jed took a step forward, chopping Jubella at the side of the neck, the struggling woman's eyes rolling back in their sockets before she lay still. "Now what?"

Grey reached across, taking both women's hands in his own before resting his head back on a straw cushion. "I have never done anything like this before, Jed. It may weaken me considerably, which will leave me vulnerable. Very vulnerable." He paused, focusing on the giant before him. "I will take both Jubella's essences, the light and the dark and then hold them within me. I will strip away the light before giving Katherine Jubella's dark power. That way, she will not be torn. She will be pure darkness, as am I. Just be ready and stay by my side. If anyone attempts to enter this place, kill them, whoever it is."

"Understood," Jed nodded.

Grey shuffled on the bunk, getting comfortable. He reached out, grasping Jubella's hand in his own, his watery eyes turning dark until they resembled blackened pits of nothingness. He began chanting, a low murmur that the giant could not make out as a fine grey mist seeped out of his clasped hand. The flickering torches around the room dimmed, barely able to withstand the pulsing blackness that was filling the chamber. Jed watched, transfixed as Jubella's chest rose and fell for the last time, her skin changing colour until it resembled extinguished embers. Grey let go of her hand, more mutterings escaping his thin lips. After several minutes, his other hand crept under the sheet covering Katherine, bony fingers becoming entwined with lifeless fingers. A blast of wind emanated from under the sheet, extinguishing all but one of the torches, Jed feeling a sense of unease creep over him as Grey continued his quiet chanting. A thick white cloud spewed from his hand, settling over the cloaked form, tiny motes of light settling on the fabric. Grey's breathing increased, his chest rising and falling rapidly, the giant noticing a faint glimmer of light coming from underneath Jubella's clothing. "Jed."

"Yes," he replied tentatively.

"I think it is done. I was right, performing this magic has sapped all of my strength. Please fetch me a shawl and wrap it around me, fore I must rest now. For how long, I do not know."

"As you wish," Jed answered, walking towards the door as the faint hue underneath Jubella's robes died away, the gold pendant that lay on her chest cooling down, its work done.

* * *

"Jake, let the three of us stretch our legs," Tamatan said, looking across the sparse cave which would serve as their quarters for the night.

"Where?"

"I have no idea, fore I do not know this place. But we are guests of Grey. I am sure we can come and go, to some extent. Wilf, are you up for a walk?"

"Why not. Emma, could the three of you stay here while we go for a wander?"

"No problem. I'm pretty tired, and the girls are dropping off."

Wilf nodded, smiling at the woman before rising stiffly from his bunk. "We should check on Kurt. Make sure that he's up to no mischief."

"Good idea," Jake said. "Although, the amount of ale he consumed earlier would put an elephant to sleep."

They left the cave, walking a few yards to an opening in the rock. Sure enough, the captain of the Tilburg lay snoring on a straw mattress. "Sleeping like an infant," the demon observed. They carried on their journey, walking along the endless hallway, flickering torches casting eerie shadows across the stone flooring. Jake was about to speak, the demon squeezing his arm gently. "Not here, Jake."

The private investigator complied, his mind starting to work overtime, knowing this was no mere walk. Robed and hooded figures shuffled past them as they continued, a large stone archway coming into view on the left. "Looks like it leads outside," Wilf said as he puffed on his pipe.

"Good. I could do with some fresh air," Jake countered.

Walking under the tall archway, they gazed in wonder at the sight before them. A large balcony gave way to a meandering river, with a waterfall in the distance. Fireflies danced around them, the smells of the encompassing forest washing over them. "A magical place if ever I saw one," Wilf breathed, looking up at the twisted tree trunks that stretched into a purply sky. He could see the faint shimmer of distant stars, adding to the ethereal scene.

Tamatan walked over to the balustrade, bending down to scratch his foot. Hidden from view, he picked up a small stone, wrapping his delicate fingers around it before waiting for the others to join him. "Neither of you talk," he whispered. "Nod if you understand."

After a moment, Wilf and Jake both nodded in unison. *What's going on,* Jake thought, noticing the expression on the demon's face.

Tamatan gripped the stone, carving a name into the balustrade. It was faint, but clearly discernible in the dim setting. *Katherine.* The demon's nails scored the surface, making it impossible to read the word before walking a few steps on. He did the same again, Wilf and Jake walking over casually, even though their hearts were beating fast. They looked down, Jake gasping. *Is here*, was clearly etched into the rock, the demon's eyes glaring at the young man.

"Such a pretty place," Jake said casually. "Hard to believe that such beauty could exist in a place like this."

Tamatan scored the rock once more, walking over to the far side of the balcony. "I did not expect to see something like this," he replied, his hand playing over the stone once more. Wilf and Jake's eyes flicked downwards in anticipation. *Trust me.* "So, what are your plans once we get back to Vrybergen?"

Jake did trust his little friend, knowing that they were probably being observed by someone or something. "We'll head back to Cornwall. Haven't really thought beyond that. And you?"

"I will return to my kin. Jake and I have planted seeds in the rear garden. Hopefully, they will have grown nicely in my absence. We will harvest them, then plant some more in preparation for the colder winds."

"Do you think Kurt will give us any trouble?"

The demon looked at Jake, shaking his head. "No. We're guests here, Kurt will do as instructed and deliver us safely back to Vrybergen. Only a fool would try and make trouble out on the open sea. By the time the next moon arrives, we'll all be back with our loved ones."

"I'll drink to that," Wilf added. "If we had something to drink."

They stood chatting as the night grew darker and cooler, a lone figure watching the exchange from another plane. A red plane, filled with menace.

Chapter Twenty-Six

A memory flickered to life. A weak flicker, with hardly any strength. However, it held, as another vision from the past joined it, entwining with it as more and more recollections gravitated inwards. Images formed, an auburn-haired woman looking down, cooing gently as two sets of pink feet pointed towards the sky. The face was familiar, a warm sensation taking hold of its host.

The scene changed, two men one with the long grey hair, the other, completely bald stood at the edge of a forest. They were joined, kin, with ruddy smiling faces. A smile formed on the host's lips, remembering the scene from another time and place. The grey-haired man puffed contentedly on a pipe, blowing a plume of smoke into the wind as the other man set a large axe on the grass. A finger twitched, just enough to disturb their shroud.

The vision blurred, changing once more as a stricken young woman appeared, her lifeless body lying on the forest floor as the two familiar men knelt over her. The woman was dead, taken by the darkness, a feeling of sorrow and pain making an arm flinch.

Another man appeared, young and vibrant, with dark hair and a fair face. The feeling of loss was replaced by a growing warmness as the man smiled at her, his tousled hair buffeted by an ocean breeze. He held his hand out, slender fingers accepting it willingly, an unyielding bond crystalizing and setting in place.

A young girl replaced the man, with bouncing ringlets of hair and an effervescent smile, tugging on her clothing with chubby pink fingers. She could smell the infant, thoughts flooding back, gaining momentum as every second ticked by.

A dark image gained shape, the baby's gummy smile replaced by a scowling face, gleaming eyes and dirty fangs filling her field of vision. She could feel her legs hanging limply before the flood rushed towards her, a white flash erupting into a thousand stars before darkness encompassed everything.

A man appeared above her once more. The same dark-haired man whose mere smile had sparked a deep warmth and love-like sensation. He was upset, tears flowing freely down his face. Time seemed to dissolve, fleeting images of forests, grassy plains with far-off mountains and finally, a spit of rock next to a raging sea, where people gathered around a hole in the ground. A deep hole, with a white-robed figure lying within. Earth landed on her upturned face, a sense of panic spreading quickly as the hole was filled in. Got to get out. I cannot scream. Please, don't bury me alive. Please, Jake, I beg you.

The transition from darkness to light was complete as the body twitched into life. Katherine's chest began to rise and fall slowly, a faint pink hue appearing on her cheeks as her lips formed a word. "Jake."

* * *

Jake stirred, rolling onto his side. His eyes fluttered open, something disturbing his fitful sleep. He rubbed his face, rising to his feet as the others slept around him. Pulling on his trainers, Jake made his way out of the cavern, heading for the Tilburg. He passed no one, the halls deathly quiet, even the wall-mounted torches seeming more subdued in the late hour. A few minutes later, he stood next to the ship, relieving himself into the sullen waters below. A memory flashed before him. *There are doorways Jake. To other places.* He tried to place who'd told him that, his mind fuzzy, as he zipped up his trousers. A deep drone from the other side of the portal made him turn around, walking towards the end of the dock. He stared in awe at the giant doorway that pulsed gently against its dark surroundings like a beacon. *Katherine is here. I can't believe it. Should I even be thinking about this. Is someone reading my thoughts?* His feet scuffed the hard ground as he made his way back to his sleeping quarters, his mind awash with thoughts, problems and possible ideas. He left the sea cave, hoping that his late-night foray had gone unnoticed. Reaching his quarters, a noise further along the corridor made him stop, his curiosity suddenly taking hold of him as the private investigator began walking quietly away from the others. After a minute of traversing the dimly lit catacomb, he came to a door. It was wooden, with black studs adorning it, a large handle just asking to be turned. A stealthily as possible, Jake depressed the wrought-iron handle, nudging the door open a crack before peering inside. His eyes tried to become accustomed to the gloomy interior, just about to make out three bunks in the middle of the low-slung space, each bunk occupied by sleeping forms. *Is that her?* Something inside Jake made him close the door, a sense of danger close by. He headed back towards his quarters, lying back down before sleep eventually took hold. Outside his quarters, Jed stood motionless, surveying the sleeping inhabitants. Satisfied that all was as it should be, the giant headed back along the corridor, past the studded door on his left before his reach an unused sarcophagus. He levered himself inside, the rocky ceiling above him within touching distance. He laid his head back on the straw cushion, wrapping his cloak around him before he too drifted off to sleep.

Chapter Twenty-Seven

"Grey sends his apologies," Jed began as they all stood at the dock. "He has some pressing matters to attend to." The giant cast a glance over at Kurt. "See to it that no harm comes to them. Grey decrees it."

"No bother," the smaller man huffed. "I just wanna get back home. This place gives me the shivers."

"The provisions provided should see you across the water," Jed said confidently.

"Well, girls, let's get aboard," Emma chirped happily, unaware of the tension at the quayside. Scarlett and Lauren hopped over the ship's rail, giggling and dancing, running through a door under the wheelhouse.

"Oi," Kurt yelled. "Don't go trashing me ship." He followed the girls hastily, Emma keeping close by, leaving Jake, Wilf, Tamatan and Jed together.

"Well, hopefully our paths will not cross again," the giant said to Jake. "I wish you swift travels and fair winds. I hope… "

The words never came as Jed looked past them, towards the sea. The others followed suit, Jake's stomach tightening as another ship appeared through the portal, a large dark-haired figure standing at the prow. "Shit. Looks like he followed you here, guys."

"Fuckenell," Wilf blurted. "He doesn't look happy."

"Leave them to me," Jed ordered, watching as the Gull nudged the dock just behind the Tilburg.

Lukash leapt onto the dock, his sword drawn. "You will pay for that, old man," he hissed at Wilf who stood his ground.

"Calm your ire," Jed commanded. "They are guests of Grey and are to set sail for Vrybergen."

"They've destroyed half of it," Longford spat back, taking a step towards the giant.

Jed wasn't frightened of the man in front of him. He was bigger, stronger and faster with powers that the dark-haired man couldn't even begin to understand. "That matters not. I'm sure Grey will compensate you for that. Jake has done us a great service and will return to his land and his kin."

At that moment, Emma, Lauren and Scarlett appeared on the deck, Kurt shooing them out of the ship's living quarters. Lauren froze, grabbing her mother's hand. "Mommy. It's him. The man who brought me here."

Emma's face contorted into a mask of anger. "Bastard," she yelled, heading for the dock.

"Let's set off," Wilf said hastily, eyeing the gang of men close by, eager for the knock.

"Good idea," Jake agreed, his mind half on the ship, half on Katherine.

Lukash wasn't to be denied, striding towards the group behind Jed. "You're a dead man," he spat at Wilf, his eyes flitting to the strange-looking creature next to him.

Tamatan's eyes sparkled red, like an evening sun as his hands came out of his pockets. "Any quarrel you have with him, you also have with me."

"Longford," Jed interjected. "Get back on your ship and leave this place. And if I hear any harm came to them on their journey, you'll have me to answer to."

Lukash held his hands up to the bigger man in resignation, half-turning towards his men. Jed turned towards Jake, the words forming on his lips. Words that never came. "Fuck you, Jed," Longford hissed, his sword embedded in the giant's chest. "I will have my sport."

Jed's eyes widened, his mouth opening and closing like a dying fish, gasping for air. "You'll…" his words trailed off as Lukash ripped the blade from his body, lopping of the bigger man's head in one swift motion.

Jake, Wilf and Tamatan watched in horror as the huge body fell to its knees, dark crimson blood spouting and spraying the stony ground. "Oh fuck," Jake breathed as Lukash wiped the blade with his dark sleeve, his eyes singling out Wilf.

With no weapon, Wilf suddenly felt his age as he looked up at the approaching man, spittle hanging from his lips, his knuckles white around the hilt.

In a blur of speed, Tamatan disarmed Longford, knocking him sideward. He lost his footing close to the Tilburg, vanishing over the side of the dock, a loud splash carrying to his men's ears. "Get on the ship. We go, now." He turned, launching himself at the hoard, his eyes glowing fiercely. Three went down quickly, the other men scattering until they regrouped around the demon, weapons ready.

"Wilf. Get her ready to sail. Do whatever it takes. Just get that ship moving."

"Where are you going?" the older man asked.

"I've left something behind," Jake shouted over his shoulder as the battle ensued.

* * *

Jake stole across the giant hall, expecting to see cloaked figures heading for the port. He never saw anyone as he sprinted towards the winding stone staircase. A minute later, he came to the door he'd previously visited, his breath ragged as he peered inside. The room was still in darkness, save for the dim glow from a flickering torch on the far side. As quiet as possible, he scurried over to the three bunks, his eyes scanning for danger. The first bunk contained what he thought was what was left of Jubella. A withered husk lay there, frozen in time. Something caught Jake's eyes, a glint of gold caught by the candle's glow. Gently, he moved Jubella's clothing aside, the heavy-set chain and pendant sitting on a sunken chest. *Poor cow*, he thought before side-stepping to the middle bunk. Grey lay there, the rise and fall of his chest barely perceptible. *Why's he still sleeping?* Hearing a noise outside the door, Jake moved to the last bunk, his gasp caught in his throat. A sleeping woman, with pale skin and long auburn hair lay underneath him. *Kath. Oh Jesus Christ it's really you.* He nudged her arm, her head lolling to one side as if in a deep sleep. "I've got to get you out of here," he whispered, an idea coming to him. He moved over to Jubella, removing the chain, the links becoming caught in her straggly hair. "I'm sorry, Grey. But she was never yours to take." He slipped the chain over the ancient man's head before lifting Katherine into his arms. *She feels so light*, He made his way to the door, a pulse of wind from the centre of the room extinguishing the candle. Jake didn't need it though. He was into the hallway a second later, walking as fast as he could, his biceps beginning to burn. Cloaked figures could now be seen as he crested the staircase. One noticed him, hissing a curse from under its hood, spurring Jake into action, his walk turning into a jog. He was ahead of the pack, noticing many flocking down the staircase, possibly to check on their master was Jake's train of thought as the heavy door that led to the dock grew ever-nearer. His arms screamed in protest as he shouldered his way through, a scene of mayhem presenting itself to him. Wilf what on the Tilburg, with Emma and the girls. The gruff old man had cut the moorings and was threatening to cut Kurt's throat unless he obeyed. The water inside the sea cave was more turbulent, seeming to curl around the perimeter in a clockwise direction. The pushed on, Wilf seeing him approach the ship as shouts and curses emanated from the Gull. "Where's Tamatan?" he called out.

"On that ship somewhere. My god! Is that..."

"Yes, but we have no time. Emma, help me."

The woman headed for the ship's rail, the water making her appear drunk as she zig-zagged left and right. "I can reach her, but you've got to be quick, we're moving away from the edge."

Jake hopped forward a few paces, placing his foot on the moving ship, bundling Katherine into Emma's arms. "I'll be back in a minute," he said, his voice shaky as he turned towards, the gull, snatching a pitchfork from the hands of Tamatan's victim.

"What are you doing?" Emma shouted as the ship began to pick up pace, the current moving her forward more rapidly.

Jake knew he only had a minute, noticing Lukash clamber out of the water fifty yards past the stern of the ship. "Shit. Tamatan!" he yelled. "Come on."

An explosion rocked the gull, the mooring ropes straining against the dock as smoke began seeping out of the door below the wheelhouse. A figure emerged, eyes blazing white as the demon floundered on the deck, a handful of men following him, coughing and cursing. He looked up at Jake, smiling mischievously. "Go. Get on the ship. I'm right behind you."

Jake nodded, taking off after the fleeing Tilburg. He spotted Longford, climbing clumsily over the last few rocks that led to the dock. "You lose," he said, locking eyes with the man from Towan Point.

"I'm gonna fucking kill all of you," he yelled, his feet gaining traction on the stone as he gave chase.

Jake turned, his eyes fixed on the departing ship. He was so focused on his goal that he didn't notice the small depression in the dock, sending him skidding across the ground. As he scrambled to his feet, Longford was on him, pinning him to the ground, his elbow across Jake's throat. *Can't die like this*, he thought as his windpipe was crushed by his attacker.

"I should have killed you back in Cornwall," Lukash spat, drawing a blade from a scabbard on his hip.

Jake's eyes widened further as the obsidian dagger arced towards his face, his hand coming up to halt its progress. "Get off me" he croaked, the words stilted.

"Die," Lukash hissed at the blade lowered, skimming Jake's upturned eyelashes.

Jake braced his leg against the ground as he let the blade almost prick his skin. He relaxed his arm slightly, making the bigger man think that his strength was ebbing away. Years before, as a trainee policeman, Jake had undergone hand-to-hand combat training, with the exact scenario as he now found himself in. Not a natural fighter, Jake had done well at the self-defence aspect of the training. He was about to play it all out again. This time, for real. He let out a breath, the blade quivering in Longford's grip before twisting his body violently to the left. The blade narrowly missed his cheek, clattering to the ground as his attacker face-planted the floor, releasing Jake from his hold. Picking up the blade, he swung a leg at his foe which connected just below the chin, snapping his head back as the man landed in a heap close to the dock.

Jake spun around, noticing how much further the ship had progressed in its bid for freedom. "Shit." He sprinted after the fleeing vessel, his legs beginning to run out of steam, his lungs screaming in protest. Got to make it, noting that the ship was at least six feet from the dock. But he was gaining. He readied himself, running in a wide arc before using the last of his reserves to fling himself across the open expanse of air and water, crashing into the ship's rail. His one hand lost purchase, Jake dangling helplessly as the Tilburg gained momentum.

"I've got you," Emma chirped from above him, Jake feeling two hands grab at his jacket and belt. She heaved, the private investigator helping out by pulling with the last of his strength before flopping onto the deck. Another explosion reverberated around the hall, the cursing and hollering turning to screams of anguish and pain.

A figure thudded into the deck next to him, the demon smacking at his flaming sleeve, snuffing out the flames. "That was close," he croaked, Jake never seeing him so ragged and unkempt. His clothing was torn, and there was an angry red welt appearing above his left eye. But he was alive.

"What happened?" Jake urged, wincing as he climbed to his feet.

"Cane spirit," the demon countered happily. "I set a few barrels alight. One below decks and one near the wheelhouse."

The ship began turning, pitching and rolling on the rough waters as Kurt began to make the turn back out towards the portal. "I'm your master now," Wilf commanded, the sword nudging the small of the captain's back. "Your friends are all dead. If you want to join them, say the word."

"I just wanna get h-home," the captain stumbled.

Jake walked over to the opposite rail, a sense of relief at the scene in front of him. The Gull was ablaze, a handful of men trying to put the gathering fire out. He spotted Longford, rallying his troops, ordering them to use buckets of sea water. His head turned ever slowly, his eyes locked on the other side before he felt the nudge of the portal, the Tilburg passing through slowly before popping out of the other side. He climbed the stairs stiffly, addressing Kurt. "Now what?"

"Once we're outside of the cave, the wind will catch. Be a couple of minutes until we're out in the open."

Jake embraced Wilf, the older man taken by surprise. "We did it, Wilf. We bloody did it!"

"We did, Son. But barely. And we're not home and dry just yet." He looked down on the deck, seeing his niece laid out on hessian sacks. "Emma. I need you."

The woman hurried up to their position, Lauren and Scarlett at her heels. "What?"

"Take the sword and watch this rogue. I need to see Kath." She took the sword, moving aside as Jake and Wilf made their way towards the robed figure. As the sea breeze caught his hair, Wilf crumpled to the deck, his resolve blown away on the wind. "Oh Kath. It's really you. Wake up, girl." Jake stood there, knowing that the older man had only cried a handful of times in his long life. He also knew that he loved Katherine like the daughter he'd never had. After a minute, the gruff old man stood up, wiping his tears away clumsily.

She remained silent and still, Jake kneeling next to her. "It may take a while for her to wake," he replied, his voice thick with emotion. "But she's comfy enough and I'll get some blankets to put over her. You sit with her. I'm hoping that Tamatan did enough damage to that ship that they'll not be on our tail straight away."

Wilf watched him head aft, sitting down next to his niece once more, taking her cool hand in his. "We've got so much to show you, Kath. Me and Jo, well, we've been together since you left us. Alicia is strong and true, a real credit to you. I will let Jake fill you in on the rest," knowing that it was not his place to talk about the younger man's private life. "Let's just get you home. Back to Cornwall, with no more adventures."

Jake appeared a few minutes later as a watery sun, bathed the deck in light. Large birds flew past the Tilburg, heading towards a clear horizon. "Weather looks decent," Jake observed. "Windy but decent. Wilf, you sit with her. I'll keep an eye on Kurt. Rest up, you've had a busy morning."

"I give you thanks, Jake. I feel weary. My bones are getting heavier and old Wilf needs the easy life again. Maybe Jo's looked after me too well, these past seasons."

"Maybe, but she's a diamond."

The older man nodded, his eyes glazing over as he stared out to see. "Aye. That she is. That she is."

Chapter Twenty-Eight

"Can we sail?" Longford asked as smoke seeped out of cracks in the Gull's deck.

The captain nodded. "Yes. But not straight away. Look at the water."

Lukash looked down, noting how the turbulent waters had calmed somewhat. "We can't stay here. I've done for Grey's henchman. He could be here any minute. And if that happens, we're all be scattered to the wind. Do we have ropes?"

"Aye. Are you thinking what I'm thinking?"

"We pull ourselves out of the cave. Once we're out at sea, we'll be right behind them."

Tybork turned to what was left of his crew, along with the smattering of men from Vrybergen. "Go below and fetch as much rope as you can."

The men scuttled off, many of them either injured, or feeling the effects of the skirmish. Longford stood there, pondering. *Why has he not made an appearance. Surely he'd have heard the commotion and I swear I saw some of his hooded goons come out of the hall?* He began pacing the dock, sweat peppering his brow as many scenarios played out in his mind. None of them good ones. Longford watched impatiently as the men tied the thick rope to the ship's rail, taking directions from Tybork, who hassled and harried them into action. "We may just make it out of here," he whispered, not wanting to tempt fate. Or anything else that was listening.

* * *

In a far-off place, a tall broad-shouldered man slipped a red cloak around his neck, fastening the clasp hastily. He looked over at his bureau, nodding simply at the objects next to his haversack. A rumble of thunder echoed across the land, a flash of lightening ripping across the dark yellow sky. Quickly, the man gathered up his belongings as the door to his quarters creaked open. A woman looked in, her raven hair and dark eyes usually pleasing to the man. "Where are you going?"

"He needs me. I can feel it."

"Have you seen it?"

"Yes. Last night. There were outlanders in Kenn. I couldn't make out their palaver, but something did not sit well with me."

"You think them trouble?"

"My instinct is telling me so, Bubera," he answered as he approached the witch.

Her eyes seemed to darken, the evening gathering pace outside as more thunder reverberated around the ancient fort. "And what of Grey? You think they've killed him?"

The man shook his head slowly. "No one can kill the father of all things. But I can sense that he's weak. Maybe they issued him a potion to slow him down. The one man looked different from the others."

"How so?"

"His garments were not like the others. I think he is from the Tekartha?"

"You think?"

"Again, my instinct tells me so. And if he is, trouble is afoot. That's why I must leave."

"It may be a fool's errand. He may have passed?"

"Well, if the doorway is open, Grey is still alive. After all, if he dies, the doorways die with him, as does this land."

"Then travel fast and do what must be done."

"I will, Bubera. I will leave the realm in your hands. Are you in agreement?"

"Yes. There is a shipment due in at dawn. The gatherers will bring all that is precious to our keep. Fear not, your land is in safe hands."

"I don't doubt it," he agreed, striding to the door. Before leaving, he turned, smiling at the witch.

She gazed at him, drinking in his features. His straight nose and almost sharp cheekbones gave the man a noble look. It was only the eyes that gave him away. Deep eyes, the colour of darkest wine. "Stay safe, Red," she breathed. "Come back to me soon."

He walked out of the keep, crossing the river as a fine rain began falling from the sullen skies. Red pulled up his hood, masking his face as he headed along the coastal path towards the settlement of Rabak. To his left, an angry sea waged war against the rocks below, coating the lone traveller in perpetual mist. He didn't feel the frigid water seep through his cloak and clothing. He didn't feel anything, except loyalty to Grey and Bubera. He took a fork in the well-trodden path, heading down towards the sea. Skipping over a small ford, Red began climbing towards Rabak. He passed the outer fortifications, the muddy streets a tumult of locals who sold food and items along with men who stood around taverns, thick smoke spilling from their pipes. As Red passed into the inner circle, people stopped what they were doing as the cloaked figure strode past. Men regarded him warily as he made his way to the largest building on the busy street, the Red Raven inn. He walked up the wooden steps, passing through the swing gate that led inside. The large room was filled with tables and men, many of whom stood next to the bar as serving girls poured them mugs of ale and drafts of sweet wine. Red removed his hood, the hubbub inside cooling as everyone in the room noticed his presence. "I'll take a jug of ale and two of your finest shigans," he asked the nearest girl politely.

"Yessir," she replied, quickly handing over the drink and smokes.

He flicked her a coin, smiling briefly before walking over to the far side, where a small enclave nestled next to a large window. "Let's see how long it takes them," he observed drily, lighting the roll-up with a snap of his fingers. He drew the strong weed into his lungs, savouring the heady aroma before blowing it out of his nostrils. He took a swig of the warm ale, liking the tangy aftertaste as three hooded figures approached. His eyes flicked up from the table, a smile transforming his face. "Good to see you."

"We offer the same sentiment, Red, King of the Keep. What brings you to Rabak?"

"I am to undertake a journey. A long journey that will require help."

"Where are you journeying to?" the lead figure asked forcefully.

Red smiled once more, putting the three figures at ease somewhat. "Why don't you sit down, Alsar. Rest your bones whilst we discuss our venture."

Alsar complied, nodding at his two companions. As they were seated, they all removed their hoods in unison, tuts and gasps from the fellow patrons drifted across the room. Their white skin and sunken black eyes were no shock to Red. He'd spent his long life in the company of demons, vampires and witches. The locals were not quite so accustomed as many filed out of the entrance, mugs of half-drunken ale clattering on the wooden boards. "So, we are seated."

"Indeed," Red agreed, looking at Alsar's two companions. Xax and Meltrom were similar in appearance, although slightly shorter in stature. Their discoloured fangs were filed to fine points, making their mouths look too big. Black mouths that reeked of death. "Grey is in trouble. What trouble he is in, I do not know. He is in a deep slumber, from which he has not yet risen."

"What event caused the slumber?" Alsar enquired, becoming more interested in the unfolding story.

"I do not know fully. I know that a powerful force was with him recently, possibly Jubella."

At mention of her name, the three vampires sucked in a collective breath. "That craven witch," Xax spat, his black eyes boring into Red's.

"For many ages, Grey has craved her, wanting her strength for himself. Not her white powers though, only the insane darkness was on Grey's mind. It's a theory I have, but nothing more than that."

"There is something that you're not telling us, Red."

"You are wise, Alsar, the wisest of your clan. There were outlanders at Grey's keep. A demon and a man from another plane, possibly Tekartha." He let the words hang in the air, the gravity of his statement plain to see.

"If you speak the truth, Grey may have fallen foul of powers that we don't understand. None of us have been there, although, we've heard fables about that strange realm."

"Tekartha has moved on from other lands," Red began. "It has machines, millions of souls and order. The place is almost completely devoid of our kind, save for a few hidden corners, where they are not as advanced. If an outlander travelled to Grey's keep, then this is a worrying development."

The three vampires nodded, understating Red's concerns. "So, what are we to do?"

The king smiled, thankful that they were willing to help. "We travel there and find out what has transpired. Hopefully, Grey will have awakened by then. If not, he may need my help." He sucked on the shigan, the tip glowing brightly, reflected in the bottomless eyes that stared back at him.

"If we help you, what recompense will you bestow upon us?" Alsar enquired, his question loaded.

"If Jubella is indeed no more, then her land is up for grabs. I will personally guarantee that you will become the custodians of the White land of Kenn."

He watched intently as the three vampires weighed up the offer, knowing that they had waged an eternal feud with the creatures of darkness that were holed up in the haunted forest. Alsar coughed, clearing his throat. "We accept. But what if Jubella is still with us? How can you guarantee us the white land?"

Red shrugged, not knowing the answer fully. "This journey will be long, with dangers on the way. I do not know how to hold up my promise. But a promise it is, even if I am to breach the castle myself and remove her head."

Alsar chuckled. "That is something that Grey has been unable to do for a thousand seasons. How do you plan on besting his magic?"

"The outlander. I find the outlander and he will remove her head for me."

Chapter Twenty-Nine

"Jake, I can feel something odd about you," Tamatan said from beneath their cover on the ship's deck.

"Like what?"

"I'm at a loss. But I noticed it when we set sail. Are you hurt?"

"I don't think so?" the man replied, wondering what had changed since their hasty departure.

"Strange. I can feel something dark emanating from you. Like before when you were sick, but much stronger."

"Hang on," Jake countered, pulling the dagger from his waistband. He saw the demon's eyes flare, his face changing from intrigue to shock.

"That's what it is. I can feel dark energy inside it. Please, may I take a look?"

"Sure," Jake offered, studying the demon closely.

Tamatan looked at the dagger, his green fingers squeezing the handmade handle, his thumb gently caressing the blunt side of the blade. "Interesting," he began. "I know not where this came from, but there is power within. See here, the red flecks in the glass." The others nodded dumbly. "This is ancient evil. Where did you get it from?"

"From Longford. He was about to take my eye out with it. When he dropped it on the dock, I grabbed hold of it. And now it's mine," a lopsided grin etched across his face.

"Strange indeed," the demon went on. "I've never seen such a thing but have heard stories over the ages of weapons with magical elements. Keep it safe, Jake. You just never know when it might come in handy. But err on the cautious side. If you cut yourself with that, the darkness will consume you. Utterly."

"Fair point," Jake replied, opting not to slip it back into his waistband. He found a piece of hessian on the deck, wrapping the dagger, over and over until satisfied that it was of no danger to him, or the others. "I'll check on the captain. Does anyone need anything?"

"We're good, thanks," Emma said, smiling at the private investigator.

He made his way across the deck, climbing the wooden stairs to the ship's wheel. "How much further?" Jake pressed, looking across the grey expanse of sea. The weather had turned, rain squalls and gusts of wind battering the Tilburg as the sun had risen on their second day aboard.

"We're close," Kurt soothed, his normal harsh tones somewhat subdued.

"What's wrong?" Jake pressed some more.

Kurt huffed, his broad shoulder sagging. "I'm finished. When I get back to Vrybergen, they will finish me off. I've gone against the Longford's and they will make sure that I pay a heavy price."

Suddenly curious, Jake probed further, the others sat underneath an awning on the deck. "Is Vrybergen your home?"

"No," the captain replied. "I'm from the north, near Kloofbai. I headed south when I was a sapling, wanting adventure and fortune."

"And did you find it?"

"Somewhat. But I settled for less than what I wanted. Yes, the Longfords have taken care of me, giving me this ship, but I wanted my own fleet of them. I wanted to trade and sail from our land to others, making my own trade and fortune. Now, that is all gone."

"How far behind us do you think they are?"

"Hard to tell. I'd say we'd have had at least a few hours head start on them as the Gull was on fire when we set sail. Plus, it's not as fast as this rig. If I were to wager, I'd say they are at least half a day behind us."

Relaxing slightly, Jake offered a thought. "Well, why don't you set sail as soon as we get off. Head back north with the ship. I have a feeling that the Longfords reign will soon be at an end."

"What makes you say that?" Kurt countered, his eyes closing slightly.

"I don't know everything, but I know they were supplying children and goods to Jubella. And Grey knows that."

"Oh no. I know that there were some kiddies that went elsewhere, but I was never privy to the information. We just unloaded them at the docks and Longford's men took care of the rest. If what you say is true, there's a storm heading their way. One that not even Berndt can weather."

"So, maybe it would be a good idea for you to get out of town, as we say in my land. If they are hours behind us, you'll be out of sight by the time they arrive in Vrybergen."

"I may take your advice, Jake. And I apologise for my rough antics when we first met. We were told that you were a dangerous outlander who was being taken to Grey for punishment. Naturally, we wanted to keep you chained and without much fight in yer guts."

Jake chuckled. "Well, you did a good job. My daughter would have offered up more of a fight, the state I was in."

"Well, it's history now. What matters is getting away from trouble. You lot and me."

Jake placed the sword on the deck, Kurt noticing the gesture. "I'm going to trust you. I think you know what will happen if you break that trust. You saw what he can do," as he pointed towards the seated figure of Tamatan.

"He's not one to tangle with. You will have no trouble from me, Jake. The tide has turned and I know that you could have killed me at any point." He was about to speak again when the spotted something. "Land!" Jake looked past the others, seeing the rocky coastline on the horizon, swathed in fog.

A few seconds later, they were joined at the wheel by Wilf and Tamatan, their expectant eyes looking for land. "I think I see it," barked Wilf, a happy expression on his face.

"We'll not dock at Vrybergen," Kurt responded coolly. "After what happened, they will be on guard. I'll change our bearings slightly. There is an inlet to the west where you can disembark. I will continue on that course, following the coast close to the unseen lands."

"Tamatan. Do you want to stay aboard? He could drop you at Sica."

The demon shook his head. "I must continue with you, my friend. There will be plenty of time for me to reach my land. But our tale is not yet told."

"Okay, as long as you're sure?" Jake added, feeling the ship change direction.

"As sure as ever," the demon chirped, his eyes a mellow shade of green.

An hour later, they bid Kurt farewell, taking the raft that he'd offered them. They paddled up the inlet as the Tilburg became lost to the sea mist, icy water slopping over the side that made both girls squeal. Jake smiled at them before looking down at Katherine. "We're going to find it hard going if we're to carry her all the way back to Amatoll."

"Is that our plan, Jake?" Wilf asked, his brow creasing.

"Well, the forest will be empty and the doorway easy to pass through. As Kurt said, Vrybergen will be on guard."

"Do you know where the doorway is in Vrybergen?"

"I think so. It's in the lighthouse. Why?"

"Kath is still asleep. And we've no idea when she will wake up. If we carry her all the way to Amatoll, it will take us days. If we head for Vrybergen, we could be back home after midnight."

Jake dipped the paddle into the water, keeping rhythm with Tamatan on the opposite side of the raft. "I know what you're thinking, but I can't see how we could make it through the doorway in one piece. They'll kill us all. Or lock us up until Longford arrives, and who knows what he'll do to us?"

The raft crunched on loose stone as they reached the shore, Tamatan, dragging them easily onto a pebbly beach. Above, high clouds wafted across the sky, the warmth from the sun a welcome addition to the otherwise chilly day. "Let us get to a more sheltered position before we discuss our plan. The sun will start its descent soon and we need to agree on our best option."

Wilf nodded before striding off towards a clump of small trees nearby. The group watched with interest as the grizzled old man began chopping branches from the trees, laying them on the coarse grass. He looked up at them, a wry smile spreading across his face. "How else are we to carry her?"

Once the frame was laid out, the men foraged for seaweed, long grass and Wilf expertly stripped long pieces of bark from the tree trunks, testing their strength with a satisfying nod. He set to work, securing the frame so it had four handholds that the others could easily grasp. After an initial steep incline, the ground levelled off, Jake noticing the copse of trees and rocky outcrop further along the coast. "That's the entrance. From there, we'll be able to see any approaching ships."

"Good idea," Wilf concurred, their pace quickening as the sun began to drop towards the horizon. He looked down at his niece, who was wrapped in two hessian blankets, her head bouncing slightly as they made their way across the rutted and uneven ground.

A while later, they laid her on the hard earth, Wilf, Jake and Emma relieved as they massaged their arms. Tamatan watched them, feeling no adverse effects from the burden he's carried. "I suggest we huddle around her. The wind is picking up and there is a chill on the breeze."

They did as instructed before Jake broached the subject regarding their voyage back home. "So, what are we going to do?"

The adults looked at each other in turn as Lauren and Scarlett snuggled into Emma. "I'll go with whatever you think is best," she added, unsure of what else to say.

"Look," Wilf announced. "They are here."

Tamatan and the others stood up, walking towards the edge of the treeline as a ship appeared on the horizon, making its way towards Vrybergen. "We're sittings ducks out here," Jake said. "If they come this way, they'll kill us. We have little ones to think of."

"Wilf, how long do you think it will take the ship to reach the dock?" Tamatan enquired, a plan forming in his mind.

"Hard to say. Just after nightfall."

"Okay. I have an idea," the demon offered. "The rest of you stay here. Jake come with me. And Wilf, light a small fire to keep everyone warm."

"But someone will see us," the old man countered.

"That's what I'm hoping for. Jake come on."

"Where?" Jake replied as uncertainty spread through him.

"Into the viper's nest."

Chapter Thirty

They came out on the rocky landing, high above Vrybergen, looking for signs of danger. Tamatan crept over to where they'd tossed the lookout's body, checking the hidden recess beyond for a lurking enemy. Finding nothing, he turned to Jake. "Look at the buildings. Most of them are occupied. My plan is to infiltrate one of them and hole up until the doorway opens."

"Okay. And how will that work?"

"The approaching ship will probably see the fire, or the smoke it gives off. I'm hoping that everyone on that ship heads this way, and that the path to the lighthouse is clear."

Jake pondered the plan, seeing a hole in it. "Okay, say that they head outside and see the fire, no one will be there, and the men will head back to the lighthouse. It won't give us much time, if any."

"What if we were to leave a trail of breadcrumbs for our friends."

"I don't follow."

Tamatan sat down beneath the wall, his eyes shimmering brightly. "I will draw them away from Vrybergen. They will see my light and will follow, thinking that we're all making our way to safety. All you need to do is hide out in one of the buildings until the coast is clear. Then, head for home."

"I'm not sure about this."

"Nor am I. But Tamatan thinks it is our best option." He looked over the wall, his eyes dimming to green embers as he pointed out some rickety buildings. "Look there. At a brisk pace, you'd be at the lighthouse in two minutes. There are windy streets and alleyways to aid your passage."

"Okay. Let's do this. I only hope you're right."

They made their way back up to the others, Wilf putting out the fire as instructed before they made their way back to the rocky ledge above the settlement. They used the shadows to edge their way down to Vrybergen, turning left at the bottom of the path, away from the lighthouse. Huddling in a side alley, Tamatan and Jake snuck around a wooden building, a faint orange glow emitting from the cracks in the shutters. "Shh," the demon said, testing the rough wooden handle, his breath held in his throat as it turned. They stepped inside, into a small lounge area complete with a large table and a small stove. Tamatan pointed towards a doorway that led towards the rear of the building, as shuffles of activity warned them that they were not alone. "On me," he whispered, as he rushed into the rear parlour, a large man spinning around at the sound of approaching footsteps.

"What..."

He fell to the floor, the demon catching the man easily before placing him on the floorboards. Flexing his fist. "The man has a chin of granite," he smiled.

"So, what do we do with him?" Jake asked.

"It has been a long time since I took a soul, and it pains me to do it now. But if he awakens, our plans will be for nothing. Stand back."

Jake leant against the doorway as the demon straddled the prone figure on the floor. A red glow emanated from Tamatan's eyes, it slowly forming into a mini vortex as it dropped towards the man's face. The private investigator watched in shocked awe as the man opened his eyes, a look of terror plain to see. He tried to call out as a white orb engulfed his face and head, slowly merging with the red twisting light before being drawn back into Tamatan's mouth. After a minute, the man lay still, the demon rising to meet Jake's stare. "Jesus," he exclaimed. "Is that how you take a soul?"

"Yes, Jake. I am truly sorry for doing so, but we cannot take any chances. Let's bring the others inside, away from prying eyes."

A minute later, all seven of them were sat in a large cupboard underneath the building's staircase, a musty smell, laced with fish permeating out of the wood. "We will stay in here, until either the right moment, or when we receive Tamatan's signal. Girls, I know it's dark, but we need to sit like this, or someone might think there is someone home." He saw the girls nod in the darkness, huddled close to Emma who gave him a reassuring nod.

Tamatan stood up, his head moving from side to side. "They are approaching. I must leave you. Jake, how long until the doorway opens?"

The private investigator checked his watch, the hands offering a slight hue. "Two hours until midnight," he stated, giving the demon a 'thumbs up.'

"Don't wait for me. If I am not there at midnight, you must think of the little ones and go through."

"Just make it back," Wilf huffed. "We don't want to leave anyone behind."

The demon scooted out of the house, his eyes almost shut as he quickly made his way to the pathway and landing above. Voices wound their way around the settlement, Tamatan recognising Longford's barks, making him quicken his step until he was high above Vrybergen. He saw the Gull bobbing gently on the water as men secured it with ropes to the dock. The dark-haired Lukash could clearly be seen, rounding up as many of the locals as possible. Tamatan picked up a pebble, tossing it along the pathway, a skittering sound making a few of the men look his way.

"There's someone up there," a large bald-headed man shouted, two dozen sets of eyes trained on the demon's position.

Longford took the lead, the men at his heels as he made his way towards the landing, his sword brandished menacingly. When they all reached the large space, Lukash looked around, checking out the hidden slither in the rock. "Let's check out in the open. If they are out there, we'll fucking find them." They made their way out into the cool night air, a faint aroma of smoke finding them.

"Over there," the bald-headed man announced, the group making their way over to the copse of trees.

"Someone was here very recently," Longford observed, his hand hovering just over the embers. "Which way do you think they went? I know it's them. I just know it."

"To the west and the forests," another man offered. If they have little ones with them, we'll soon catch them on open ground."

"Look," another man yelled. "Over there."

Longford looked across the open ground, two faint orange orbs cutting through the night. "That's the demon. His eyes. After them." The orbs vanished as the men gave chase, Longford leading the charge across the grasslands.

Tamatan was counting as he ran, "one hour and forty-five to go. Got to keep them at my heels until they're all spent." He ran on, his green feet barely touching the stubbly grass.

* * *

"How much longer?" Wilf grunted, the floorboards failing to keep the old man comfortable.

"Thirty minutes," Jake replied. "It doesn't look like Kath will wake up any time soon. So, we should set off shortly. I think he managed to lure them away, as we've heard for about an hour or so."

"Okay. Let's get ready."

They came out of the under stairs closet, the two girls looking pensive. Jake knelt next to them, his smile hoping to calm them. "Now listen, girls. When we go, stay right next to us. Whatever happens, don't run off anywhere. Okay?"

Lauren and Scarlett both nodded emphatically. "We promise."

"Good. Okay, I'll take the rear of Kath's stretcher. You two take up the front as you'll have a free hand in case anyone gives us trouble."

"I'm ready for anything," Wilf replied gravely, Jake noting the steely resolve in the old man's eyes.

"Okay. Let's go."

They made their way out of the building, taking the alley at the side that led to another street. Vrybergen was quiet, many of the wooden structures in darkness, save for a few, the inn and the lighthouse. Their progress was slow, the group falling into the shadows as a lone sentry passed them by, pitchfork in hand. "Almost there," Wilf said, offering encouragement to the others as they made their way out onto the street.

"Shit. We need to avoid the inn," Jake rasped, his arms burning. "Go down the next alleyway. And we'll come out right by the lighthouse." As they turned into the confined walkway, Jake could see a few patrons stood at the bar, a few flickering torches giving the interior an almost welcoming vibe. The alley was strewn with remnants of food, a few dead cats greedily chewing on the remains of someone's supper as they made their way past silently. They came to the end of the passage, the pathway to the outside on their right, the lighthouse to their left like a lone beacon, carved from the cave itself.

"On three," Wilf instructed. "One, two, three." Jake lurched forward as they covered the ground quickly. *This is too easy*, he thought, expecting a barrage of locals to come storming at them. None came as they reached an arched doorway that led inside. To their right, a stone staircase wound its way ever-upwards, a similar staircase to their left leading down into the massive structure's foundations.

"Go left," Jake whispered, the convoy heading ever-downwards until they reached a dusty storeroom, high-level windows offering a brief slither of light from the moon outside.

"This must be it," Wilf hoped, looking for somewhere to place his niece. "Let's put her down over there. Once the doorway opens, we can carry her through."

They laid her on two large chests, Jake walking over to the centre of the room, noting a thin line on the floor, as if the stone had been scorched. "That's where the doorway opens. Be ready for anything. We have ten minutes."

* * *

Tamatan slowed to a stop, turning around towards the coast, his eyes sparkling in the darkness. "Ten minutes to go. I hope you all made it." He saw them before he heard them, a line of men emerging from the darkness, converging on his position.

Longford slowed to a stop, his breathing laboured. "Where are the rest?" he croaked, his usual suave look replaced by one of dishevelment, his dark hair plastered to his forehead.

"They are well ahead of me. You're too late. You'll never catch them."

"Yes, we will, once we've sent you to hell, demon. Have at him, lads."

Nine minutes. He stood stock-still, his legs tingling as he readied himself. The men formed a tight circle around him, swords, pikes and pitchforks ready to skewer the diminutive demon. Tamatan opened his mouth, a green jet of fire engulfing the nearest man. Others screamed as the man went down on the earth, the green flames searing his skin and hair. He made a break, skipping over the fallen man as the hoard dispersed.

"Get the bastard!" Longford screamed, his long legs propelling him forward as a few braver souls rallied behind him.

They gave chase, many of them not lasting more than a few hundred feet as the demon ate up the ground. "I'm coming, Jake," he hooted, his speed increasing rapidly as an orange glow streaked towards the coast.

Chapter Thirty-One

"The doorway is appearing," Emma exclaimed, relief flooding over the woman.

The others looked on, the girls laughing as the faint glow took hold in the darkened room. "Come on," Jake urged. "Let's get through before our luck runs out."

"What about Tamatan?" Wilf replied gravely.

"He said not to wait for him," Jake stated a little too forcefully. He saw the older man's expression, the private investigator's shoulders slumping in defeat. "Let's get them through. I will go back through the door and wait for him."

They bustled through the doorway, the familiar surroundings of Towan Point's lighthouse greeting them. "Jake," Wilf began. "I will go back and wait for him. You have too much to lose."

"No way," Jake argued. "I'm not drawing straws against you. You must stay with…"

"Don't worry," Tamatan addressed them, panting slightly. "I know you wouldn't have left me. We have made it through, the others are far behind us."

Jake, Wilf and Tamatan all embraced as the Emma and the two girls looked on happily. "We're home," Emma croaked, tears falling from her eyes. "I have my little girl back home. And Scarlett too. Thank you. All of you. I never thought I'd see her again."

Jake broke the embrace, enfolding Emma in a bear hug. "It was a bumpy road, but we've made it. Now come, let's get out of here before that oaf Malcolm shows up. You must come home with us, Emma. Your house is not safe."

"Okay. Good point. Let's get out of here."

After a few attempts, Jake kicked open the door, the dull thuds reverberating through the stone structure. They made their way outside, all of them taking in the fresh sea air as though it was the sweetest aroma they'd ever smelt. "How far to your car?" Wilf asked expectantly.

"Hopefully it's where I left it. Shouldn't take too long. Let's each grab a handle."

The going was slow, Wilf and Emma almost losing their footing in the darkness as they climbed away from Towan Point, the coastal path dipping and meandering. The pressed on, step-by-step as the Atlantic battered the coastline to their left. After what seemed like hours, lights appeared as they rounded a bend, the small village Jake remembered coming into view. "Is that where you left the car?" Emma asked, her arm and shoulder burning.

"Yes. There is a playground near the car. If we set Kath down there, I'll drive up to you, just in case any nosy villagers are watching. The last thing we need is the police on our tail."

"Good point," Emma agreed, her spirits bubbling over despite the pain in her body.

When they reached the playground, they balanced the stretcher on a park bench, Jake leaving them to locate his Volvo along the winding streets. "There you are," he chirped, Jogging towards the black SUV. Once inside, he pressed the ignition, the car firing up as LED headlights illuminated the desolate side street. Less than a minute later, he killed the lights, coasting to a stop next to the huddled group. "Right. Let's put Katherine in the back," he instructed, removing Alicia's car seat. "Wilf, you ride up top," the older man hurrying stiffly to the other side of the car.

The others took their cue, Scarlett's face a mask of awe as she climbed into the dark steel contraption. "What is this?"

"It's a car," Lauren stated. "This is how we ride around in our world. Don't worry, you'll get used to it."

Tamatan squeezed in next to the girls, his sparkly orange eyes making them giggle. "Tis a wondrous thing. The last time I was in this realm, wooden carts were pulled by horses. They have moved on, and then some."

"Okay, everyone. Let's go home. I hope we can wake Jo and Alicia."

"I have missed them both," Wilf whispered, his voice trembly, his eyes misting over.

"I'm sure they've missed you too. And think of the stories you'll have to tell."

* * *

A gentle noise from somewhere in the house woke Jo. She rubbed at her heavy lids, Shifting herself onto one elbow. What's that? She rubbed her eyes, looking over at the alarm clock. It was well after midnight, the woman sliding out of bed, finding her slippers close to the wardrobe. Another noise from downstairs made her flinch. "What the bloody hell is it?" she said to herself, walking out of the bedroom towards the top of the stairs. A brief glimpse around another door told Jo that Alicia was sound asleep. She padded downstairs, grabbing a large walking stick from next to the shoe rack. She could see movement on the step, her breath catching in her throat. "Wilf!" Fumbling fingers tried to unlock the door and remove the security chain, the woman yanking the front door open as two men smiled back at her.

"Is it too late for a cuppa?" Jake asked as Wilf took a step forward, taking Jo in his arms.

"Oh God," he cried. "I can't believe it's you."

Wilf moved her into the hallway, burying his head in her long brown hair. "I'm home, love." Salty tears wetting the woman's skin. They stood together, sobs and laughs prompting movement from upstairs.

The landing light came on as a young girl appeared. "Daddy?"

"Hello, princess," he breathed, his own tears beginning to fall freely as the girl bounded down the carpeted staircase. At the fourth step, she leapt into his arms, giggling and kissing Jake's bearded face.

"I knew you'd come back. I just knew it. Jo's been so worried, but I've been telling her that everything will be okay."

"Yes, she has," Jo blurted in reply. "I don't know what I'd have done without her." Something occurred to her. "Did just the two of you come back?"

"No, love. The others are at Jake's house. Before we go around, there is something that you need to know."

Both Jo and Alicia stopped, staring at Wilf and Jake. "What?" Jo quizzed.

"Let's go into the lounge for a minute." They filed in, Jo switching on a side lamp, the added glow from the streetlights giving the room a cosy feel.

Jake sat on the settee, motioning for Alicia to sit next to him. Wilf stood next to Jo, who had seated herself in an armchair, a worried look in her eyes. "Okay. How do I say this?" He looked at his daughter, her glistening eyes looking up at him. "You remember when we had our last adventure and we found your Mum's grave had been dug up?"

"I do."

"Well, someone wanted to bring your Mum back to life."

"What" Jo gasped from the other side of the lounge, Wilf placing a calming hand on her shoulder.

"The same nasty people who took the little girl, took your Mum. They gave her to someone called Grey."

"Who's Grey?" Alicia enquired as any little girl would.

"An old man, a bit like a wizard. Anyway, to cut a long story short, Grey brought Mum back to life. She's at home now, sleeping in her bed." He let the words sink in as Jo let out a cry, Wilf stooping to hug her.

"You mean, Mummy is back? She's alive?"

"Yes, princess. Although, she's not woken up yet. I hope she is the same Katherine that we remembered?"

She flung her arms around his neck, Jake falling backwards into the cushions. "Oh Daddy! Mummy's home." Alicia cried in his arms, Jake smiling at the others, their relief and joy spreading across the lounge towards him. "Can I see her?"

"If you want to?"

"More than anything in the whole world."

"Come on then. Let's go and join the others."

Five minutes later, the bedroom door opened slowly, soft light from outside illuminating the sleeping form. "Mummy," Alicia whispered before padding over towards the bed.

Jake followed, sitting down next to Katherine. "It's your Mum," he croaked, his voice shaky.

"I can't believe it, Daddy. Is she really home for good?"

"Yes, princess. Can I tell you something?"

"Yes, Daddy," she nodded.

Jake pulled the girl onto his lap, looking down at the sleeping dark-haired woman. "The last time you saw her, she was lay in this bed. We'd just lost her, but I wanted you to see her one last time." Tears ran down the man's cheeks as the memory flooded back to him. "You were only a baby, but I remember that you gave her a cuddle and a kiss before we took her back to her world"

"I don't remember."

"I know. You were too young, princess. But let's hope she wakes up soon. Let's hope that you have many more memories to share with her."

"I hope so, Daddy," she replied, bending forward to kiss her mother's forehead. "Night night, Mummy. See you in the morning."

Jake bent forward too, planting a soft kiss on Katherine's lips. "I love you." He stood up, letting his sleepy daughter wrap her legs around him as he carried her back to bed. After cuddles and kisses, Jake was back in his bedroom, not realising that it was their bedroom once again. He draped a fleecy blanket over Katherine, easing himself onto to the bed beside her. "Wake up soon, babe. I've got so much to tell you." He lay there, watching the rise and fall of her chest, his eyes transfixed on the woman that he'd not seen for many years. Gradually, fatigue and a heavy head got the better of him as he succumbed to a deep sleep. His breathing slowed, his body relaxing fully as a gentle breeze drifted in from the open window. A slim hand moved out from under the blanket, fingers intertwining his as they were joined once more.

Chapter Thirty-Two

They came out of the pool, the four figures shaking water from their capes as Red took in the room around them. Their journey had been without incident, the foursome commenting how quiet the white forest had been. They had skirted the settlements, seeing the humans mill around in a state of lethargy. They all knew something had recently happened as they pressed on towards their destination. “I can feel him,” Red stated. “He is close by.”

“Then let’s find him,” Alsar replied, his lifeless eyes scanning the darkened space.

They proceeded out of the room, skirting a long corridor with doors on one side. Torches flickered on the walls, casting lengthy shadows across the stone floor as a gentle breeze ruffled the back on their wet cloaks. After a few minutes, they came to a stout door, Red sensing a presence on the other side. His gloved hand pushed the door inwards, the space beyond dank and gloomy. “Grey!” he called, seeing the ancient man seated on a large iron chair, an aide at his side.

“Red! Is that really you?” Grey croaked as he lowered the mug from his chapped lips.

“It is. I saw them, Grey. I saw outlanders here and I sensed danger had befallen you. What news from Kenn?”

Grey handed his aide the mug, the shuffling figure leaving the room silently. The ancient man sagged, his watery eyes downcast as he held his arms out. “It is all gone. My plans have gone awry.”

“How so?”

Grey looked at the vampires behind Red, nodding his head. “It has been many moons since I last saw you. I trust you are keeping well.”

“We are,” Alsar confirmed. “It is good to see you, Grey.”

Grey smiled, albeit tightly. He turned back to Red. "I had finally found a mate. A special one, who was to join me as winter approaches."

"Who was she?"

"A simple girl who had passed on through. However, she had vampire blood in her veins. In another realm, Korgan and Reggan ruled the plains and forests. This girl was caught up in a great battle between the vampires and the outlander. The outlander won through. The woman was called Katherine. She was special."

"And where is she now?" Red asked.

"Taken by the outlander, Jake. I thought him an ally, albeit on my terms. I gave him an impossible task. To bring Jubella to my keep. However, he won through and he delivered on his promise. I used her essence to bring Katherine back to life. However, Jubella's dark essence weakened me and whilst I was sleeping there was a skirmish down by the dock. Jake took Katherine and stole her away for his own."

"And where is she now?"

Grey sighed. "Best guess, Tekartha. There is a doorway in Vrybergen that is linked to their realm. I've never travelled through it, but I'm sure that Jake took my prize back to his land."

Red nodded, turning towards the others. "You said that this Jake delivered Jubella to you. What news of her land? We passed through, but it seemed quiet."

"Jubella is gone, her minions scattered and leaderless."

Red addressed the three vampires. "The white forest is yours. You may take your leave and travel to her castle. I have upheld my promise to you."

The three vampires nodded, Alsar's blackened eyes seeming to sparkle. "Very well. And thank you, Red, King of the Keep. I wish you luck in your quest for retribution."

Grey nodded as the vampires left the room, his focus on the impressive cloaked figure before him. "When did you know, my brother?"

"I saw an image when I looked into the waters within the Keep. I could see the outlander and his friends. I could feel that you were weakened, so I travelled to Rabak to seek the help of Alsar and his kin. In truth, I could have travelled here alone. I was expecting trouble, but found none. All is good though. They have a new land to rule over and we have strong allies within the white forest."

"You are wise, Red. And I need your help."

"I am at your service, Grey. Tell me what you need."

"We will travel to Vrybergen. There is a treacherous fiend there who you can deal with before we pass through to Tekartha."

"And then what?"

"We take back my prize and lay waste to their realm. You have the power to do that."

"You mean…"

"Yes, I do. The Red wind."

* * *

Jake's eyes fluttered open, the sound of the sea rousing him from his slumber. He took a moment to gain his bearings, his head turning towards the window. *She's still asleep*, his heart sinking slightly. He sat up, looking at Katherine who was still covered in the fleecy blanket, her left hand protruding from the edge. Squeezing it briefly, Jake moved it back under the covers before climbing stiffly out of bed. The summer had moved into autumn, although the north Cornish coast was still enjoying the sun's warmth. He watched silently as waves crashed into the rocks a few hundred yards away, the sound of nearby seagulls telling Jake that he was home. Home at last. He made his way downstairs, the house silent as he padded into the kitchen. Flicking on the kettle, a thought registered in his mind. *What day is it?* As the kettle began to boil, he found his phone on the counter, unplugging it and activating the screen. "Saturday," he said to himself as footsteps drifted along the hallway.

"Good morning, Jake."

"Tamatan," he replied. "Did you sleep well?"

The demon walked over to the window, his orange eyes muted as the sun's rays beamed through the glass. "I did. Your crib was very comfortable. I rose a while ago and have been sat looking at your wondrous land from the window. It is indeed magical."

"Well, this part of the UK is. Did you not venture here before?"

He chuckled. "No. I only saw the smog-ridden streets of your cities. It was that long ago that I can barely remember anything. The smell I remember though. And it is not a pleasant memory. No, this is something else, Jake. To wake up every morning and see what you see is a special gift."

"Well, I never thought about it like that. But I guess you're right. I grew up far from the sea and never really thought about it. Living here now, I cannot imagine leaving here. This is my home." The kettle clicked off, steam rising towards the kitchen window. "Can I make you a drink?"

"Splendid. I will have whatever you're having."

Jake busied himself with the drinks as the demon seated himself at the table, his eyes scanning the strange room. "Bikabak would love this. It's so shiny, with many machines. If she lived here, I am sure that she would never leave this room."

Jake chuckled as he placed a mug of coffee before his friend. "Well, maybe one day I will finally get to meet her. And it would be great to see Veltan and Jake again."

"Then it shall be so. I do not know when I will make my way home, or even how I go about that?"

Jake pondered it for a moment, taking a sip of his coffee. "I would think it best if I took you back to the Lickey Hills. Vrybergen is not safe. If you go through the doorway where I used to live, you'll be back in Amatoll."

"Very well, although, I do not want to head back immediately, but please tell me if I am imposing on you."

"Of course not. You can stay as long as you like, my friend. You've saved my bacon on more than one occasion. I owe you my life."

The demon's eyes sparked to life, changing from orange to green as he hefted the mug to his lips. "Thank you, Jake. I do have one request."

"Sure."

"I know I will draw attention to myself looking like this."

"Only a little," Jake replied wryly, looking at the demon across the table with his glowing eyes, green skin and twin horns that were perched on the top of his forehead.

"You're too kind. Anyway, I would really like to explore some of your land. Even if I get a chance to dip my toes in your sea. Could I do that?"

"I think we could do that. I will have to get some clothes for you to wear, and a pair of sunglasses. It's Saturday today, so Alicia isn't at school. I'm sure once everyone's awake, we can make some plans."

"That sounds wonderful."

"Now, do you fancy some breakfast?"

"I would. I am rather famished. What did you have in mind?"

Jake smiled as he stood up. "I think a Full English will do you the world of good, my friend."

Chapter Thirty-Three

"Nothing, Father," Lukash said as he looked at the old warlock.

Berndt Longford looked out at the Atlantic Ocean, his rheumy eyes focusing on a single bird that floated on the thermals. He sighed, shuffling back over to a large chair next to the lighthouse's many glass windows. He'd been back for only a day and already he missed the familiar surroundings of Vrybergen. He felt old. Old and vulnerable as his son stood before him. "You're sure?"

"Yes. We searched the grounds and gained access by the bathroom window. The Thorne woman and her welp are not there."

"So, where could they be?"

"Honestly, they could be anywhere. I've done some digging and it looks like this Jake lives in Tintagel, which is not far from here. He would not be hard to find. Or, we wait until the Thorne woman arrives home and go from there."

"I suppose you're right, Lukash. But that does not concern me as much as our other problem."

"It's all in hand. I know someone close by. They will be here later today with their wagon. It will only take an hour or so and then it will be blocked off, forever." The younger man had listened to his father's worries, seeing fear in the head of the family's eyes. He was concerned that Grey would follow them to this land and take his revenge for breaking their agreement.

"You're sure that this…"

"Concrete, Father."

"Yes, this concrete will seal the doorway forever?"

"No one will ever be able to pass through once it's set."

"You may be right, Son. However, there are other doorways to this land. Grey could find an alternative route."

"He could, but I'm guessing that any other doorways are miles away from here. He will be vulnerable. Yes, he's powerful, but he cannot fly, nor can he jump in a car and drive to Towan Point. So, I think we're as safe as we can be."

"Okay. However, if Vrybergen is lost to us, so is all its treasures. All its trade. We have had a good thing going on for centuries. If that is now lost to us, we'll have to find other ways to sustain the family."

"Leave that to me, Father. I know people around these parts. All it will take is a few calls and favours called in for us to flourish once more."

Berndt looked at his son, seeing the similarities of his younger self. Lukash was brash and cocky, strutting around the top of the lighthouse like he was a god amongst men. But Berndt knew he wasn't he was fallible, much of Berndt's powers diluting into his offspring. "Leave the woman be, Son. She's been through enough."

"I can't do that. I have scores to settle, Father. I cannot let this lie."

"No. Once the doorway is blocked, we're stuck here. If what you say is true, there are lawmen and rules here. If we come out of the shadows, we may end up in trouble. And our escape route is lost forever."

"Okay," the younger man relented. "I will leave her be. But if I ever set eyes on Jake, or that old bastard that goes around with him, I will deal with them, in my own way."

"Just be mindful. You said he's a resourceful man. I would be wary before engaging him in battle. Son, tell me, what became of the blade I gave you?"

Lukash baulked, remembering how it was taken from him. "I lost it, Father. During the scuffle at the dock."

"Foolish boy!" Berndt spat. "That was the only weapon that we could ever hope to use against Grey. If he finds us, we'll be blown away on the breeze."

"Relax, Father. You worry too much. I will head downstairs and call Seth. Once the concrete is in place, Grey can spend eternity trying to dig through it."

Seth stood next to the lighthouse's rear entrance, hosing concrete remnants from the path that circled the massive structure. As Lukash approached, the Cornishman looked up and smiled. "All done."

"Good. How long until it's set?"

"It will have gone off somewhat by tonight. However, it takes years for the concrete to achieve its full strength."

"That's fine. There is no rush," he lied smoothly. He wanted the concrete plug to be as solid as possible. He looked the man up and down, feeling infinitely superior to the scrawny individual before him with his unkempt hair and tattooed arms. Lukash took a wad of notes out of his pocket, handing them over. "For your trouble."

"Oh, cheers for that." The man counted the notes, a frown appearing on his face. "This is too much."

"There is something else I would like you to do for me," he replied, moving closer. His handsome face and large frame were his main asset. He knew people usually bent to his will.

"Sure," Seth replied evenly.

"There is a man I want you to find. His name is Jake Stevenson."

"Okay. Who is he?"

"A bothersome chap that needs to be taken care of. I am tied up here for the foreseeable future and need someone with keen eyes to locate him for me. Could you do that?"

"I suppose so. Where do I start?"

Lukash smiled, making the other man reciprocate, albeit warily. "I'm pretty sure he lives in Tintagel. And he drives a black Volvo SUV. It's only a small place and I'm sure you'll be able to seek him out."

"Okay. What does this fella look like?"

Lukash shrugged. "Early forties. Tall, with dark hair."

Seth nodded, making a mental note. "I do if I find him? You want me and some of my mates to give him a slap?"

"No. Just tell me where I can find him and I'll pay him a visit. I might take Malcolm with me for a bit of added muscle."

"No probs," Seth replied before reeling his hose away.

Two minutes later, Lukash leant against the stone lighthouse as the truck made its way towards the main village. He looked out at the ocean, a smile spreading across his face. *I'll find you. And I'll finish the job this time.*

* * *

Several miles away, Jake and Tamatan walked across the open ground towards the sea. The late summer warmth beat down on them, the demon enjoying every moment of his adventure. They joined the coastal path, walking in silence as the sea below hammered the rocks. "This way," Jake offered, heading across the stubbly grass towards the edge of a sheer drop. "Mind your feet," he warned, gingerly heading down towards the ocean as the demon followed gamely. They sat down, Tamatan removing his glasses but leaving his hood up. "See over there?"

"Where am I looking, Jake?"

"The cave by the sea. That's Merlin's cave."

"Merlin. Who is that?"

Jake was suddenly at a loss for words, not knowing how to proceed. "Erm, he was a mythical wizard in the time of King Arthur. His stories are part of our history."

"A wizard, you say. He must have been very powerful."

"I don't really know. It's all myth and legends." He looked at the demon, a lightbulb moment occurring to him. "But based on what I know now, maybe he really was a wizard."

"That's the problem with your world, Jake. All of the magic has disappeared from it. You've moved on, which I'm sure folk are now used to. If only they knew the truth."

"I know. There would be utter carnage."

"When can I return to my land?"

The question was abrupt, taking Jake off-guard. "I thought you weren't in any hurry to leave?"

"I'm not, truth be told, but I miss my kin. And something about this world doesn't agree with me. I felt it long ago, almost as if my strength was ebbing away with every step I made. I feel weary, Jake. It's time for Tamatan to return home. To sail to the Unseen Lands and beyond."

"Well, I can take you whenever you want to go."

"Tomorrow night. I will spend one more night with you, then I will take the long journey home."

"I will miss you, Tamatan. I've not seen you in such a long time. And now you're going to leave me again."

He chuckled, a soft lyrical sound. "Dear Jake. You have Katherine back. When she wakes, you'll have more than enough to keep yourself busy. Old Tamatan will always be with you. Remember that."

"I will. Who knows, maybe one day I'll visit you."

"My home will always have an open door for you, and your kin. Even old Wilf. I'm sure Bikabak will keep him in check."

Jake smiled, knowing that the demon spoke the truth. "Okay. If you're going home tomorrow, then we'll have a farewell party tonight. I will do a barbeque for us all."

"A bar-bar-cue? What in heaven's name is one of those?"

"Trust me. You'll love it. And there will be plenty of ale to go with it."

"Then let us carry on our adventure and head home for the feast, my dear friend." The turned, heading back past the castle towards a small cove a few hundred metres along the coast. Ten minutes later, they were stood on a rocky beach, Tamatan removing his socks before walking into the water, his baggy trousers rolled up to his green knees. "What a feeling, the cool waters feel so invigorating."

Jake smiled, watching as the demon took a few paces forward, his ill-fitting clothes making him look like a cartoon character. "Just don't fall in. Or you'll be dragged out to sea."

Tamatan dug his feet into the sandy floor, looking up at the clear blue sky. The closed his eyes, the sound of the ocean filling his ears. He was at peace once more. His friend was safe, and his kin were counting the days until he returned home. "Thank you, Jake. I have done what I came here to do. Let's go home and prepare for the festivities."

"As you wish, my old friend." They looked at each other, the sound of the sea dissipating. Man and demon, from different worlds smiled. They both loved the other like a brother. And they knew that their bond would remain forever.

Chapter Thirty-Four

Jake's fire pit stood near to his wooden shed, the wooden logs inside beginning to settle as a warm breeze blew across the enclosed garden. He took his faithful bamboo stick, rustling the burning wood as Alicia, Lauren and Scarlett hooted and giggled at the bottom of the garden. "Not long now," he stated happily. "Give it a few minutes and I'll put the chicken on."

"Don't leave it too long," Wilf countered. "My belly is grumbling."

"Your belly is always grumbling," Jo quipped, punching her man lightly on the shoulder. "Emma, shall we go and get the salad ready? Leave these brutes outside to tend the fire."

"Sounds like a plan," Emma replied. "I need a refill anyway."

The two women headed back inside, leaving the men by the wrought iron fire pit. Tamatan had ditched the hooded top and glasses, Jake telling him that his neighbours were on holiday and no one would be able to see the diminutive demon in the rear garden. He hefted the glass of beer, smacking his green lips together in delight. "I will miss this. Nowhere in my land is the ale so fair."

"You have a point, my friend," Wilf agreed. "The ale is fine, and the weed is the best I've ever had," he said, puffing on his wooden pipe.

Jake took the empty beer bottles, heading through to the carport where his recycling bins sat. The sound of an engine nearby made him look out into the street, seeing an old concrete wagon parked a few doors away. As he stood there, the truck moved away slowly, the driver peering at Jake as the vehicle trundled past. The private investigator turned and walked back towards the back garden, blissfully unaware that he'd been found. He made his way to the kitchen, sliding a large tray of chicken drumsticks and thighs out of the fridge, before strategically placing them over the crackling wood a few seconds later.

"Right. Give them ten minutes or so and then I'll pop the rest on." He lifted a bottle of Lowenbrau lager out of an ice-filled bucket next to the shed, popping the lid off with his bottle opener. "Cheers."

The others lifted their glasses before taking a swig of their ale, the sound of nearby seagulls drifted over them. "So, we're heading back to the doorway tomorrow?" Wilf asked.

"Are you coming too?"

"Of course. I want to say my final farewells to this old rascal."

Tamatan smiled, enjoying the balmy sun that caressed his bare legs. "It will be a fond farewell, but not a final goodbye. I have a feeling that our paths will cross again. Hopefully, under happier circumstances. We've come a long way since I first met you both. Many moons and seasons have come and gone since then. And many monsters have fallen at our hands."

"Aye," Wilf added. "I never dreamed that I'd end up in a far-off land, living by the sea. I thought I would see out my days under dark clouds. Funny how life turns out."

Jake nodded. "You're not wrong there. I…"

Jake's words were cut-off as a scream came from the kitchen, followed by the clattering of cutlery on the floor. They dashed inside, the chicken forgotten. Jo was stood next to the sink, her hand over her mouth. Emma was standing by the fridge, knives and forks strewn around her feet. A third woman stood in the doorway, her auburn hair framing her passive face. "Jake," Katherine whispered.

He crossed the kitchen in three steps, taking Katherine in his arms. "You're awake," he croaked as tears began to form in the corners of his eyes. The others looked on as Jake sobbed openly, burying his head in the crook of her neck, the world momentarily forgotten. Finally, he pulled away, his eyes red-rimmed. "I can't believe you're back."

Katherine smiled at him as an older man appeared before her. "Uncle Wilf?" Now it was her turn to cry as the old man strode towards her, putting his arm around both of them.

"Aye Kath. Welcome back."

At the sight of the older man weeping, Jo leant against the sink, her tears flowing freely. Three sets of footsteps grew louder down the garden path, the girls spilling into the kitchen. "Mummy," Alicia cried, joining the others in a group embrace.

Katherine knelt down, holding the girls face in her hands. "Alicia? Is it really you?"

"Yes, Mummy. I'm a big girl now," she chirped jubilantly.

Jake pulled up a kitchen chair, seating Katherine as their daughter vied for position on her mother's lap. "I'll get you a drink," he said clumsily, not knowing what else to say.

"I've missed you, Mummy. Every day, I wished you were here, and now you are."

Katherine hugged her daughter, her weak arms barely able to squeeze the little girl on her lap. She looked up at Wilf, Jake and Tamatan, smiling. "I don't understand what's happening?"

The demon placed a green hand on her shoulder. "It will all come out, Katherine Bathurst. Have something to drink and you will feel stronger."

She took a sip of water, the liquid seeming to revive her slightly. "It's so good to see you, Tamatan. What are you doing this far from home?"

Before the demon could answer, the chicken began spitting and sizzling on the grill. "I'll sort that," Emma offered. "I'll put the rest on too. Lauren, Scarlett. Come with me outside for a bit." They filed out, the girls looking over at the unknown woman before continuing their games in the garden.

Tamatan smiled at her, his eyes a mellow orange. "My friends needed me."

"Jake, what happened?"

He knelt in front of her, wiping his face with the back of his hand. "What do you remember, babe?"

Her eyes clouded over, trying to dig up the past. "We were out on the rocks. The vampires were there. We were fighting them. I remember being held by one. Then, it all went black. What happened after that? And how long have I been asleep for?"

Jake swallowed, trying to find the right words, realising there was no easy way to proceed. "You died, babe."

"I died," she repeated.

"Yes. After the fight, we brought you back here, then took you home to Shetland, where we buried you."

"But… how is that possible?"

"It's true, Kath," Wilf interjected. "We laid you in the ground many seasons ago. We said our goodbyes and came back to Cornwall to raise Alicia. This is

Jo. She's my..." At a loss for words, Wilf looked over at the woman who was still perched by the sink.

"I'm his partner," Jo added, her voice shaky. "It's wonderful to meet you, Katherine. Sorry if we startled you when you came in."

Katherine stood up, walking over to the counter. She enveloped Jo in a hug, kissing her cheek. "Hello, Jo. It's lovely to meet you too. I always wanted Uncle Wilf to meet the right woman. I'm so pleased he finally has."

Jo broke down, racking sobs echoing around the kitchen as Wilf put a steadying hand on her shoulder. "She's a fine woman," the old man said. "Worth waiting all this time for."

They all embraced, more tears flowing as Jake stood there, his legs feeling rubbery. "How do you feel?" he asked.

She turned to him, her face pale. "A little weak. I think I need to sit down."

He took her arm, guiding her back to the chair before handing her some more water. "We're preparing some food, although it might be a good idea to just do you something light."

"I'll put some toast on," Jo said hurriedly.

Jake leant against the wall, smiling at Tamatan who handed him his beer. "We've lived here ever since" *Shit, what do I say about Alana? I'll save that for another time.* "Then, the lady outside, Emma contacted me. Her daughter went missing last year. It's a very complicated story, babe, which I'll fill you in on later. Anyway, there is a doorway close by. One that comes out not too far from Shetland. It's called Vrybergen."

"Vrybergen," she mouthed.

"Yes. There is a family called the Longfords, who live in the lighthouse. They took Lauren and kinda sold her to someone in another world. I know this all sounds a bit crazy, but we all know how crazy things can get. I found Lauren and we brought her back home, but during all this, we discovered that the Longfords had visited Shetland and taken your body."

Her eyes widened. "What? Why would they do that? I must have been a pile of bones?"

"Believe me, there is more at play here. I met someone called Grey. He's an ancient being, who has powers over all the doorways. We all thought it was Korgan and Reggan that did that, but no. It's Grey. He lives across the sea from Vrybergen, through a massive portal. I ended up his prisoner if you like. I did a job for him and he then released me. Little did I know, the person that I found for him was to be used to bring you back to life. Crazy huh."

"Who was it?"

Jake took a swig of his beer, his throat feeling dry and raspy. "Someone called Jubella. I'm not really sure who she was. Grey said she was an old enemy of his, who he'd never been able to capture. So, I was sent to bring her to him. It wasn't easy. There were vampires. Lots of them."

Katherine shook her head, trying to piece together all that had transpired. "So, if this woman's essence was used to bring me back, why do I still feel like me?"

"From what I was told, Jubella was half-darkness, half-light. I think Grey took her light and somehow, I don't know how to explain it. He transmitted her light into you, babe."

Katherine understood what he meant, peering around the familiar kitchen. A kitchen where she'd spent many happy times, with the man who knelt before her now. "Thank you, Jake. Thank you for bringing me home, finally."

They kissed, Wilf looking away as Jo placed a hand on her chest at the sight before her. As their lips parted, something occurred to Jake. "This might not be over yet, babe. The Longfords chased us all the way to Vrybergen. They are also powerful, and may want revenge."

"So, what shall we do?" She asked nervously. "I just got back. I don't want any more trouble, Jake. I want to live a quiet life, with you, Alicia, and all our new kin."

Jake looked out into the garden, smiling as Emma tended the barbeque. "Whatever happens, nothing bad will ever happen to you again, babe. I swear."

"So do I," Wilf added, embracing his niece. "I had to bear the burden of losing two nieces. To have one back is a blessing from the gods, whoever they are."

"Uncle Wilf. It's so wonderful to be here with you. I'm sorry I've been away so long."

Wilf's tears were clear to see, the gruff old man, crying freely. "Kath, you're home. My old heart is happy. I've always loved you like the daughter I never had. Cedric would be so proud of you."

"Jake. What do you want me to do with these drumsticks? They're nearly ready."

"Sorry babe," Jake said smiling. "Trust you to turn up when we're cooking a feast."

She smiled, her eyes lighting up her pale complexion. "Then go and do what must be done. I'm home and everything is just as it should be."

The barbeque was served and eaten with gusto, Tamatan devouring enough food to see him all the way home. He sat there, a glass of ale on his knee as the girls played on the lawned area. Katherine sat in the sun, enjoying the warmth on her skin and the attentiveness of her man. Wilf and Jo chatted with Emma, the older man replenishing drinks when the ladies were down to the dregs as the sun slowly made its way towards the Atlantic.

Far away, a ship ploughed through rough seas, two figures standing at the bowsprit as the vessel fought against the coming storm. Both were hooded, their cloaks covering them from the driving rain. One cloak was grey, the other red as the two figures focused on the task before them. Revenge.

Chapter Thirty-Five

"How are you feeling, babe?" Jake asked as he snuggled into the woman next to him.

"I feel a lot stronger today, Jake," she replied, a warm smile spreading across her face.

Jake could see the first blossom of colour on her cheeks, Katherine appearing more vibrant than when he'd first set eyes on her in the kitchen below. "Well, I know you said that you wanted to come with us later, but why don't you stay here and rest with the others."

"I'm not letting you out of my sight, Jake Stevenson. The last time I did that, you ended up being chased by a witch."

"Okay," he relented. "But you need to get some rest before we set off. Are you hungry?"

"I guess so, although I think I had one-to-many burgers last night."

"Okay. I'll be back in a minute with a coffee, then we can think about breakfast."

A few minutes later, he placed a mug next to her side of the bed, bending down to kiss her lips. She snaked a hand around the back of his neck, crushing their lips together as her eyes closed. "Hmm. Jake Stevenson. I have missed those."

"Well there is an endless supply, babe," he replied before his face dropped slightly.

"What is it?"

"Okay, there is something I need to tell you. I wanted to yesterday, but the time wasn't right."

Katherine sat up in bed slowly, taking a sip of her coffee as Jake made his way around the bed. "Okay. What is on your mind?"

"Okay. After you died, Alana stayed with us. You might not remember, but she was also hurt during the fight with the vamps. She lay on the sofa downstairs for days, until her strength came back. I never planned for it, but we kinda ended up together. Not straight away. It was a good while later."

Katherine digested the information, nodding her head. "So, where is she now?"

Jake sighed, looking up at the ceiling. "She died during childbirth. The baby died too."

"Oh, Jake. I am so sorry. I did like her. She saved your life and if she made you happy after I had died then I can hold no ill-feelings. When did she die?"

"Six years ago. It's 2019 now. You've been gone for almost eight years."

"Well, I am very sorry, Jake. And to lose the baby too, that must have been heart-breaking."

"It was. But I guess I'm used to heartbreak."

She understood, knowing that he'd lost his wife and daughter years before. She pulled him towards her, letting his head settle on her breast. "No more hurt. No more pain and adventures, Jake. We have a second chance at life, and I want to spend every waking moment watching Alicia grow. And I want to do that with you, Jake."

"Then let's celebrate those words with a Full English."

She giggled, stroking the top of his head, noticing the silver strands intermingled with his dark hair. "Always the joker, Jake Stevenson. I have missed your wit."

* * *

The day went quickly, Emma and the girls coming over to say their farewells to Tamatan. The demon's eyes shone brightly, salty tears running down his emerald skin as they waved their goodbyes. In the afternoon, Jake popped out to the local chip shop, struggling back to his car with a double-armful of treats for both households. Just after seven, they all stood in the carport, Jo giving Wilf a fierce hug. "What time will you be home?"

"Ask the captain," he grinned, pointing at Jake.

"I'd say about three. There will be no traffic and we'll come straight back after Tamatan goes through the doorway."

Alicia, leapt into the demon's arms, planting a kiss on his lips. "I will miss you. I've never met a demon before, but I'm sure you are the nicest on in the world."

He beamed at her, more tears beginning to cascade down his face. "I need you to look after them both. You are a very special little girl, Alicia, and I wish you a long and prosperous future."

"What does that mean?" the girl enquired.

"He means that he wants you to be happy," Jake added smoothly.

"Oh, I will. I have two new friends to play with. Some of my classmates are a bit boring, so it will be nice to hang out with Lauren and Scarlett. They are not boring. They are cool."

"I'm sure they are," Tamatan agreed heartily, placing the girl on the ground. "Farewell, little one. Stay safe and live long."

"Bye bye, Tamatan. Thank you for saving my Mummy and Daddy."

"I'm not used to hugging demons," Jo giggled, wrapping her arms around him, Tamatan's head barely reaching her chin. "Thank you for everything. I know I've not known you for long, but I know these two rouges think the world of you."

As he broke the embrace, wiping his eyes, Tamatan smiled once more. "It takes a strong woman to keep Wilf Bathurst in check. I have never seen the old monster looking so happy. I can rest easy, knowing that his belly will always be full and his smile will never be far away."

"Stop all that soppy nonsense," Wilf croaked, his own tears threatening to tumble down his ruddy cheeks. "We should be hitting the road as you say in these parts."

Hugs and kisses were exchanged before they all climbed into Jake's Volvo, the SUV backing out of the driveway before heading off down the road, leaving Jo and Alicia waving after it. Jo said a silent prayer, hoping that her man and the others would be home before the sun rose once more.

* * *

Vrybergen was silent, save for the waves that lapped at the dock. Men, women and children were scattered around the narrow streets and alleyways, as rodents, cats and dogs scurried through the streets. All the bodies bore puncture marks or large gaping wounds, dried blood clinging to the walls and seeping across the rough ground. Something had laid waste to the settlement and no one had escaped its clutches. Inside the lighthouse, Grey and Red were seated close to the doorway, waiting for the sun to leave the land for another day. "Are you sure something is different?" Red asked.

"I am. I can almost reach out and touch it. They have barred our progress back to their world. Even when the doorways are closed, my mind's eye can see the other side. Here, I can see nothing but darkness. It's as if the ground on the other side has swallowed up the entrance."

"How long do we have?"

"A few hours, Red. And that is all the time I need to prepare myself for when the doorway opens."

"What do you have in mind?"

"I will gather all the strength needed and make sure that we can pass through. Leave me now, Red. I will be no company for the next few hours."

"As you wish, Grey. There is a tavern close by. I will sate myself for a while and take a look around this desolate hole before the door opens."

"Very well. I will give you a signal to return. Go, sample what those pitiful souls have on offer."

Grey sat there, his milky eyes turning white as he sat rocking in Berndt Longford's chair. Out at sea, lightning hissed as it struck the dark waters, a growing storm converging on the once-thriving port, the sea beginning to batter the coastline as the ancient being's magic began to manifest.

* * *

Jake sat with the others, his fingers entwined into Katherine's as the Lickey Hills lay silent. The temperature had not dropped too much since the sun had set, the evening air pleasant despite autumn's approach. He checked his watch for the umpteenth time, his heart beginning to increase as the hour approached. "How long will it take you to get home?"

"If I travel at a steady pace, I'll be back with my kin in one of your Earth months."

The private investigator nodded, knowing that the demon knew the far-flung reaches of the lands beyond like the back of his green hand. "Okay. That's good to know, my friend. There should be enough food and drink in your pack to last you a while. Sorry I couldn't give you more."

"You are most kind, Jake. I am sure that your offering will keep old Tamatan going strong. And once I reach Sica, he will fill my belly with cyder and griddled fish steaks."

"Good to know. Hopefully, we'll be home in the early hours. Then, we can return to normal soon, I hope. We still need to make sure that Emma and the girls are in no danger."

"Aye," Wilf added in between puffs on his pipe. "Those Longfords are probably back by now. We need to make sure that they don't come after any of us."

"I know. But I don't know how we go about that. They are connected, and with social media, they may start looking for us."

Wilf and Tamatan frowned, not understanding how this world had moved on so fast. The older man huffed. "Well, however we go about it, those bastards are not going to ruin what we now have."

"Agreed," Jake replied. "We will think of something."

Silence fell over the group as the seconds ticked away. Jake noticed it before anyone else as leaves and bracken began to skitter along the hillside. "Is it time?" Katherine asked.

"Yes," Jake replied as a blue outline began to form in between two familiar trees.

"We have said our goodbyes," Tamatan stated. "I do not want more tears. You need to get home to your kin, as do I."

They all climbed to their feet, dusting leaves and twigs from their clothing as the doorway pulsed in front of them. "Goodbye, my dear friend," Jake began. "I hope you…"

His words died in his throat as a strong wind crashed into them, almost knocking them all over. "What's happening?" Wilf shouted as the doorway grew brighter, lighting up the darkened forest. They all watched in frozen horror as the trees bent towards the portal, debris flying into it before becoming lost to sight.

"Go," Tamatan hollered. "Run as fast as…"

Katherine screamed as the foursome were sucked through the doorway, disappearing, into the unknown.

* * *

"It's as I thought, someone has blocked up the doorway. We only have a few moments before it closes for another night."

"Are you ready?" Red asked, wondering what Grey had up with long sleeves.

Lightning crackled nearby, a fierce wind invading every opening of the lighthouse. "Stand aside," Grey commanded, his bony fingers pointing towards the doorway. Sparks began to appear at his fingertips, reaching out until a steady stream of them encompassed the glowing portal.

Red looked on as a white aura surrounded the ancient being, as chips of stone began flying through the doorway. "Come on, Grey. You have the power."

Grey's other hand shot out, more shards of light pulsing against its target before he twisted his body, casting his arms to one side in a blur of speed. The doorway bulged, its frame distorting as a huge chunk of dirty-grey rock shot out of it, smashing through the lighthouse wall. Grey's arms fell to his side, as wind and rain poured in from outside. "Hurry. It will collapse. Let us be on our way."

Red needed no further encouragement as the stone structure began to groan around him, dust and chunks of rock falling from above. He followed the cloaked figure, into a new world.

Chapter Thirty-Six

"What the hell happened?" Jake said as he tried to scramble to his feet. Before him, the doorway disappeared, the forest becoming silent.

Tamatan writhed on the floor, the demon groaning in pain as if attacked by an unseen entity. "Noooo!" he wailed, Jake and Wilf lifting him to his feet.

"Tamatan. What's wrong?" the older man asked before looking around for his niece. He smiled thinly when he saw Katherine gingerly rise from the forest floor, making her way unsteadily towards them.

"I felt it," the demon began. "He has passed through the doorway and he has someone with him."

"Who?" Jake urged. "Grey?"

"Yes, yes. I felt their power as we were drawn through the doorway. They must have crossed over from Vrybergen into your world at the same moment we came through. I think something terrible is about to happen."

"Well, we're bloody-well stuck here until tomorrow night," Wilf spat, thumping a nearby tree in anger.

Jake slumped against a tree, his shoulder drooping. "He's right. Vrybergen is three days away. We may as well stay here and hope that Tamatan is wrong. Although, I think he's right." Jake turned towards the demon whose eyes glistened with a purple hue. "You are more than welcome to stay with us, my friend. But I know you are keen to get back to your family."

Tamatan shook his head solemnly. "I am keen to return to my kin. But you need me, Jake. I am staying with you until this is finished."

* * *

"What the hell was that?" Lukash hollered as the ran down the lighthouse steps. Barging through the door to the cellar area, the man flicked the light switch on the wall, barely bathing the bottom of the lighthouse in light. He stopped mid-step, a tight sensation squeezing his chest.

"Lukash," Grey proclaimed from below him. "Looks like your attempts to stop us following you have indeed failed."

Longford noted the red-cloaked figure next to Grey, his stomach turning to ice when he realised who he was looking at. "Red," he breathed.

"Yes," Grey replied. "He left his land to help out his brother. When I needed him most, he was right by my side. I can trust him, and only him, as I'm sure you're aware."

"Grey, please, I never meant to break our agreement," Lukash said hesitantly.

"Come down here," Red offered. "It is straining our necks looking up at you like this."

Longford began descending the stairs, the wood creaking loudly under his footfalls. "You have to believe me," he offered, his voice hollow.

"Now now, I think we are past that now. What's done is done, Lukash. I am not here for you. I am here for my woman. Jake took her and I want her back. Now!" His eyes glowed in the darkness, the last vestiges of his power surge still within the ancient being.

"I will bring her to you," he announced confidently as he came to the bottom of the stairs.

Red approached him, matching height with the dark-haired man. "Do you think I was born yesterday? I can see your soul, Longford. I know you are lying."

"I'm not. You've gotta believe me. I know where Jake lives. He's not far from here. I could have them all here by tomorrow night."

"Sounds like an agreeable plan," Grey agreed. "But first, take us to your father."

"My f-father?" Longford stammered. "Why?"

"Because we have many things to discuss," Grey countered. "Lead on."

Lukash climbed the stairs, feeling two sets of eyes burning into his back. He tried to think, scenarios flitting across his mind. "Even thinking about defying us will end with your head leaving your shoulder," Red admonished. "Now, take us to Berndt."

As they climbed ever-upwards, they eventually came to the top of the structure, a large bed in one corner. Grey looked at the large glass beacon, his eyes scanning the round space. "Impressive. Much nicer outlook than the one in Vrybergen. Tell me, what sea is that?"

"It's called the Atlantic Ocean."

"Atlantic, I like the sound of that."

"Lukash?" A male voice called out. "Is that you?" Berndt flicked on the bedside lamp, flinching at the sight in front of him.

"Berndt. So good to see you," Grey smiled. "Sorry to call unannounced. But as you can imagine, we have much to discuss."

The old warlock was not fooled. He knew what was coming. The sheets of his bed shot across the room, the older Longford rising up from the mattress, his bunched fists emitting red sparks. "Get out. Both of you."

"Now now, is that any way to welcome an old friend?" Grey held a pointed finger, lightning striking the roof above them. His eyes began to glow until his head was engulfed in light, the warlock holding his ground in front of them. "You are old, Berndt Longford. And it is time you took the long sleep." His finger jabbed forward, Berndt screaming in pain as white light struck him in waves. Lukash looked on in horror as his father's eyes melted into his skull, the warlock's skin drizzling away from the bone until as an acrid stench filled the room. The top of the lighthouse suddenly returned to normal, save for a steaming pile of melted flesh and charred bones on the floor. "That's for breaking our accord."

"You bastard!" Lukash screamed, rushing the grey-cloaked figure.

A fist connected with his jaw, knocking the man to the floor. As he lay there groggily, a large hand encircled his throat, lifting the large man into the air. "Pitiful scrote," Red spat. The only reason you're still breathing is because we want the others. Try anything, and I will take you back to my land and let you loose with the local rabble. Pretty lad like you will be very popular. Think carefully. Do as we bid, and you might just survive. Betray us, and I'll personally see to it that you are sodomized until the wind will whistle up your back passage. Do you hear me, boy?"

"Y-yes," he croaked, the large fingers crushing his throat.

Red dropped him to the floor, Longford wheezing and gasping for air as the cloaked figures regarded him pitifully. "Now. There are many hours until the sun comes up," Grey started. "We'll not sleep in this room, the stench is not to my liking. Prepare our quarters and do it quickly. Remember, he will be watching. Even when he's asleep," he warned, pointing at Red.

"Okay," Longford sighed, looking down at the remains of his great father. With dragging feet, the new head of the Longford clan led them downstairs.

Chapter Thirty-Seven

"Are you sure?" Red asked as Lukash placed two large plates of toast and coffee before the two men.

"Yes. When we passed through the portal, I caught sight of others passing in the opposite direction. One of them was a demon, with green skin and glistening eyes. That was Tamatan, I am sure of it."

"How many were there?"

"Alas, I could not tell you," Grey lamented. "I was focused on the demon, but there were others. Of that I am sure."

"So, let's just say that this Tamatan passed through with Jake. Maybe Jake was taking him back to the doorway to let the demon return to his homeland. If that's the case, he is stuck there until midnight. And… "

"My prize may be close by, ripe for the picking. And Jake is beyond her reach."

"So, what are we going to do?"

"It's quite simple. At midnight, no doors will open. I control them and I alone can do with them as I please."

Red smiled as Lukash stood by nervously. "I like your plan." He turned. "Longford. You need to locate this woman. Today, with no exceptions."

"I'm on it. One of my contacts is pretty sure he found Jake's house. All we have to do is drive over there and bring the woman back here."

"Then make it happen. Immediately."

"Yes. I will leave you to your breakfast and I'll be back later."

"Oh, and Lukash," Grey called as the dark-haired man began retreating.

"Yes, Grey."

"I am watching. Do not fail me."

Lukash headed down to the lighthouse's front door, the warning seared into his mind.

Longford pressed the phone to his ear as he picked at a piece of loose skin on his thumb. He was nervous, and the thumb picking was a sign that he was ruffled. "Seth. I need your help. Bring your van to the lighthouse. And hurry."

The van arrived ten minutes later. A white panel van that had seen better days. The smaller man climbed out of the cab, ambling over towards Lukash who had a tense expression etched on his face. "What do you need?"

"You know the man I asked you to find?"

"Uh-huh."

"He's out of town, but I need you to bring anyone else you find in the house here."

"You mean kidnap them?"

"If that's what you want to call it."

"I don't know, Lukash. That's pushing it a bit. With my record, I'd be back in the slammer pretty quick."

"I'll make it worth your while."

"How much?"

Longford knew that it was no time for bartering. He could intimidate the man into submission. However, if he got this wrong, he'd end up like his father. A pile of steaming bones. "Five thousand."

The man's eyes opened, a dumbfounded look washing over him before he regained some composure. "Okay. But this is risky."

"Relax. The people who you will take will not go to the police. You'll have to trust me on that, Seth. They will be far from our laws."

The other man frowned, not fully understanding what Longford meant. "Okay. If you say so."

"Go to the Narwhal. Tell Malcolm that I want him to help you. Things may get a little rough. If he tags along you'll be fine."

"Fair enough. You want me to go now?"

"I do." He took a roll of notes out of his pocket. "Here's two thousand," he said a few seconds later. "I will give you rest when you get back here."

The van pulled away from the lighthouse, leaving Longford there alone. He peered out at the ocean, wondering how many times he would see it after today.

* * *

"Right. Are you clear on the plan?"

"Arr," Malcolm nodded, his head almost touching the ceiling of the cab.

"Okay. Tell me."

"I knock on the door. I ask them if they need their drive re-laying. Then I barge in. You will reverse the van up the drive, and we will tie them up in the house and put them in the back."

"Okay. That's good, Malcolm. That's very good," he replied nervously.

"What if they kick-off?" the giant asked.

"Just give them a slap. A slap from you would knock a horse over. But don't slap too hard."

"Understood. Not too hard."

"Okay. Let's do it."

Malcolm levered himself out of the cab, the van's suspension righting itself. He walked up the road, turning right onto the driveway, his feet kicking pebbles as he made his way to the door. He knocked twice, turning to see the van edge closer. "Not too hard," he repeated as the door opened. He was greeted by a forty-something woman with a kind face. She peered up at him, her expression edgy as she looked beyond him.

"Hello, can I help you?" Jo asked.

"We're asking if people need their drives relaying. Are you interested?"

Jo smiled, noticing the van approaching. "I'm sorry. I don't own the house, love. They will be back later. Do you have a card?"

"Have no card," Malcolm replied dumbly. *It's not her house. Maybe we get wrong house?* He was unsure of what to do. He didn't want to hurt anyone, let alone the wrong person.

"Jo, who is it?" a female voice called from inside.

"Just someone doing driveways. It's not…"

"Oh fuck. He's one of them," Emma shouted as she came out of the kitchen.

Before Jo could think, her world went black, the giant chopping her below the ear. As Malcolm grabbed at Emma, he heard the van reversing before a door slammed. "Keep quiet," he said softly.

"Get out! Help, please h…"

She crashed into the wall, another blow delivered as Seth barged into the hallway. "Bloody hell! I said not too hard."

"It wasn't hard. She was screaming."

"Never mind. Gag and tie their arms. Like in the movies."

Malcolm did as he was asked as Seth made his way into the kitchen. In the garden, three girls were playing on the lawn, completely unaware of the two men's presence. "Get them in the van. There're three kids out here. I will sort it."

"Arr," Malcolm replied behind him.

Seth walked to the kitchen door, waving at the girls. "Hi. I'm a friend of Jake's. You need to come with me. They have found you and we need to hide."

Scarlett and Lauren edged closer, coming to within arms-length of Seth, who tried his best reassuring smile. Alicia hung back, eyeing the stranger. "Where's Jo and Emma?"

"Out the front. In the minibus. Hurry. They will be here any minute." The two girls scooted past him, Seth hearing muffled cries a moment later as Malcolm gathered them up.

Alicia shook her head. "My Dad told me never to go with strangers."

"I don't have time for this. Either you stay, or you come with us. They're all outside waiting for you."

"I'm staying here. My Dad would want me to." She turned away from him, looking for something on the lawn as Seth made his move. He grabbed her around the waist, his hand clamping over her mouth. "Put me down," she tried to scream, Seth holding her tightly as he ran through the house to the waiting van.

He opened the rear doors, flinging the girl onto the metal floor. "Keep an eye on them," he urged, Malcolm sat on the wheel arch, two terrified girls in his grasp. The van lurched off the driveway, turning sharply before heading out of Tintagel. Towards Towan Point.

Chapter Thirty-Eight

"Feels weird to be back here," Katherine said as she walked around the remains of her former home. Heronveld lay dormant, the wooden buildings either dilapidated or burnt-out.

"You're not wrong there, Kath," Wilf observed drily as he sat on the steps of his old cabin. "It was once so full of life. Now look at it. It's a refuge for insects and vermin."

Jake sat down, a memory flooding back to him. "I remember being chased out of her by the Cravens. Jesus! That was a close call."

"And yet here you are, Jake," Tamatan replied. "We've all faced horrors and hardships, yet we have won through to this moment in time. We will get back home and put things right, once and for all."

"It's never-ending," Jake sighed. "For the past ten years, our lives have been a rollercoaster. I just want for all this to end."

"And it will. Tell me, Jake. What did you do with the weapon that you took from Longford?" Tamatan asked.

"It's in my garage, why?"

"Because, you will need it. If there are two of them to deal with, you must use the blade when you get the chance."

"I'll remember that. Jesus! You couldn't make this shit up. First vampires, now ancient demons. Sorry, my friend. I didn't mean you."

Tamatan chuckled, making the others smile. "No offence taken. Yes, I am ancient. But not like them. They must have been alive when the mountain were mere hills. Grey has hidden himself well throughout the ages. No one knew about him. Not even the vampires."

"Well, let's hope that we can get through this," Katherine added. "I've only just come back to you and I'm not ready to die yet."

"Nothing will happen to you, Kath," Wilf countered as he lit his pipe. "You have countless seasons to live out. With this ugly bugger and Alicia."

Jake smiled, knowing the man loved him as a son. "And you have Jo. Although what she sees in you is anyone's guess."

"Then we are agreed. We have much to lose but so much to gain," the demon stated. "Let us spend the day at our leisure and wait for the doorway to open."

"Amen to that," Jake replied, wrapping his arm around Katherine.

* * *

Grey and Red stood before the five captives, each of them bound to a wooden chair by cable ties. The three girls hung their heads, their laps dotted with tears as the two women tried to remain strong. Jo eyed the strange men, while Emma tried her best to hold their gaze. Lukash and Malcolm slouched at the rear of the basement area, Longford pretending to be interested whilst checking out social media. Grey spoke, his voice light and friendly. "Come come. There is no need for any unpleasantness. Just tell me where they are, and you can all go home safely."

"Up yours," Emma spat. "Why should we tell you anything? You're in our world now and there are laws against this kind of thing."

Grey sighed, standing back as Red approached the woman. She didn't see the backhand coming, her vision exploding into a thousand stars as the others cried out in fear. Even Jo was fearful, clamping her legs together to stop the seep of urine that was threatening to trickle out onto the dusty floor. "As I said, there is no need for this," Grey continued. "Just tell me where they are, or Red will become very unhappy. Believe me, it's not a wise decision to make the Red King unhappy."

Red took a blade from his waistband, grabbing Emma by the face as the pointed tip closed to within inches of her left eye. "Tell me," he soothed. "Give us what we need, and no harm will come to you. Defy me, and I'll skewer each eye in-turn and feed them to the rats."

Emma cried out in anguish as the blade made a small incision just below the eye, a droplet of blood mingling with her tears. "Nooooo."

"Okay. Please stop," Jo urged. "I will tell you."

Red stepped back, slipping the knife under his cloak. "Talk."

She swallowed, her throat feeling as dry as the basement floor. "They have taken Tamatan back to the doorway. They should have been back by now?"

"What doorway?" Grey asked expectantly.

"It's up in the Midlands, a few hundred miles away. They were due back this morning but never showed up."

"Alas, that was my doing. I will have to alter my plans. The doorway will open tonight, and I'm hoping that they will return."

"We hope so too," Jo added. "Please don't hurt them. Jake's been through a lot and has only just been reunited with Katherine."

"I'm sorry to say, Katherine was not Jake's to take. I had claimed her, given her a new lease of life. She is to come home with me and sit by my side."

"W-what?" Jo blurted. "You can't do that. She's not yours to just do with as you please."

"Oh, but she is. I am Grey and even in this world, I have the power to do what I want. Jake is a resourceful man. I am sure that he will come for you. And we'll be waiting for him. Won't we, Red."

"You speak the truth," the red-cloaked figure stated.

"The police will also come for you. Do you think that you can get away with this? They are probably looking for you right now. We have cameras everywhere. Someone will have spotted our abduction and can trace the van here."

Grey looked at Red, not wanting any diversions from his plan. "You know what to do." The larger man nodded, leaving the basement with Lukash. He beckoned Malcolm over, the giant approaching hesitantly. "I may be many things, but I am not a complete monster. Watch over them and provide them with sustenance. I will return to my quarters and wait for our friends to arrive." He turned to the five prisoners. "Do not try to escape. This oaf looks like he packs a mighty punch. Stay here and you'll be safe."

Malcolm stood there as the Grey made his way up the stairs, watching every step the ancient being took before turning his attention back to the captives. "I can bring water and biscuits."

"We'll need to use the toilet," Emma stated.

"Bucket over there. I will untie you, one by one and let you go. Try anything and I will snap the blonde girl's neck."

The two women nodded, tears falling freely as they both wondered if they would make it out of the lighthouse alive.

* * *

Red walked into the village of Towan Point, drawing stares from the locals who went about their business. Longford stood next to him, without a clue as to what was about to happen. "So, what are we doing here?"

"I've heard many fables about Tekartha. That is what we call your plane. I was expecting something grander, more fantastical. And yet, it appears not much different than other places I've visited."

"This is just a small village," Lukash countered. "There are big cities with millions of people living there. It's quiet here. And that's how I like it."

Red reached out, taking the man's hand. He held it firmly, Lukash not seeing the crimson mist that danced over his skin before embedding itself and vanishing. "This is what I want you to do. Go to every household. Tell them that the lighthouse is off-limits to everyone. Do it now and Grey will look upon you favourably."

"Is that all?"

"Yes. But you must tell everyone. Leave no pebble unturned. I will walk back to the lighthouse and leave you to it."

Longford watched as the hooded figure strode away, wondering if he was off the hook. Scratching his hand, he began walking from house-to-house, telling the villagers to stay away from the massive stone structure next to the sea. At one house, a little boy smiled up at him, grasping his finger in his tiny hand, the child's mother's eyes lingering on him as he walked back down the path. For the next ninety minutes, he traversed Towan Point, delivering Red's message, without questions from the villagers. They all knew not to cross Lukash Longford, with many glad to close their front doors, none seeing the red mist that crept underneath their door jambs. Satisfied that the whole village had been instructed to stay away, Lukash sat down on a park bench next to the convenience store as a van pulled up nearby. A man got out, smiling at the bigger man. "Morning, Mr Longford."

Lukash looked up, offering a thin smile. "Morning, Tony," he said almost happily. "Are there any packages for the lighthouse?"

"Hang on, I'll check," the courier replied jovially, rummaging through the rear of his van. "Here we go," he said, handing over a small parcel. "Something nice?"

"Just some wireless phone buds," the dark-haired man said. "Here, I'll take it. The lighthouse is having some restoration work done, so it's probably best if you don't venture down there."

"Fair point. I'm almost finished for the morning. Got one more drop off before heading back to Plymouth."

"Okay, well, have a good day," Longford replied, an unusual warmness creeping over his skin. He sat back down as Tony carried a few parcels to various houses before leaving the village. The Sunday morning solitude was shattered as one resident flung their front door open before collapsing in the small front garden. Longford rose from the bench, his legs feeling heavy as sweat began peppering his brow.

"My baby," a female voice shrieked. "Someone call an ambulance. My baby is sick."

The woman's neighbour, a woman in the mid-fifties pulled a phone out of her dressing gown pocket, dialling the emergency services.

What the fuck is going on? Lukash thought as he saw smoke begin to seep from the windows of another house. He looked at his hand, the one that Red has held, his stomach turning to lead as an angry red rash had crept into his sleeve. "Shit. What the hell have you done?" He took a step forward, his legs buckling underneath him as he floundered on the road. Longford looked up into the pale blue sky, his vision beginning to darken with a red tinge at the peripheries. He clutched at his throat as oxygen was stifled to the point of suffocation. The man tried to scream, the sound a hacking gurgle before darkness consumed him. He lay still. The first victim of the Red Wind.

Chapter Thirty-Nine

Roger Harris hit his hazard button, slowing down to the hard-shoulder of the dual-carriageway. A few hundred yards ahead, a van had left the road, a plume of smoke rising into the blue sky. In his early fifties, the silver-haired Roger exited his Audi, running towards the van as another car pulled in further on from the crash site. Flames began to rise from the crumpled bonnet, Roger managing to prize the drivers' door open, dragging the barely conscious man along the carriageway before depositing him on the grass verge, safe distance from the smouldering vehicle. He looked up at the approaching man as the van exploded, almost knocking the man over. "Call an ambulance," Roger shouted. He looked down at the man on the grass, baulking slightly at his appearance. His skin was pallid, a fine sheen coating his face. Tendrils of red were creeping towards his face, like crimson fingers crawling up his body. "An ambulance is on its way. What's your name?"

"Tony," the man croaked.

"Okay, Tony. What happened?"

"Not. Sure," he replied, barely able to get the words out of his mouth as his windpipe began closing. "Can't breathe!"

"Okay. Help is on its way," Roger soothed, looking up at the man standing over him.

"Ambulance is on its way. What happened?"

"Not sure. He doesn't look good though."

"No, he doesn't," the man replied, taking a step backwards as he spotted the angry red marks on the van driver's skin. "Should you be so close? Whatever he's got maybe infectious."

Roger stood up, heeding the warning. "I suppose you're right. I wonder what happened to him?"

"Who knows. Let's hope the paramedics can sort him out."

A hacking scream erupted from Tony's mouth before he lay still, his blood-shot eyes glazing over as they stared upwards at the blue sky. "Shit," Roger exclaimed. "I think he's dead." They both stood there, unsure of what to do as sirens drifted towards them.

A few minutes later, two paramedics arrived at the scene. The female spoke to the men, asking the usual questions as the male tended to the man on the ground. Finally, he stood up, shaking his head solemnly. "Nothing I could do. He's gone."

"Shit," Roger said, checking his watch. "Look. I need to dash. I'm flying to Amsterdam and I don't want to miss it." He pulled a business out of his wallet, handing it to the female paramedic. "Here. Give this to the police in case they need to speak to me."

The other man shook his head. "Don't you think you should get checked over? He may have some kind of virus?"

"I'll be okay," Roger countered, looking at the paramedics who were unsure of what to say.

"We don't know the cause of death, so it's hard to know what this man was suffering from. Only an autopsy will clarify that. If you start feeling unwell, call the emergency services, wherever you are."

"Okay," Roger agreed before jogging back to his waiting Audi. The two paramedics watched as the car pulled away, gathering speed before disappearing into the distance.

After a few seconds, the other man spoke. "What do you need me to do?"

"What's your name?" the woman asked.

"Giles. Giles Kennedy."

"Okay, Giles. Well, the police will be here shortly, along with the Highways Agency and the Fire and Rescue service. They will want to speak to you. I suggest you sit on the verge, as far up as you can. We will take the deceased back to Plymouth."

"What do you think killed him?"

The woman massaged the back of her neck, her expression pinched. "Not sure. Could have been an allergic reaction to something."

"What, like peanuts?"

The male paramedic shook his head. “No. This is something else. Not seen anything like this before.” The words hung in the air.

“Okay. Well, this isn’t how I was expecting to spend the morning. I was heading for my girlfriends in Bristol. I’d better give her a call and tell her I’ll be delayed.” He looked over at the van as the paramedics went about their business, lifting the dead man onto a stretcher before pushing it towards the ambulance. Flames and black smoke drifted across the carriageway, as the Highways Agency arrived, cars on the opposite side of the road slowing down to see what had transpired. Giles dialled a number on his phone, sitting down on the grass. “Hi, babe. I’m going to be a little late. I’ll fill you in when I get there. Love you.” He ended the call as two policemen approached him. He scratched his bare forearm, not seeing the red marks on the skin as he trotted down the verge towards them.

* * *

Ninety minutes after leaving the crash site, Roger sat down at the busy arrivals lounge at Schiphol airport. He placed his coffee on the floor next to his seat, knowing that something was wrong. A few minutes earlier, he’d felt unsteady on his feet as the smiling barista handed him his latte. It had started as the plane began its approach to the airport, prickly heat spreading across his upper body. Now as he sat on the chair, he felt his breathing become laboured, beads of sweat dripping from his hairline. Ex-military, with no wife or family to speak of, Roger closed his eyes, trying to ride out the sensation coursing through his body. Passengers and airport staff ignored the silver-haired man as they headed for their destinations or carried on their duties, completely unaware of the silent plague that had invaded the airport.

* * *

Giles never made it to Bristol. His girlfriend getting the call hours later as she sat on the sofa watching the news channels. He’d stopped off at the motorway services, hoping to grab a bunch of flowers for Tina. He died as people stood around him as nearby fruit machines pinged and played tunes, the man from Cornwall falling into a black abyss from which he would never return. As the emergency services arrived, concerned shoppers and travellers continued their journeys, heading north, south, east and west to be with family, loved ones and colleagues, also unaware that they were taking something with them. Something red, from a distant world.

Chapter Forty

They came through the doorway, standing in the forest for a few moments before Jake spoke. "Right. Let's head home and finish this."

Wilf puffed on his pipe, as alien sounds drifted over the Lickey Hills. "What's that noise?"

"Just a siren," Jake replied. "Probably an ambulance or police car. Nothing for you to worry about. I'm going to get the car. Kath, if you all head towards the road over there, I'll meet you in about ten minutes."

"Okay, Jake," she replied, the far-off noise unsettling her. "Just hurry."

He gave her a kiss before heading down the gravelly path towards his car. More sirens could be heard in the distance, Jake looking out across the city of Birmingham. *Strange. Something's going on somewhere.* He stood for a minute, seeing blue flashes of light as emergency vehicles sped across Britain's second city, the private investigator completely unaware of what had taken place in their absence. He carried on, jogging down a steep path towards a quiet lane, his car only a few hundred yards away. A minute later, the Volvo's headlights came to life, Jake pulling away from the kerb as he drove towards the others. As he came to the junction close to the Hare and Hounds public house, a police car shot past him, heading down the dual-carriageway towards the suburb of Longbridge. "Something is really going on. I hope it's not serious." He crossed the dual-carriageway, heading down to a roundabout where he turned right before driving along a tree-lined road. He spotted movement to his right, Wilf coming out of the shadows, a plume of smoke above his head. "Get in," Jake called through the open window, the others doing so with some urgency. "Right, let's go." A few minutes later, the Volvo pulled onto the M5, the SUV picking up speed briskly on the empty motorway. By the time they'd reached the junction for Droitwich, Jake spoke again. "There's hardly any traffic. And there's flashing blue lights every few minutes. Something bad has happened?"

"Like what?" Katherine said, her voice edged with concern.

"No idea. Hang on. I'll put the radio on." He selected BBC Radio 5; the others sat in silence as a male voice filled the car.

"We're staying with the breaking news that is unfolding across the country and on the continent, where hundreds of people have died from an unknown illness. Emergency services have been attending calls across the country, with hospitals on high alert as accident and emergency departments receive patients on an unprecedented level. The prime minister is due to chair a meeting of the COBRA Committee later this morning, with a press conference due at around 11am. It is yet unclear as to how and where the illness originated, with unconfirmed reports claiming that the first case occurred in the West Country. A statement from Public Health England has instructed people to remain indoors with a further statement expected from the prime minister in the coming hours."

Jake switched the radio off, a stunned silence inside the car they drove towards the West Country. "This cannot be a coincidence," Jake said, breaking the silence. "This is Grey's doing."

"I'm scared, Jake," Katherine said, tears streaming down her face. "I don't understand what is happening, but Alicia and the others are down there."

"I know. I'm trying to think about what we do."

"Head to your home first, Jake. And we'll go from there."

"Okay," Jake replied. "Hundreds of people dead. Maybe more. Jesus Christ!"

"Has this ever happened before?" Tamatan asked from the back seat.

"Well, we had the Black Death hundreds of years ago. That killed millions. And more recently, we've had something called SARS and bird flu, which were pretty serious. But things like this are very few and far between, and usually start in other parts of the world. If what they say is true, it could have started in Cornwall. If that's the case, it must have been done by Grey. Or Red." Silence descended over the car as it headed south-west, Jake noticing more blue lights and some abandoned vehicles at the side of the motorway. "I think I know what we should do. But I don't know how we're going to manage it?"

"What?" Katherine asked expectantly.

"We need to get the others and go back through the doorway. At least until all this blows over."

"We'll have one hell of a fight on our hands before we can do that," Wilf added.

"I know. As I said, I don't know how we're going to manage it," Jake replied, wondering if the others were safe. He tried to stop a thought invading his mind. *What if they're all dead?*

Chapter Forty-One

Low cloud hung like a blanket over Towan Point, the lighthouse shrouded in sea mist. Rumbles of thunder echoed along the coast, strobes of blue lightning illuminating the night. Inside the lighthouse, five females lay together near the top of the stone steps, Malcolm trying his best to watch over them as tiredness assailed him. The three girls had succumbed to exhaustion, gently snoring on an old tarpaulin sheet. Jo and Emma had woken up minutes before as a rumble of thunder nearby had roused them. “I can’t hear any more sirens,” Emma whispered.

“No. I’m not sure what is going on out there, but I’m scared.”

“Keep it down,” Malcolm ordered from his wooden chair.

“Or what?” Emma said. “No one has been down here for hours. Don’t you think that’s a bit odd? You’ve heard the sirens. And your boss is nowhere to be seen.”

He didn’t want to admit it, but the giant was also scared. Although huge in stature, Malcolm was what some folk called ‘simple’. Approaching his fortieth year, he could barely read or write, staying off the grid of what people would consider a normal life. He rarely ventured outside the village, with Lukash taking care of him. And now, his protector was nowhere to be seen. He sensed something bad had happened but was too scared to admit it to himself. “He’ll be back. Lukash takes care of me.”

“Err, hello!” Emma retorted. “It looks like he’s met his match. These two monsters are dangerous and who knows what they’re going to do with us, you included.”

“Lukash will sort it all out. You’ll see.”

"Well, I don't share your optimism. I just hope that Jake and the others will find us. And soon."

"Let's hope they are on our way to us," Jo said quietly. "What time is it?"

"Just after four," Emma replied, rubbing her eyes. "I'd say that they must be back home by now. And they will figure out what happened."

"Makes no odds," Malcolm countered. "They cannot help you. Go to sleep before you wake them folks upstairs."

"I couldn't give a shit about them folks upstairs," Emma hissed. "We've been kidnapped. Once the police find out, you'll all be for the high jump."

Malcolm lowered his head, his large feet moving backwards and forwards on the stone floor as he fidgeted nervously. "No police here. Lukash sees to that."

"Well, not this time. As soon as we're out of here I'm going to report this."

"Do you really think something bad has happened to Lukash?" Malcolm asked.

"Yes. Yes I do," Emma stated. "He's been gone for hours. I'm betting that's not like him?"

"No."

"Are you scared, Malcolm?"

"A little."

"Not nice, is it?"

"No, Mrs Thorne."

"Well, that's how I felt when Lauren went missing. That's how she must have felt when someone snatched her from our garden and took her to another world."

"I'm really sorry. I took her."

"I guessed as much, you heartless bastard. Why?"

"Because Lukash told me to. He said it was revenge for what your husband did with Ciara. Said you all needed to be taught a lesson."

"Well, you should have punished my ex-husband, not my little girl," Emma spat, causing Lauren to stir next to her. She stroked the little girl's hair before addressing the man across the room. "You've stolen a piece of her childhood. She must have seen things and done things that no child should endure. Are you proud of yourself?"

"No," Malcolm whispered. "I never wanted to take her, but Lukash said it had to be done. I don't know what happens on the other side of the doorway, but I was told not to think about it. I just do what I'm told and Lukash looks after me."

Emma's expression softened, seeing that the man was torn. She could see that the giant in front of her was not evil like his master. Looking at him, she could see his frailties. *He's just a boy, locked in a man's body,* she thought. "Look. We're all tired. We'll try and get some sleep. You should too. Don't worry, we're not going anywhere. With any luck, Jake and the others will be here soon." She nodded at Jo, who smiled weakly. Both women lay down, closing their eyes, hoping beyond hope that help was on its way.

* * *

Jake's car pulled up outside the house, the man striding into the hallway, his expression grave. "There's no one there either. I think they've all been taken to Towan Point."

Wilf banged his fist against the wall, Tamatan and Katherine standing in the kitchen, unsure of what to say. "I'll put the kettle on," the older man said. "We can think better with a hot coffee inside us."

A few minutes later, they all sat around the kitchen table, mugs of steaming coffee in front of them. "We need to think," Jake started. "Regardless of their predicament, there is an unknown plague sweeping the country. We need to make sure that we don't come into contact with anyone. If we do, we may get it."

"So, what are you thinking?" Wilf asked.

"I still think we need to head through the doorway. But we cannot do that until tonight. Grey is here for Katherine and won't leave without her. He won't care what happens to the rest of us. I'm guessing he has plans, which doesn't bear thinking about."

"So, we need to go to the lighthouse and kill the bastards," Wilf replied.

Despite the situation, Jake smiled. "Yes. But I'm not sure it will quite that simple?"

"But it is, Jake. It's no different than how we dealt with Korgan and Reggan. They had something of ours, and we took it back. There's no need to go around the houses, as Jo would say." He stopped, thinking about his woman. "If anything has happened to her."

"Try not to think about that, Wilf. We need to focus on what we need to do. Not worry about what may or may not have happened."

"You're right," the older man relented, taking a sip of his brew.

"Jake. Where is the dagger?"

"Oh, good point. I'll go and get it." He walked out into the carport, opening the garage door as quietly as he could. After locating the weapon, Jake made his way back into the kitchen, unwrapping the hessian carefully.

They all stared at the ancient dagger, Katherine noticing the red flecks that shimmered under the kitchen lights. "Where did this come from?"

"I took it from Longford," Jake replied. "It must have been his."

Tamatan picked it up, turning the blade over as he inspected the obsidian blade. "This is as old as time itself. The blade is razor-sharp, but brittle. You'll only get one chance to use it."

"But there are two of them," Wilf said, the others pondering his statement.

"Then it must be used only on Grey," the demon replied. "We will have to find another way to take care of his friend."

"Well, I think stakes and garlic are out of the question. He's not a vampire. I'm not even sure what he is?"

Tamatan put the blade down, spreading his green hands on the table. "I'm not totally sure either. He could be a maygr, or a warlock. Maybe even an ancient conjurer? All I know, is that he's powerful. Almost as powerful as Grey himself. Tackling him won't be easy. What weapons do we have?"

"Not much. I had some firearms but got rid of most of them. I still have the shotgun though. It's hidden away in the garage."

"Well that's a start," Tamatan nodded. "I can take care of Longford and his goons myself. We have the dagger for Grey, that just leaves Red. Hopefully, your shotgun may slow him down a bit?"

"Hope so. I'll dig it out in a bit. We need to figure out what time to go. You heard the radio, we're all being told to stay inside. We may be stopped by the police if we venture out."

"Then we need to wait until the time is right," Wilf said. "The doorway opens at midnight. We should arrive maybe an hour before. What do you think?"

Jake pondered the question, nodding his head in agreement. "Sounds good. If we're too early, we'll be stood waiting with Grey and Red to contend with. If we leave it too late, we may not find them in time."

Katherine stood up, walking over to the window. The others looked over at her, Tamatan sensing something was wrong. She turned, her eyes pulsing gently against the darkness. They all flinched before she spoke. "Someone is talking to me, Jake. Someone inside my head is calling out."

"Who?"

"It's Jubella. I can hear her words as clearly as yours. She can hear our plight." They all approached slowly, Jake holding out a hand which she took readily. "She says that her darkness has gone, but a little spark of light remains." Her glowing eyes closed slightly as if she were concentrating on an unseen message. "She is not bitter. She knew her time had come and Jubella bears no malice, for she is on another plane now. Free of pain."

"So, how is she still inside you?" Wilf asked nervously as the furniture around the room started to vibrate. The framed pictures on the wall began to shift, the older man feeling the room grow cooler.

Katherine relayed the message, listening for the reply. "Her duty. She cannot fully leave my spirit until she has banished the darkness." More words echoed around Katherine's mind, the other watching on expectantly. "She does not have the power to banish them both, but she wants to help."

They all stood there, Tamatan taking her other hand gently. "Tell her we give her thanks. When the moment is right, she can cast her power at the red one. I only hope it is enough."

"It will be enough," a distorted voice stated, the others taking a step back. Katherine's expression changed, the frown-lines in her forehead disappearing. She appeared almost robotic, her movements stilted as her head snapped towards Jake. "I met my match with you and can have no complaints. Just do the right thing when you get the chance. It will be a fleeting moment. Do not hesitate. If you do, all is lost."

Jake nodded, goosebumps breaking out over his skin. "I won't hesitate. I promise."

The glow dissipated until Katherine shook herself free of the spell. "Jubella has gone but remains close by. She will rise again when the moment comes." The furniture stopped vibrating, the room returning to normal as the woman smiled at them.

"Then let's prepare," Wilf said. "We've got many things to do and my belly is grumbling. Jake, I think this calls for one of your hearty breakfasts."

The younger man clapped Wilf on the shoulder. "Never change, Wilf. Never change."

Chapter Forty-Two

The sun kissed the Atlantic, the shadows lengthening in the front garden as Jake peered through the window. He'd just walked through from the kitchen, switching off the radio as news of the unknown plague was all over the news channels. The others sat on the sofas, Tamatan looking up at his friend. "Ill news?"

"Yes," Jake breathed. "No one has a clue what's going on. We've seen pandemics before, but not like this. Thousands of people are dead, here and on the continent. The prime minister has evoked a full lockdown. No one is to go out, except for the police and armed forces, who are patrolling certain parts of the country. From what they've said, everyone who has been infected has died. Even the hospitals are locked down. Many doctors and nurses have also died when trying to treat the sick. This is unbelievable!"

"And yet, you should know by now, that anything is believable," Tamatan countered.

"I know," Jake huffed. "After what I've been through, anything is possible. But to have it here, in my world is scary. No one knows about the other worlds that we've seen, and yet, it looks like someone from those worlds is intent on wiping us all out."

"I'm sure it won't come to that," Katherine replied, her words hollow and without conviction. "You have medicines here and scientists that will find a way to fight it."

"I really hope so, or we're all screwed."

"Let's not dwell on the ifs and buts," Wilf cautioned. "Let's just go and do what needs to be done. They must be scared witless, wondering if anyone is coming to help them. I just hope Jo and Emma are keeping cool. Emma has a strong spirit, which may bring her trouble."

"I know, but Jo is level-headed. I'm sure they're all okay at the moment. Grey will know that we're coming. So, anything could happen tonight. We need to watch each other's backs. We do that, and we might just make it through this."

The Volvo pulled off the drive, the sleepy village of Tintagel deserted as they wove their way towards the main highway. None spoke as they saw fires in the distance and cars strewn across the verges. "Look out!" Katherine exclaimed, nudging Jake's shoulder.

"Shit," he cursed, steering around an abandoned lorry as the car came around a tight bend in the road. "Sorry, babe. Took my eyes off the road for a sec."

"Well, keep them on the road, Jake Stevenson. We need to get there, and in one piece."

Jake smiled at the chastisement, squeezing Katherine's knee as she grinned back at him. "God, look at this," he started, seeing more cars and lorries that had either crashed or been abandoned. "It's like something from a movie."

"Do you think it's like this in other parts?" Wilf asked from the back seat.

"Probably worse. The big cities could be hit harder. Cornwall and Devon are not as populated, and yet we can see what Grey has unleashed. It could take years for us to recover."

"Well, let's get to the lighthouse and finish this madness," Tamatan said forcefully. "Too many people have suffered. It's time it stopped. Once and for all."

They rode on in silence until a flashing blue light caused Jake to swear. "Bollocks. We've got company."

"Lawmen?" Wilf asked.

"Yes. And we're not going to outrun them. It's only a few miles to the where we need to park."

"Then let them follow," Wilf offered. "We'll think of something when we stop. If things go badly, we make a break for the lighthouse."

The blue lights drew nearer, the police car's siren filling their ears as they continually flashed Jake to pull over. "We're almost there," he said over the noise that was bombarding the interior of the SUV. "Best case scenario, they order us to drive home. Worst case, they arrest us."

"Don't worry, Jake," Tamatan chirped. "They will not hinder our passage."

The car pulled in at the end of the quiet street, the bridle path to the lighthouse and Towan Point only a few yards from the black bonnet. They sat there in silence, as two police officers climbed out of the unmarked BMW. Two torches flicked on, Jake seeing that both officers were wearing face masks and gloves. "Here we go," he whispered, buzzing his window down.

"Good evening," the officer started, Jake noticing that he was stood a few metres away from the car.

"Hello, officer."

"You are aware that you're breaking the lockdown order?"

"Yes, sorry. We were just taking my father home. He's been with us in Tintagel for the past few days but wanted to be in his own house while this is going on."

"Has any of you started feeling unwell, or shown any unusual symptoms?"

"No, we're all feeling fine thanks."

The other policeman walked around the rear of the car, casting his torch into the interior. A pair of glowing orange eyes peered back at him, making him start. "Bloody hell! What the hell is that?"

"Shit," Jake hissed as the officer strode around the car to the passenger side. "Looks like we do this the hard way," he said climbing out of the car.

"What have you got on the back seat?" the smaller officer shouted, Jake noticing the terror in his eyes.

"It's not what you think," Jake soothed, baulking as one of the men reached for their taser. "Please, we don't need to do this."

The rear passenger door opened, Tamatan stepping out into the cool night air, his orange eyes regarding the two men with intrigue. "I mean you no harm," he said lightly. "But we have pressing matters to attend to, and you must let us carry on our way."

"Fucking hell!" the lead officer shouted. "Stay back." He pulled his taser, aiming at the demon's chest.

"Now now, dear man. I suggest you put that down and forget you ever..."

"No!" Jake cried as two prongs shot from the weapon, imbedding themselves into his friend, a crackling sound emitting from the device.

Tamatan looked down at his chest, a frown appearing on his face before he glared at the two men, his eyes turning from orange to red. "AAAAAGGGHH!" he hollered, a jet of white flames engulfing the taser.

The officer dropped it as the other policeman turned on his heels towards the nearest house, his colleague following a few steps behind. "Are you okay?" Jake asked as he approached Tamatan.

"Why yes. Whatever it was, it rather tickled. I think we need to be on our way. They will probably alert others."

"I agree," Jake replied as Wilf and Katherine rushed over to them. "Let's get the stuff out of the boot and get out of here. We've drawn an audience." Several front doors began opening, frightened people staring out at the foursome.

"Come on," Katherine urged. "Or we'll never make it."

Jake locked the Volvo, the foursome setting off away from the streetlights onto the dark headland, Towan Point's lights guiding them in the darkness. "How much time do we have?" Wilf asked as he trudged through the grass while adjusting his backpack.

"Forty minutes. We'll be there in fifteen, which gives us twenty-five to find the others and deal with Grey and Red."

"We'll be cutting it fine," the older man grumbled from behind Jake as they pressed on through the darkness.

"Jake. Do you have the dagger?" the demon asked.

"Yes. It's safely tucked away, but easily accessible should I need it."

"When you need it. Be ready."

"Kath, is she with you?" Jake asked.

"I'm not sure? I can't hear any voices inside me. Let's hope she's in there somewhere and is ready to help us."

"I'm sure Jubella is close by," Tamatan offered.

A short time later, they arrived at the lighthouse, a churning dark cloud hovering above it. Lightning flashed out at sea, rumbles of thunder echoing along the coastline. They removed their packs and started sorting through their arsenal. "Wilf, take this lump hammer. It may come in handy." He removed the sawn-off shotgun, sliding two cartridges into the breach before snapping it shut and placing it on the stony ground. Jake looked at Tamatan and Katherine, who both held long kitchen knives, the demon also holding a baseball bat. "Okay. Let's get in there. We have less than fifteen minutes."

"I'll get the door open," Wilf said, hefting his hammer before walking over to the door. As he felt for the bolt, the door swung inwards, the older man jumping back a few steps, hammer ready for use. Light filtered out from inside, a large silhouette casting its shadow across the ground.

"Come in," Malcolm whispered, Wilf spotting Jo inside, her pleading eyes reaching out towards him.

"Wilf, wait," Jake said, hurrying over to the door as the older man entered the lighthouse, Katherine and Tamatan a few steps behind him.

They piled in, Wilf striding over to the huddled group. "You're okay," he blurted, tears streaming down his cheeks as Jo wrapped her arms around him.

"I knew you'd come," she cried, burying her head into the crook of his neck.

Jake sized up Malcolm, noting the giant looked sheepish – almost scared. "Where are they?"

He poked a finger upwards. "Up there, somewhere. We've not seen them since this morning."

"Where is Lukash?" Jake pressed.

The giant looked at the floor. "Dunno. He went out this morning and never came back."

"Jake," Jo piped up. "What is going on out there? We've heard sirens and even a few loud bangs."

The private investigator leaned against the wall, his shoulders drooping. "We're not totally sure, but thousands of people have been struck down by some kind of virus. If I were a betting man, I'd say that it's the work of those two upstairs."

Jo and Emma's eyes widened, their mouths falling open. "Jesus," Emma gasped. "How bad is it?"

"Pretty bad. It's even spread to Europe, with major cities on lockdown."

A voice from the top of the stairs made them all look up, save for the girls, who were stirring from their slumber. "They have felt the Red Wind," the crimson-cloaked figure proclaimed. Red and Grey began descending the stairs, the others backing away towards the door. The two robed figures stood side-by-side, staring at the gathering in front on them. "Now come," Grey announced. "We have much to talk about and so little time to do it."

Chapter Forty-Three

The woman dropped the phone on the sofa in growing frustration, her stomach churning as a tumult of thoughts ran through her mind. She ran a hand through her long brown hair as footsteps approached from the hallway. "Still nothing," she huffed as the youth leaned against the door jamb, his dark wavy hair matching his mother's.

"So, what do we do, Mum?"

Vicky stood up, pacing the cosy lounge as Jasper looked on. "I don't know, love. We've been ordered to stay inside. You've seen the news. The latest death toll is in the hundreds of thousands. And it's only been a day since the outbreak." She looked at her son, tears forming at the corners of her eyes, her heart thumping rapidly.

"You think…"

She cut him off, not wanting to hear his words. "I don't know. They were in Birmingham yesterday until things turned crazy. You heard them on the phone last night, Son. They seemed okay. But I've tried them about a dozen times today and nothing. Mum's not even been on Facebook, which is unheard of. I just don't know what to think or do."

"I'm scared, Mum. I don't want to get sick, like all the people I've seen on the news."

"I'm scared too. I've never seen anything like this before. It's just incredible." Vicky stopped pacing, turning to look at her son. She remembered the little boy he once was. With his curly brown hair and mischievous grin. Since the whirlwind of events that had rocked them many years before, Vicky and Jasper had grown ever-closer, their tight bond unbreakable after losing the rest of their family in a tragic car accident. A face appeared in her mind's eye, a dark-haired man with a kind face. She smiled at the memory, looking at the clock on the mantlepiece. "It's eleven-thirty. Run upstairs and pack as much as you can into your backpack. I'll do the same once I've sorted some snacks and drinks. We need to leave in ten minutes."

"What? We're supposed to stay indoors, Mum? If we go out, we could get sick, or die?"

"You need to trust me. Now hurry." The teenager left the room, hurried footsteps filtering down the stairs as Vicky made her way into her kitchen. Two minutes later, she had a collection of energy bars, crisps and Lucozade on the table in front of her. "I hope that's enough," she said before running upstairs. She dropped her backpack on the bed, frantically stuffing underwear and anything else that she could think of before tossing the pack over her shoulder. "Come on, Jaspy," she called. "Downstairs now!"

"Coming," he called from his room as Vicky ran downstairs, almost tripping over her son's trainers.

As he entered the kitchen, Vicky was fastening her pack closed, checking that the back door was locked before turning off the lights. "Meet me outside. We have about twenty-five minutes."

"Where are we going, Mum?"

"Through the doorway. It's our only chance."

* * *

Jake looked at the two figures in front of them, a creeping cold washing over him. The girls had woken up and now stood huddled behind Jo and Emma. He looked at Red, his shotgun held in the crook of his arm. "So, what is the Red Wind?"

"It is a cleanser. I have used it over the ages to restore balance."

"Balance? You've killed thousands of people, maybe millions."

"Well, it is done, a punishment laid on your world due to Longford's treachery and your pilfering."

"Fuck off!" Jake spat. "Katherine is not yours. She's a free person, who can go where she likes."

"I'm afraid you're mistaken, Jake," Grey replied. "She was bones in the ground until I brought her back from an eternal sleep. I own her essence and she will join me in the Grey halls. If you disagree, you can all perish here."

"With the Red Wind?" Jake countered, his index finger curling around the trigger.

"No. The Red Wind is now spent. But we have other means of taking care of you," Red cautioned, his eyes fixed on the private investigator.

"Jake," Katherine whispered, taking his hand. "Grey is right, I do owe him," she said, turning towards him."

"What?" Jake blurted. "You want to go with them and leave us behind?"

Her eyes bored into his, a faint glow appearing around the edges. "If not, we'll all die here. I've been gone for so long, Jake. You will move on from this, of that I'm sure."

Jake didn't know whether she was serious, or if she was merely creating a ruse. As he was about to speak, she smiled at him, her eyes shimmering. "But I've only just found you again, Kath," he replied, his voice shaky. "I don't want to go on without you."

"But you must, Jake. I am sorry." She turned from the group, Wilf looking on in shock as she walked over to her new kin.

"The doorway is about to open," Grey proclaimed. "We will pass through without intervention from any of you. Once we're through, I will leave it up to you to make your choice. But heed my words, Jake Stevenson. If you attempt to come after us, you will all suffer the same fate as this forsaken realm."

"What happened to Lukash?" Malcolm asked, taking a step forward, a length of timber grasped in his huge hand.

Red's eyes flicked towards him. "He is no more. Your master has paid for his craven ways."

"You killed him, and everyone else in Towan Point." It was not a question. It was a statement as the giant took another step forward, the others becoming edgy.

"Take another step and I will kill you where you stand," Red ordered.

"Relax," Katherine said, tugging on the crimson robes. "He will not cause us harm."

Red turned his head towards her, seeing the shimmering light in her eyes. He was about to speak, his words never coming as Malcolm smashed the length of timber into the side of his face. The wood snapped clean in two, Red taking a step back, seemingly unhurt. Before he could launch an attack, the giant fell on him, the two crashing to the ground in a tangle of limbs. Jake turned to the others. "Get down the stairs. Now!" he shouted, pushing Jo and Emma towards their escape route. Screaming filled the lighthouse, the three girls wailing as Grey shot lightning from his fingers, scoring the wall above their heads as they ducked down the stone steps.

Wilf drew his knife, advancing on Grey. "Time to die, you bastard." More lightning emitted from Grey's fingers, propelling Wilf across the room, crashing into the wall. He slumped forward, toppling down the steps as Tamatan crashed into the ancient being.

Katherine stood there, impassive as Red rose from the ground, holding Malcolm aloft with one hand. Red lightning pulsed across the room, the giant crashing into the wall, his neck snapping loudly before he crumpled to the floor. "Red. We need to go," she urged. Take my hand."

He did so, knowing that Grey would make light work of the demon as they fought on the dusty floor. They hurried over to the stairs, the Red King falling to his knees as Jake unloaded the shotgun into his back. "Fool," he hollered, feeling strong hands turn him over as he looked up at Jake who pointed the weapon at his face.

Jake saw his adversary's eyes begin to shine, pulling the trigger again before the red lightning at Red's fingertips could do their work. At almost point-blank range, Jake expected the man's head to dissolve into a mass of brains and shattered bones. His stomach clenched as the Red King smiled up at him, knowing that his time had truly come. "Oh no," he breathed, as Red's eyes grew ever-brighter, Jake closing his eyes, accepting the inevitable.

"Hello Red," a distorted voice announced as Katherine stepped between the two men.

"What?" Red uttered, a look of confusion spreading across his blackened face. "Katherine?"

"No," she replied. "Katherine is now in the shadows. I have risen, one last time. And you will bear witness to it." White light emitted from her eyes, piercing Red's as he writhed and screamed underneath her. He tried to push her away, a new-found strength inside Katherine holding him easily.

Jake watched on in horror as a voice came to his ears. "Jake, the doorway is opening. Wilf's hurt."

"Go through it, now! Don't wait for us."

He was blasted into the wall as white light filled the lighthouse, dust and debris falling from the ceiling as Tamatan was hurtled across the basement. He landed heavily, Jake scurrying over to him as Grey began climbing to his feet.

"Tamatan, wake up," he urged, tears falling from his eyes. The demon didn't respond, Jake's heart constricting at the sight before him. The ancient demon who Jake considered his brother lay on the ground in a broken heap. "No," he cried, placing his hand on Tamatan's chest. "I'm so sorry, my friend."

"Jake," Katherine screamed as the walls began to splinter and shift. "We need to go."

He looked up, his vision blurred with tears to see Grey standing close by, his eyes burning with fury. "Run Kath. I'm right behind you." He dived forward as lightning blasted the ground behind him. He crouched behind an old crate as more dust and rock crashed to the floor nearby.

"You will now die, Jake. Know this. I will take Katherine but kill the others slowly and painfully. Take that thought with you."

Jake spotted Katherine, motioning for him to follow. He tensed his legs, holding his breath before launching himself towards the lip of the staircase. He felt an intense sensation as his legs were caught by Grey's salvo, Jake toppling down the staircase, taking Katherine with him. They scrambled to their feet as Grey loomed over them. "Go!" he shouted as she barged through the doorway into another world. Jake stepped through, coming out in the remains of the lighthouse, wind and rain assaulting him instantly. The others were close by, Jo tending to Wilf who looked up at him, a thin smile telling Jake that the older man would pull through. A noise behind him made him spin around, Grey standing inside the doorway, eyes seeking out their quarry.

"Now, you will all die," Grey stated coldly as the doorway began to blink and fade. As the light in his eyes grew brighter, a figure appeared next to him.

"Tamatan," Jake blurted as the demon pinned Grey to the side of the doorway, red light streaming from his eyes into his adversary's face.

"Jake, the dagger," he shouted, his voice pained as white light merged with red, pulsing out across the flagstone floor. Jake pulled the ancient weapon out of his jacket, tossing it towards Tamatan who caught it deftly, despite his injuries. Time seemed to slow down, the red light in the demon's eyes diminishing to nothing. He stared at Jake and smiled, the searing glow diminishing for a few seconds. "I love you, my brother," he called, thrusting the obsidian blade into Grey's throat, the ancient being uttering a garbled scream as Tamatan sliced deeply into withered flesh and sinew. A flash of light erupted from the doorway, a deafening shockwave knocking Jake and Katherine over. They lay there for a few seconds, their ears ringing as Vrybergen fell silent. Clumsily, they climbed to their feet, staring at the rubble that had fallen through from the Cornish lighthouse.

"He's gone," Jake whispered. The doorway had disappeared, along with Grey and Tamatan. Motes of red and white light floating in the air before being dispersed as strong winds whipped across the desolated settlement.

"Jake, are you okay?" Katherine said, taking his hand.

"He's gone, babe," he cried, burying his face into the crook of her neck. She held him, the others looking on in stunned silence as Jake wept.

"He died so that we could live," she soothed. "I'm so sorry, Jake. I'm so very sorry."

Two hands separated them, Wilf standing between them, his face stony, tears falling on his ruddy cheeks. "He will live on through us. I loved him as you did, Jake. And there will be a time to mourn his passing. But for now, we have to get out of here. It's not safe."

The others came over, the girls clinging to Jo and Emma, scared expressions staring up at Jake. "Where shall we go?" Jo asked.

"Shetland," Wilf replied. "It should be safe there. Let's go."

They made their way across the rubble that was once the Vrybergen's lighthouse, stumbling over loose rock before making skirting the settlement. The girls cried out, noticing the dead that lay strewn across the street, Jo and Emma turning their little heads away. Five minutes later, they came out into open ground, a strong wind at their backs as they began the long journey. To their new home.

Chapter Forty-Four

A week later

"We'll need more tools from Fingles," Wilf said as he puffed on his pipe. "Are you sure about this, Toby?"

The younger man nodded. "It's your home, Wilf. As you said, we can stay there until the other buildings are restored. We'll all muck in together. I've already discussed it with Dee. She is in agreement.

"I give thanks and I am truly sorry for what evils you had to endure." He looked out at the grey sea, smiling at the sight of the three girls who played on the stubbly grass. He turned towards the advancing couple. "Any luck?"

"Some," Jake said, his dark hair ruffled by the breeze. "There is plenty still to salvage from Fingles. Toby did a good job of restoring some of Shetland, but with our help, we can have it looking like it once did."

"That's good, Jake. Kath, are you okay?"

The woman smiled, lifting the old man's spirits. "I'm good, Uncle. Although the walk was a challenge. I need to get my hands dirty and build up some strength."

"Aye, but that will come. We will have this place back to normal before the winter arrives. And with any luck, we can herd some livestock from the mainland. Old George lived out here for years. We can sustain ourselves as he once did."

"Where are the others?" Jake asked.

"Emma and Jo are inside with Toby's wife and son. They are sorting out where we all sleep. I'm letting them get on with it. Old Wilf will just get in the way."

"Okay," Jake replied. He breathed out, looking at the others. "I wonder what's happening on the other side?"

"No idea," the older man huffed. "Hopefully, your people would have found a way to stop Red's plague."

"And if not?"

"Best not to think about it, Jake. What's done is done. You have your kin here with you. That's the most important thing."

"I know. It's just easier said than done. For all I know, the whole world could have been affected."

"Maybe. But don't dwell on that. Come on, let's go and if there is a mug of nettle tea going."

An hour later, Wilf and Jake were stood at the tip of Shetland, looking out at the grey sea. The older man sighed. "It could almost be Cornwall," he mused. "I know I said not to dwell on it, but I'll miss your ale, Jake."

The younger man smiled, turning to his old friend when something in the distance caught his eye. "Look," he urged. "Someone is heading our way."

Wilf strained his eyes, noticing two small figures walking towards Shetland. He could barely make out that one was much taller than the other, both with dark hair. "Strange. Don't get people out this far very often. Come on, let's go take a look."

They headed across the headland, striding past the farmhouse as the figures approached. "Jesus," Jake blurted. "Is that who I think it is?"

"Who?" Wilf asked, struggling to keep up with the younger man.

"It's Vicky and Jasper," he said, waving at the oncoming duo.

"Fuckenell! What the hell are they doing this far from home?"

"Let's find out," Jake laughed, scooting down towards the bridge, the couple cresting the summit on the path above them. "Vicky," he called.

"Jake!" a female voice cried out, the woman running down towards him, the lanky teenager in hot pursuit.

They came together, Vicky bursting into tears as Jake spun her around in his embrace. "What the hell happened?" After a few seconds, he lowered Vicky to the ground, embracing Jasper in a tight hug. Wilf followed suit, clapping the young man on the shoulder before giving his mother a bone-crunching hug.

"Oh Jake," she croaked, her voice breaking. "I can't believe we found you." She began hyperventilating, the former private investigator placing a calming hand on her shoulder.

"It's okay. Just breathe. You're safe now. Did you come through the doorway at the Lickey's?"

"Yes," Jasper replied, the light lyrical voice that Jake remembered had been replaced by a deep rumble.

"Jasper, what happened?"

"How long have you been here?" the teenager replied.

"About a week."

"So, you must have seen what was going on back home?"

Jake's face dropped. "Yes. We were caught up in it. The person that did that was called Red. He unleashed some sort of plague on us." He was about to continue, his words halted as Vicky broke down, Wilf catching her before she fell backwards onto the stubbly grass.

"It's okay, love," he soothed. "You're safe now."

She wailed in his grip, her breathing coming out in pained gasps as she tried to get her words out. "My parents. I. th-think they're dead."

"What happened?" Jake asked, feeling the woman's pain.

"I called them on the Sunday morning, but there was no answer. We couldn't go out because everyone was told to stay indoors. I tried them again later that night. But no one answered. They'd been shopping the day before. In the city. I saw the news, Jake. People in some of the major cities were dying, including Birmingham. I can't believe they're gone."

He walked over and embraced her, his eyes welling up with tears. "I'm so sorry, Vicky." He reached out, grasping Jasper's shoulder who stood there forlornly. "But you're safe now." He felt her strength as she hugged him back, knowing that she was strong. "So, it took you a week to get to us?"

"Yes," Jasper replied.

"And you knew the way?" Wilf asked.

"I remembered it from when I was a boy," he blushed, giving a lopsided grin.

"Come," Jake said. "Let's introduce you to the others."

They headed back down the slope, across the bridge towards the farmhouse as the sun broke through the clouds. Vicky looked at the headland, wondering if this was now their new home.

* * *

Joseph Thorne looked at the moped, regarding it strangely. It was lay on its side, the engine gently ticking away. A loud bang in the distance should have made him start. But it didn't. He was calm. He knew that things were coming to a close. His beloved village was bathed in the warm Mediterranean sun, an image that would normally make tourists stop and take in their surroundings, marvelling at the cobbled streets and white-washed higgledy-piggledy buildings. But not today. His eyes moved away from the moped, his vision taking in the scene around him. People lay in heaps on the pavement and road, a car protruding from a shop doorway as smoke drifted across the small settlement, high up in the mountains.

I'm so sorry Emma. I hope you're at peace. Lauren, Daddy will always love you. His vision began to cloud over as the sound of birds passing over the white-washed morgue gently drifted to his ears. He welcomed the darkness, knowing that something better was waiting. He hoped.

Chapter Forty-Five

Two Months Later

The journey back from Tamatan's homeland had been uneventful. They encountered very little people or beings, even Sica offered little conversation as he sailed them back to Mantz forest. From the jetty, they had maintained a steady pace, sleeping under the thick canopy every night until they emerged at the eastern fringes as the sun fell away once more. The two men had eaten frugally, sitting in the log cabin where they had met up with Father Stephen, the vicar that Jake had known most of his life. They'd pushed on, coming into Amatoll forest as the sun had begun its descent on the following evening. As the two men sat around a small fire, Jake looked at Wilf. "Do you think it will open?"

"Dunno," the older man shrugged, puffing on his pipe. "If I were to lay a wager, I'd say not. Tamatan did what he did, knowing that killing Grey would kill the doorways with him. Let us hope our friend did not die in vain."

"I know. His family took it better than I thought."

"They are demons. A hardly breed. Jake will take care of them. He's grown strong and will carry his kin forward in his father's absence."

They sat, eating the last of Sica's smoked fish, knowing that their packs were growing ever-lighter. "It's almost time," Jake said, checking his watch.

They both walked over to the trees, waiting for the day to pass. "Nothing yet," Wilf observed as no blue outline appeared.

After a few minutes, Jake clapped Wilf on the shoulder. "Well, that settles it. Whatever happened on the other side, we'll never get to see it."

"It could all be gone," Jake uttered solemnly.

"Aye. But we're still kicking. And I truly think that this is the end. No more adventures, no more troubles. Our kin are waiting for us and can finally put down roots."

"You're right. We have Katherine back. Plus, we have Vicky and Jasper too."

"We do. And they will make a fine addition to our little family. Come now. Let's bed down and get some rest. Old Wilf needs his beauty sleep."

"I'm sure Jo would agree," Jake smiled before they settled down in the quiet forest, knowing that their loved ones were only a few days away.

* * *

The family came out of the treeline, tentatively looking at the open area next to the river. The large machinery lay still, carcasses of the workers lying next to the dead carrion that had feasted on them. The man stood a step forward, jabbing his spear into the soft brown earth. No one spoke, the mother and son hanging back by a thick tree as the man moved closer to the macabre scene in front of them. The skull of a man peered up at the sky, a silver tin hat still attached as it lay at a jaunty angle. The remains of his withered skin had blackened, resembling the bark of the nearby trees. The dark-skinned man, prodded the corpse with an outstretched toe, flinching slightly as a large spider crawled out of the gaping mouth. He moved away, instructing his family to stay where they were as he made his way over to a large steel cabin, taking a blade out of his faded khaki shorts. He peered around the door, a husk of a man peering back at him from a wooden chair. The man spat on the floor, opening his sack before rooting around for anything of use or value. Five minutes later he waved his family back into the treeline, his sack bulging with cutlery, tobacco and a wad of notes. He knew what money was. On occasion, he'd traded with it as strangers from far and wide had passed through his village. It would be of little use to them now, but the man didn't know that. His primitive mind just thought that the men had died in an ambush, or of a local disease or an animal bite. He had never travelled more than thirty miles from his birthplace, completely unaware of the Red Wind that had engulfed the planet in which he lived. As they headed back to their village, they never thought about the rest of the world. Never gave a moment's thought to the other indigenous people across the globe who were beginning to venture towards the edges of their worlds, all of them seeing the same thing. Death. On a scale never seen before and never to be seen again.

Chapter Forty-Six

A Year Later

A large black gull flapped its wings leisurely, aided by the gentle breeze that blew out to sea. It glided effortlessly over the spit of land, looking down as it flew over a large collection of buildings huddled next to the sea. Its keen eyes scanned the area, looking for something to eat. Nothing could be seen though, the sight of a gathering of people underneath making up the gull's mind to head out to sea to the lands beyond. On Shetland, there was a fervour of activity. Lauren, Scarlett and Alicia, skipped across the grass, the golden ribbons in their hair flapping in the wind. They made their way over to a wooden archway, Lauren running her palm over the smooth wood and lattice framework.

"It's so exciting," Alicia chirped, her hair bouncing up and down as she hopped from one foot to the other.

"I know. I've never been to one before," Lauren added. "It will be fun."

"When will we see her?" Scarlett enquired expectantly.

"Soon. She's inside with the others. I'm sure they will let us know." They skipped away, heading over towards the new animal pens to look at the pigs and chickens that they had gradually acquired from passing traders and far-off villages.

As they ran past the furthest cabin, two men regarded them fondly from the veranda. "Settled they are," Wilf said happily.

"Yes, they certainly are. Who would have thought it after what they've been through?"

"I know, Son," the older man agreed. "Part of Alicia is from this land. Maybe that's why she has taken to it so much."

"True. I thought she would be missing her life back home. TV, music and her iPad, but no. It's almost as if she's always lived here. The others have settled down too. I suppose it's easier for Scarlett. She grew up not far from here, but Lauren has done well."

"She has. Got a strong spirit has that one. Like her mother."

Jake turned, looking at his old friend as a smile spread across his face. "Anyway, how are you feeling? Nervous?"

The older man scoffed. "Me, nervous! Never." He puffed out his chest, tapping his pipe on his chin before his shoulders sagged. "Okay. Maybe just a little. I've never done this before, Jake."

"Relax. Getting married is the easy part. It's keeping them that is the challenge," he replied winking mischievously.

Wilf guffawed, clapping the younger man on the shoulder. "Don't worry, Jo's going nowhere. It's not like she's got a lot choose from, truth be told."

"Well, you're not wrong there. There's only three men out here, four if you count Jasper."

"He might be a little bit young for her."

"Seriously, I'm so happy for you, you old rogue. I never thought you would ever pop the question."

Wilf adjusted his belt, the newly made britches feeling ever-so-slightly snug around his waistline. His freshly washed shirt had been pressed, giving him a noble appearance. Even his usual unruly hair was tied back into a ponytail. "Well, I'm getting on in seasons, Jake. I don't know how much longer old Wilf will be kicking around this piece of rock?"

"Bollocks," Jake countered dryly. "You've got plenty of life left in you. And you've many happy years ahead. She's a wonderful woman. A real catch."

"Aye," he agreed, the embers of his pipe lighting up as he sucked heartily. "Did you ever imagine we'd end up like this?"

"Never in my craziest dreams."

"Nor mine. To think, I spent nearly all my life in that forest, barely venturing anywhere until you turned up. It was the best thing that ever happened to this land, Jake."

"Don't get all soppy on me," the younger man said, feeling a lump forming in his throat.

"I mean it. I remember it well. We'd just lost Alice and folk were scared. Scared that the monsters would come for them in the dead of night. And then, you turn up on your motorcycle. Cedric must have seen the steel in you, Son. That's why he sent you out here to us."

"I remember it well. A right game of cat and mouse. I had no idea what I was doing. My life had turned upside-down in a few short days after losing Daz and meeting Elias. And before you know it, we're being chased off this rock by a pair of vampire pigs. They should have made a movie about it."

"Oh, I would have liked that. Could have sat on Jo's sofa and watched it with that popcorn stuff she likes."

Jake chuckled at the thought. "One day, eh? Anyway, we've made it through. Yes, we've lost loved ones along the way, but they would have wanted us to be happy."

"They would, especially Tamatan."

At hearing the name, Jake's face dropped slightly, the older man seeing the sorrow in his eyes. "Yes, he would. I really miss him. When he died, a little part of me did too."

"A little part of all of us did. He was bound to us and always will be, of that I have no doubt."

He was about to go on when Emma appeared on the veranda. "She's ready."

Wilf stood stock-still as Jake nodded his head. "Okay, we'll head over. Is everything else ready?"

"Leave it to the girls," she smiled. "We've got it all in hand." She headed away from them, towards the main house.

"Come on then. Let's get you wed," Jake said straightening his shirt.

The two men walked across the grass towards the archway as the three girls hurried over, Lauren and Scarlett holding a little boy's hands. Jake smiled at them, Toby and Dee's son grinning broadly, thinking it was all a fun game. A gentle melody carried on the air. It sounded to Jake like a mandolin as he noticed a woman with short dark hair heading towards them, her white dress flapping as the sea breeze stiffened slightly. He smiled at Dee, the woman reciprocating, her warm friendly face radiant in the early afternoon light. The tune continued as Jake and Wilf stood facing out to sea, the girls behind them, giggling and waiting for the bride to appear. "Girls," Jake said calmly. "Eyes this way." They all complied, standing patiently as Vicky and Jasper appeared at Wilf's left-hand-side.

"Good luck," Vicky beamed, her dark hair braided into matching tails, her newly created summer dress almost touching the stubbly grass.

"Break a leg," Jasper added, smiling at the older man who nodded happily.

"Look" Alicia called, both men turning towards the main house.

Wilf's words caught in his throat, tears forming at the corners of his eyes at the approaching sight. "Oh bloody hell!" he blurted. "My Jo."

Jake looked at the three women, Katherine and Emma a few paces behind the bride, their blue dresses flowing behind them, their dark hair the same as Vicky's. A lump formed in Jake's throat, his woman beaming back at him. However, the day belonged to Jo. Her red-framed glasses did their best to mask the tears that were threatening to spill from her eyes, a wide grin etched on her face as she drew nearer. Her brown hair was tied up, white flowers woven into the braid that spanned the top of her head. Her white dress completed the look, with lacy arms and neckline that had taken Dee many weeks to lovingly create. "She looks beautiful," he whispered, the older man nodding dumbly. On cue, Jake left Wilf, walking towards Jo who threaded her arm through his. "Hello," he said. "You look amazing."

"Don't," she laughed. "I've been in bloody tears most of the day. You'll start me off again." As Jake turned, he noticed Toby standing underneath the archway, his unruly hair plastered to his head. Jake could see that he was nervous. They'd stayed up late the night before, going over Toby's lines, Jake explaining what a registrar did and what lines he'd need. As they reached Wilf, Jake took Jo's hand, passing it to Wilf's outstretched arm, which she took willingly. As they all took their places and waited for Dee's melody to conclude, Toby cleared his throat loudly.

"People of Shetland, we are here to bear witness to the marriage of Jo and Wilf. Do any of you folk have any objections?"

They all shook their heads silently, except for his son, Eden, who nodding happily. Toby smiled at the sight, relaxing slightly before continuing. "Jo, do you love the man before you?"

"I do," Jo breathed.

"Wilf, do you love this woman before you?"

"I do," Wilf croaked, holding back the tears.

"Jo. Do you promise to love him, honour and cherish him for the rest of your days?"

"Kinda," she winked, turning towards Toby. "Yes, I do."

"Wilf. Do you promise to love her, honour and provide for her for the rest of your days?"

"Aye," he agreed.

"Who has the rings?" Toby asked. Jake went into his pocket, retrieving two silver-coloured rings that Toby had spent many weeks crafting. They shimmered in the sunlight as Jake handed them over to the man. He handed the smaller on to Wilf. "Repeat after me. With this ring."

"With this ring," he said, staring into Jo's eyes.

"I give you my life."

"I give you my life," he repeated, seeing his bride's eyes sparkle as a stray tear slipped underneath her glasses.

"It will bind us together."

"It will bind us together."

"As long as we both shall live."

"As long as we both shall live." He winked at Jo, whose toothy grin made his chest constrict.

"Jo, repeat after me," Toby instructed, handing her the larger ring. "With this ring."

"With this ring."

"I give you my soul."

"I give you my soul," her voice quavering.

"It will bind us together."

"It will bind us together."

"Long past when we are old."

"Long past when we are old."

Toby held both their hands, raising his head to the others. "They have given solemn vows and exchanged rings. By the powers vented in me…"

Jake suppressed a giggle, looking at the floor as Toby concluded the ceremony, unaware of his mistake.

"I proclaim that they are man and wife. You may kiss your bride."

Wilf pulled Jo towards him, their lips meeting as everyone cheered and clapped. They both cried, tears mingling as they held onto each other. "We did it, girl," Wilf rasped, his voice hoarse.

"We sure did, husband," Jo concurred, kissing him once more before they were mobbed by the others. Hugs and kisses were exchanged, the women admiring Jo's wedding band, the men shaking hands and patting the children on the head as they ran around them.

Dee walked over to Jake, embracing him. "We give thanks, Jake. We've endured so much loss, but having you here with us is so wonderful."

"Thank you, Dee," he replied, planting a kiss on the woman's cheek. "We have much to build here, and we'll all do it together."

Her face lit up as the sea breeze ruffled her dark hair. "I give thanks."

Jake turned towards Jo and Emma, failing to notice Katherine walk the other way, nodding at Toby as she covertly slipped something into his hand.

"Folk, we are not yet finished," Toby announced authoritatively.

"What?" Jake said, his brow creasing. "I thought that was it?" The laughter died down until Shetland stood quiet, Jake looking at the others, a confused expression on his face.

"Jake."

He turned around, seeing Katherine kneeling behind him, a silvery ring in her hand. "Kath?"

"Marry me," she said, her dark eyes staring up at him.

"W-what?"

"I love you, Jake Stevenson. Will you be my husband?"

He looked at Jo and Wilf, who both winked at him mischievously, huge smiles on their faces. He couldn't speak, his dry throat closing up as he walked towards her. "I-I…"

"Just say yes," Katherine said playfully. "Say yes and be my man, forever."

He scooped her into his arms, kissing her fiercely. "Yes," he replied, tears streaming down his face as the others cheered. He buried his face into her dark hair. "I love you, Katherine Bathurst."

"I love you too, Jake Stevenson. And I always will."

The gull glided back towards the land, dark clouds out at sea making the bird change course. As it glided over the spit of rock, it looked down at the gathering, completely unaware of what was taking place. It glided over the buildings, in search of a tasty treat to keep hunger at bay as more cheering drifted up towards it.

The End

Dear reader,

We hope you enjoyed reading *The Secrets Beneath The Sea.* Please take a moment to leave a review, even if it's a short one. Your opinion is important to us.

Discover more books by Phil Price at https://www.nextchapter.pub/authors/phil-price-horror-author-united-kingdom

Want to know when one of our books is free or discounted? Join the newsletter at http://eepurl.com/bqqB3H

Best regards,
Phil Price and the Next Chapter Team

Lightning Source UK Ltd.
Milton Keynes UK
UKHW040232121020
371334UK00022B/163

9 781715 582272